SWEENEY SISTERS SERIES

Saturdays at Sweeney's

ASHLEY FARLEY

Copyright © 2017 by Ashley Farley

All rights reserved.

Cover design: damonza.com

Formatting: damonza.com

Editor: Patricia Peters at A Word Affair LLC

Leisure Time Books, a division of AHF Publishing All rights reserved. No part of this book may be used or reproduced in any manner without written permission from the author.

This book is a work of fiction. Names, characters, establishments, organizations, and incidents are either products of the author's imagination or are used fictitiously to give a sense of authenticity. Any resemblance to actual persons, living or dead, events, or locales is entirely coincidental.

Newsletter Signup

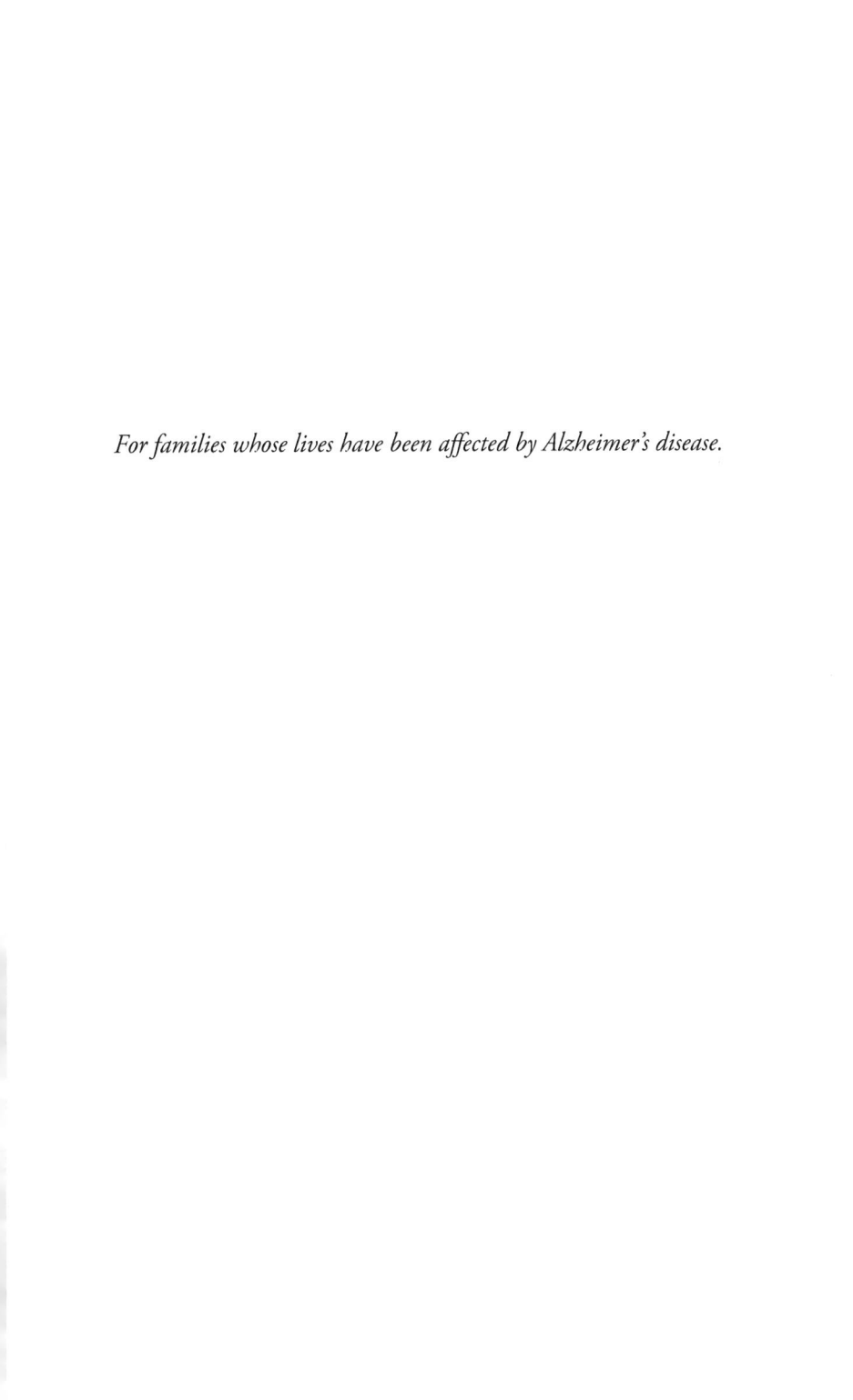

For families whose lives have been affected by Alzheimer's disease.

ALSO BY ASHLEY FARLEY

Magnolia Nights
Sweet Tea Tuesdays
Saving Ben

Sweeney Sisters Series

Tangle of Strings
Boots and Bedlam
Lowcountry Stranger
Her Sister's Shoes

Adventures of Scottie

Breaking the Story
Merry Mary

ONE

SAM

The shrill ringing of Sam's cell phone jolted her upright in bed a few minutes before twelve on a stormy Wednesday night in early May. Blinking his eyes open, Eli propped himself up on one elbow beside her. She snatched the phone up from her nightstand. Sam could barely hear the man's voice over the wail of sirens in the background.

She pressed the phone closer to her ear. "You need to speak louder, sir. I can't hear you."

"I . . . said . . . I'm Lester James . . . from the local fire—" In spite of his attempts to enunciate, the sirens drowned out his voice.

Sam turned her back on her husband's worried gray eyes. "Can you repeat that, please? I'm having trouble understanding you."

This time, she heard every word when Lester James yelled into the phone, "Captain Sweeney's Seafood Market is on fire!"

"I'm on my way." Sam ended the call as her feet hit the ground. "The market is on fire! I need to get down there. Fast."

Eli struggled to free himself of the tangled covers. "I'm coming with you."

She glanced down at her nightclothes—a gray Carolina Baseball tee over an old pair of Eli's plaid boxers. She wouldn't take time to change. It was the middle of the night, and no one cared about her attire. "I'll meet you in the car. But hurry."

She stuffed her feet into the rain boots she'd left beside the front door when she'd arrived home from work earlier. She stared down at their two sets of keys on the hall table and grabbed Eli's. His strobe lights would come in handy. She hurried out to his unmarked sedan and started the car from the passenger seat. She turned up the volume on the police radio and was listening to the dispatcher bark orders to officers about the fire when Eli emerged from the house, struggling to zip up his jeans over his pajama bottoms.

Eli slid behind the steering wheel and peeled out down their driveway. He skidded onto Creekside Drive and engaged his lights—sans siren so as not to wake the neighbors—as he raced toward the center of town. The police had cordoned off the intersection of Creekside and Main Streets in their small coastal town of Prospect. A uniformed officer signaled them into the parking lot of the Inlet View Marina across the street from the market. Eli and Sam jumped out of the car and ran to the sidewalk, staring at the small square building engulfed in flames. Smoke filled her nose and mouth and made her eyes water. Eli tugged his red bandanna free of his back pocket and handed it to her.

She wiped her eyes and then covered her mouth with the bandanna. "Do you think they can save it?"

"I don't know, honestly. Anything that isn't destroyed by the flames will be ruined by smoke and water damage." He drew her in for a half hug. "I'm so sorry, babe. This is a tough break for your family."

She rested her head on his shoulder. "I can't believe this is happening."

He kissed the top of her cropped blonde head. "Not that it's any consolation, but at least you have insurance. You'll rebuild even better than before."

She couldn't bring herself to think about that now.

Sam squinted at a familiar figure standing with one of the firemen next to the hook-and-ladder truck in the market parking lot. "Is that Mom over there?"

Eli followed her gaze. "It certainly looks like Lovie. I wonder how she beat us here."

"I have no idea, unless the fire department called her first." She ducked out from beneath his arm, and before he could stop her, she darted across the road to her mother. As she drew near, she recognized the fireman as Jared Rhodes, an old friend from high school who stopped by the market two or three times a week for lunch. A look of relief spread across his craggy face when he spotted Sam.

She placed a hand on her mother's trembling shoulder. "Are you okay, Mom?"

Lovie tightened her grip on the blanket draped over her cotton nightgown. Her legs and feet were bare, the soles filthy dirty.

"How did you know about the fire?" Sam asked. "Did someone from the fire department call you?"

Lovie stared at Sam with a bewildered expression, the fire reflected in her glazed eyes.

Jared leaned in close to Sam's ear. "She was already here when we arrived. She seems confused. She keeps mumbling something about a dream."

Sam squeezed her mother's shoulder. "Aw, Mama, did you have a bad dream?"

Lovie bit down on her lip as she bobbed her gray head up and down. "I had a dream about Oscar Sweeney. He told me to hustle on down here, that we had trouble at the market."

Sam was at a loss for words. *Oscar Sweeney?* Why was her mother referring to her husband as one might an acquaintance?

Never mind that Sam's father had been dead for eight years. Lovie was prone to periods of forgetfulness and confusion, but this sounded more like a premonition than dementia.

Sam turned to the fireman. "Thank you for taking care of her, Jared. Do you have any idea how the fire started?"

He lifted a shoulder. "My guess is a lightning strike. But we won't know for sure until we conduct our investigation."

"That was my first thought as well," Sam said. "But how is that possible when the storm ended hours ago?"

"It's not uncommon for lightning to ignite a fire that doesn't become a full-on blaze until several hours later." He squeezed Sam's elbow. "I'm sorry for your loss, Sam. I know how much this place means to your family."

An explosion inside the burning building shook the ground beneath their feet. Sam stepped in front of her mother to shield her from the fire.

Lovie placed her hands over her ears and cried, "Lord in heaven, we're being bombed!"

Sam shot Jared an apologetic look. The dream about Oscar Sweeney or the fire or a combination of both had triggered one of her mother's spells.

Jared gestured at the cluster of pedestrians gathered in the marina parking lot. "It'd be safer for y'all across the street."

Sam tugged off her rain boots and set them on the ground in front of Lovie. "Here, Mom, put these on." She held tight to her arm while her mother slipped her tiny feet into the boots. They'd once had the same shoe size, but Lovie's feet had shrunk like the rest of her body in recent years.

Sam prodded her mother forward. "Let's get out of Jared's way so he can do his work. We need to call Faith anyway."

She trod gingerly on bare feet as they crossed the rocky pavement. Once they were safely back at Eli's car, she placed the call to her younger sister.

Faith answered on the fourth ring. "What's wrong?" she asked, her voice hoarse from sleep.

"The market's on fire. You better get down here. And bring me some shoes, please."

Eli conversed with a group of his coworkers while Sam sat with her mother on the hood of his car, watching fifty-nine years of Sweeney family history go up in smoke. Her mother had started the business on a Saturday in late June of 1958 at an umbrella stand she'd set up in this very parking lot. She'd sold fish caught by her husband and his lifelong best friend, Captain Mack Bowman, on their commercial fishing boat, the *Dreamer*. Her baked goods and charming personality contributed to her overnight success. A year later she'd leased, and eventually purchased, the small building at the main intersection of town where the market had been located ever since. Lovie was a legend throughout the Lowcountry, with customers traveling from miles away to buy her goods and consult with her for cooking tips.

Faith's red SUV came to a screeching halt beside them fifteen minutes later. "What a nightmare," she said, unable to take her eyes off the fire. "Any idea how it started?"

"Lightning maybe, but they won't know for certain until after the investigation." Sam eyed her sister's flannel pajamas—an odd choice for a steamy night—under her yellow rain slicker. "I see you received the memo about the attire."

Faith gave them the once-over and rolled her eyes. "I hate theme parties."

"Mom left her house in such a hurry she forgot to put on her shoes. I gave her my boots."

"That explains why you wanted these." Faith removed a pair of flip-flops from the pocket of her raincoat and handed them to Sam. As she climbed onto the hood next to her, she whispered, "Mom's awfully quiet. Is she okay?"

"I'll let you be the judge." Sam nudged their mother. "Mom, tell Faith about your dream."

Lovie pried her eyes away from the fire. "What dream?" she asked, her gray brows knitted together.

"Remember what you told Jared and me? That Oscar Sweeney visited you in a dream and told you we had trouble at the market?"

Lovie shook her head. "I don't know what you're talking about," she said, and returned her attention to the scene across the street.

Faith shot her sister a look of concern. "Oscar Sweeney?" she mouthed.

"Let it go for now," Sam whispered. "The fire is enough to addle anybody, let alone an eighty-five-year-old woman."

Flames licked the night sky as Sam considered the loss in profits. How would her family survive without the income? Summertime had always been their busiest season, but in recent years the fall months, particularly the holiday season, had proven equally profitable. She knew little about commercial construction. How long would it take to rebuild? *If* they decided to go that path? She leaned into Faith. "Please tell me our insurance premium is current."

"I made the quarterly payment last month," Faith said.

All three Sweeney sisters had grown up helping their mother at the market, but only Faith and Sam had chosen to make it a career. Over the years, they'd slowly taken over management of the business. Faith was in charge of financials, while Sam handled everything else.

"We'll have to decide if rebuilding is even the right choice for our family. You're retiring soon. Without my income Eli and I would have to cut back, but we'd survive. The decision will affect Jamie the most."

"You don't need to worry about your son. With his outgoing personality and hospitality degree, he will have his choice of jobs. Maybe not in Prospect, but there are plenty of great restaurants and hotels in Charleston." Faith lowered her voice. "Mom is the one we need to be concerned about."

"Are you kidding me?" Sam said in a loud whisper. "She's been saving ever since she was forty so she could retire when she reached sixty-five. And that was twenty years ago."

Faith shifted toward her sister, placing her back to their mother. "I realize that, Sammie, but we have no way of knowing what to expect of Mom's health. She could rip through her entire savings as fast as this fire is burning through the market."

"But—"

Eli approached them, putting an end to their discussion for the moment. He gave Faith a peck on the cheek. "I don't know what to say, other than I'm sorry."

Faith swiped at her eyes. "There were a lot of memories in that old building. I'm just thankful no one was hurt."

"That's the most important thing to remember at a time like this." Eli winked at Sam, a reminder for her to stay focused on the positive. She'd suffered a big loss tonight, but it could've been so much worse. He pulled her to her feet. "Let's go home. It won't do any of us any good to stay until the bitter end."

Sam hesitated, knowing it was time to go but not willing to leave, as if her staying could somehow bring about a miracle that would save the market. She felt as though she were saying goodbye to an old friend, as when she'd visited her Uncle Mack in the hospital the night he died.

"I guess you're right," she said finally, and looped her arm through her mother's. "You're coming home with us."

"Oh no I'm not!" Lovie yanked her arm free. "I'm going home to my own bed."

Sam sighed. She knew better than to argue with her mother in her current state of mind. "Then Eli and I will drive you home. Where's your car? I'll bring it to you tomorrow."

Sam followed her mother's finger to the burning building. Lovie had driven her old Buick right up to her usual parking spot at the back door as though reporting for work. Sam viewed this as evidence that her mother had arrived before the fire was in full blaze. Once metallic blue in color, the sedan was now charred black. Sam and her sisters had worried for years about their mother's driving, but they'd had no concrete reason to take away her license until now. The fire's destruction of the car solved that problem while presenting yet another. Sam and Faith would now be at the beck and call of their active mother, a woman accustomed to coming and going at will. Lovie would not take kindly to having this major change of lifestyle forced upon her. It would cramp Sam's style as well. Then again, now that she no longer had a workplace to go to every day, what else did she have to do?

Sam said goodbye to her sister and climbed in the back seat beside her mother. She watched out the back window as the blaze disappeared. Captain Sweeney's Seafood Market was no more.

She waited until they were out of sight of the market before she said, "Tonight has been hard on all of us, Mama. Let's pack up some of your things, and you can come stay with Eli and me for a few days."

Lovie pinned Sam against the seat with her death glare. "I told you, Samantha. I'm going home to my husband, and I don't want to hear another word about it."

Sam studied her mother's face through the darkness. The steely determination she hadn't seen in years, if not decades, was apparent in the firm set of Lovie's chin and the defiant look in her hazel eyes. *I'm going home to my husband?* She was no longer dreaming about Oscar. She spoke as if she expected him to be waiting for her at her front door.

When Eli pulled up in front of Lovie's town house, Sam hurried around to her mother's side of the car. She opened the door, but when she offered her hand, Lovie brushed it away and marched toward the town house. Sam followed her up the brick steps. "Is there anything I can say to change your mind? I would feel better if you stayed with us, at least for the night."

"Stop your fussing now." Lovie inserted her key in the lock. "Your father is inside waiting for his supper. Run along home to Allen. I'm sure your husband is wondering where on earth you are."

Allen? Sam's heart skipped a beat. She'd never married Jamie's father, and even if she had, he'd died of liver cancer the summer before last. And what about Eli? Lovie adored him. She'd just ridden home in the car with him, for crying out loud.

"Fine, Mom. But I'm going to call you when I get home, and you'd better pick up."

Lovie slammed the door on her in response.

"I don't feel right about leaving her alone," she said to Eli when she got back in the car. "She's seriously lost it this time. She won't even let me in the house. She thinks my dad is inside waiting for her."

"Your mom's a tough old bird," Eli said, putting the car in reverse. "She'll be fine in the morning."

"I can't take that chance," Sam said. "Drop me off at home. I'll get my car and come back. I'll sleep in the parking lot if I have to."

"No need to do that." Eli backed the sedan out of the parking space. "I'll have one of the guys drive by periodically to check on her."

Sam thought about the situation and Eli's proposal. "I guess that'll have to do. We both need some sleep." She stared out the window as he pulled back onto Creekside Drive. "I'm worried, Eli. I've never seen her this bad before."

Eli stroked Sam's thigh. "Give her some time, honey. She'll come around."

They rode in silence the rest of the way home. Eli wove through the back streets of town to avoid the market. But no detour could erase the image of the fire from her mind. Just as no amount of detergent, shampoo, and soap could rid her clothes, hair, and skin of the stench of smoke.

"If I didn't know better, I'd think that Curtis was responsible for setting the fire," Sam said as they drove down the long driveway to their bungalow.

Three years ago, when Faith had finally summoned the nerve to leave her abusive husband, Curtis had come after her family with a vengeance. He blamed Sam for breaking up his marriage and went on a rampage, torturing her for weeks on end.

"But you do know better, because Curtis is in prison." Eli put the car in park and killed the engine. "Besides, the fellas are convinced that lightning caused the fire."

"Jared said the same thing. And it makes sense considering the storm we had earlier. But I can't shake this creepy feeling the fire was intentionally set."

Eli tilted her chin and looked deep into her eyes. "Put your overactive imagination back in its cage. There's no point in looking for trouble when there isn't any."

She held his gaze for a long minute before shaking off her concern. "I'm sure you're right. It's been a long night."

He put his arms around her and held her tight. "Lean on me, babe."

As recovering alcoholics, they both instinctively knew when one was close to the breaking point. "Lean on me" was their motto, their way of comforting each other when one of them was in trouble.

She buried her face in his neck. "Believe it or not, I'm more concerned about my mother than the market. I need to stay strong for her, which means staying sober. I'll be fine if I focus on her. I promise my head is in the right place. At least for now. If that changes, you'll be the first to know."

TWO

JAMIE

Jamie's cell phone, beside his face on the desktop, vibrated and startled him out of a sound sleep. He cracked an eyelid and saw his mom's image on the home screen. He fell back against the chair and raked his fingers through his greasy black curls. When was the last time he'd taken a shower? Yesterday? The day before? He stared across the room at the silver-rimmed wall clock that had marked his time for the past three years. Seven o'clock. Was that a.m. or p.m.? He'd spent so much time in the library during the last week, his days and nights were all mixed up.

He picked up the phone. "What day is it, Mom?"

She hesitated as though she didn't know either. "It's Thursday morning."

Right. He'd pulled an all-nighter studying for his last exam. He must have fallen asleep during the last set of accounting problems.

He whispered into the phone, "Why are you calling so early? Did someone die?"

"No, son. It's nothing like that, thank heavens. But I do have some bad news. I wanted you to hear it from me before you saw it on Facebook or Snap whatchamacallit," she said, speaking so fast her words came out all garbled.

"Slow down, Mom. You're not making any sense. I can't really talk right now anyway. I'm in the library, and people are trying to study." He glanced around at the sea of empty desks. "Can I call you back in ten minutes?"

"Sure, honey. But don't forget. This is important."

He stuffed his books and computer into his backpack and took the escalator to the main floor. He stopped by Cooper's Corner to pick up a coffee in the lobby before exiting the building. A chill in the air reminded him it was still spring, even though many of the students had already left campus for the summer. Locating an empty bench near the fountain, he set down his coffee and backpack and tugged his hooded sweatshirt over his head. He stretched out on the bench, propping his head on his backpack, and called his mother back. "Are you better now?"

"Not really, no. I'm sorry to have to tell you this while you're in the middle of exams. There was a fire at the market last night. We lost everything."

Jamie scrambled to sit up without spilling his coffee. "Wait, Mom. I'm not sure I heard you right. Did you just say that our market, Captain Sweeney's Seafood, burned to the ground last night?"

Her voice sounded choked. "Yes, son, that's exactly what I said."

Jamie thought about the artifacts that had hung on the walls marking decades of the family's business. "Were they able to save anything?"

"I don't know. I'll have to sift through the rubble today."

"What about Gran's recipe box? Please tell me it was locked in the fire safe." Jamie held his breath when his mother hesitated, envisioning her pinching her lower lip. Those recipes were the foundation on which his grandmother had built the business. Some she shared with customers, others she didn't.

"That's a good question, now that you mention it. Roberto had the box out yesterday. I hope he put it back in the safe when he locked up last night."

He got off the bench and began pacing in tight circles. "What caused the fire? Do they know?"

"Lightning, most likely, although we won't know for sure until the firemen conduct their investigation."

He heard a loud slurp coming from the other end of the line. "Are you okay, Mom? You're not drinking, are you?"

"As a matter of fact, I am. I'm drinking coffee, and I've had way too much. I'm pretty strung out between being up half the night and the caffeine. As for me drinking anything stronger than coffee, you have nothing to worry about."

"Good." He let out a deep breath. "I'm going to hold you to it." His mother had been sober for nearly two years, but he worried constantly that something would set her off. "We have insurance for this kind of thing, don't we? I mean, we're going to rebuild, right?"

"I wish it were that easy, Jamie. We have the loss of income to consider, and there's no guarantee the insurance will cover the full cost of construction. We may have to raise money from another source. We can count Faith out since she's retiring. And your grandmother . . . Well, Lovie had another one of her spells last night, the worst one yet. I'm afraid her days of working at Sweeney's are in the past."

Jamie felt an aching in his chest. "Is Gran gonna be okay?"

"I honestly don't know. Time will tell. But even if she snaps out of it, I wouldn't feel right asking her to invest. She has her health to consider. She needs to save her money. She may be facing a long stay in a nursing home."

"Don't give up on her yet. She's a trouper. She'll bounce back." Jamie dropped down to the bench as the repercussions of the situation hit home. "I guess I'm out of a job for the summer. Hell, I'm out of a career if we don't rebuild."

"In the short term, the Pelican's Roost may have something. They always beef up their staff during the summer months. You've done well for yourself, Jamie, with a near-perfect GPA in a field that makes you highly marketable, not only in the restaurant business but in the hotel industry as well. If we decide not to reopen, you may have to move to Charleston to find a position that is suited for you, but that's right up the road."

Jamie got to his feet and slung his backpack over his shoulder. "I'm not moving to Charleston, Mom." He dumped his coffee in a nearby trash can and set off toward Sumter Street. "I've told you this a million times. I have no burning desire to discover the world. Prospect is where I plan to live. End of discussion."

"Calm down, sweetheart. I was merely pointing out that you have choices."

The sound of Jamie's heavy breathing filled the line as he hustled his way across campus.

"All this can wait until you get home," Sam said. "For now you need to concentrate on your exams."

The sadness in his mother's voice tugged at his heartstrings. The family business meant everything to her. "I love you, Mom, and I'm sorry about Sweeney's. I'll be home sometime late tomorrow afternoon, maybe sooner depending on how long it will take me to move out of my dorm. We'll grill out and have a long talk over dinner. We'll put our heads together and figure out a plan."

Jamie ended the call and pocketed his phone. He took a left onto Williams Street and walked down a block to Founders Park, where he often sought refuge when he needed a break from studying or to clear his head. He'd come to the University of South Carolina on a baseball scholarship, and had played the best baseball of his career during the spring season of his sophomore year. The following September, this past fall, he'd resigned from the team. The decision to quit had not come easy, but his determination to graduate early, in December of his senior year instead of May, necessitated an insane number of hours each semester. Ultimately the rigorous demands of his academics had taken priority. Baseball had played a major role in his life and he missed the camaraderie with his teammates as well as the physical activity. He still worked out four or five times a week in the campus fitness center, lifting weights and running on the treadmill, but he didn't get the same satisfaction as he did when training for a sport.

Jamie entered the stadium and sat down on the bleachers near the dugout behind home plate. The team was having batting practice, and the pitcher who had taken Jamie's starting position appeared to be doing an okay job. A sophomore from Greenville, South Carolina, Tomas was likable and coachable. Jamie had offered him suggestions that had improved his pitch.

George Hodges, Jamie's favorite coach, slid onto the bleacher beside him. "You're here early. Something on your mind?"

Coach Hodges had lent a sympathetic ear when Jamie was struggling with his decision to quit the team. The coach's counsel had convinced Jamie to follow his heart. "Your career and your family are what matter. Down the road twenty years, baseball will be a dim memory."

Jamie hung his head. "My mom called. Our family business burned to the ground last night."

"Oh man. I'm so sorry to hear that." Hodges laid a hand on his shoulder and squeezed. "I know how much that place means to you. Will you be able to rebuild?"

"I'm not sure. A lot depends on the insurance company."

"I have faith in you, Jamie. I've rarely known someone as passionate as you are about your future. You believe in yourself and you believe in your family. You'll find a way to rebuild."

Jamie's head shot up. "Do you really think so?"

"Hell yes, I think so. I know so." Coach huddled up close to

Jamie. "I have a saying that I tell my own children. When life throws you a curveball, you stay focused and hit the ball out of the park. Don't look at this as a setback. Look at it as an opportunity to make your business bigger and better than before."

"Thanks, Coach. I really needed to hear that," Jamie said, feeling a glimmer of hope for the first time since hearing the news from his mom.

"You're welcome, son. You come talk to me anytime about anything."

For the next few minutes they discussed the team's potential for success in the upcoming playoffs. Coach eventually excused himself and returned to the field to help a player who was struggling with his swing.

Jamie's cell phone vibrated in his pocket, and he was surprised to see Annie's name on the caller ID. "Long time no hear, sis!" he said, even though she was technically his half sister. "How are things in New York?"

Annie giggled. "I wouldn't know. I'm back in Charleston now."

"What happened to traveling the world and studying under the top chefs?"

"Nine months of living in the Big Apple cured me of that. Why follow someone else's path when I can chart my own course?"

Her words hit close to home. "I applaud that mentality and enthusiasm."

"I'm glad I went, though," Annie said. "The experience was amazing. I learned all the skills I need at the culinary institute. The rest, the creative part, is up to me."

"Are you planning to stay in Charleston?"

"I think so. Heidi needs me here. Her business has taken off like you wouldn't believe."

The excitement in her voice brought a smile to his face. "Sounds like the two of you are getting along well."

"We are, Jamie. Heidi and I make a good team."

Annie and Jamie shared the same father. Jamie's mother had been engaged to Allen, but he left her at the altar when he found out she was pregnant with Jamie. When his next girlfriend, Heidi, found herself in the same predicament, Allen decided to stick around and help raise the kid. Six months after he married her, she headed for Hollywood, leaving him to raise their baby girl, Annie. But Heidi never became the movie star she'd always hoped to be. She became a caterer to the stars instead.

Brother and sister had met for the first time two summers earlier, when Annie came to Prospect desperate for the slice of Jamie's liver needed to save their father's life. But Allen died before the doctors could arrange the transplant. The one positive outcome of the sad situation was learning about and connecting with his only sibling. When Heidi moved to Charleston from California six months later, she used their shared love of food to try to worm her way into her daughter's heart. Annie had been neither accepting nor forgiving of this woman who had abandoned her as a baby. It had taken a near-death experience before she was willing to give her mother a chance.

"I saw the fire at Sweeney's on Instagram just now," Annie said. "I'm so sorry for your family. Do you know what happened?"

"A lightning strike. At least it looks that way."

"How long will it take to rebuild?"

"You mean *if* we decide to go that route. Mom's freaking out on me." Jamie told Annie about his conversation with Sam.

"I wouldn't worry too much. Sam without Sweeney's is like a schizophrenic without her meds. I know your mom. She'll lose her mind without a job to go to every day. And I don't mean any job. I mean her life's work, her pride and joy. She needs that seafood market like she needs air to breathe."

He chuckled. "I hope you're right."

"When are you done with exams?" Annie asked.

"Today. I'm packing up tonight and heading home tomorrow sometime."

"If I can get away, I'd love to drive down and see your family. Can you pencil me in for lunch on Monday?"

"It's a date."

THREE

JACKIE

Jackie looked out across her backyard from the second-story bedroom window of her house on Lamboll Street in downtown Charleston. She watched her young designers, Liza and Cecilia, transport lamps, rugs, and other accessories from her design studio to their delivery truck in preparation for a large installation later that morning. Jackie was on edge about the project. She'd spent a large amount of her client's money based on a few photographs torn from a magazine. She usually interacted more with clients when decorating an entire house, but Ellie Hagood seemed content to let Jackie make all the choices. What if Ellie wasn't satisfied? Would Jackie be forced to eat a percentage of her profits? She couldn't bring herself to think about that now.

Her eyes roamed across her courtyard garden to her pool, where two blue jays splashed about in the water. Leaves and other debris floated on the surface of the pool from last night's storm. Lightning had caused her power to go out and stay out for most of the night. But she'd fared well in Charleston compared to her family in Prospect. She envisioned the seafood market ablaze while her sisters and mother watched in helpless despair. She'd never cared much for the business, but Captain Sweeney's was the heart and soul of her family. She respected how hard her mother and sisters worked, and applauded Sam for the steps she'd taken to expand the business into an upscale market that offered everything from raw oysters and clams to salmon cakes. If Sam kept her head together and didn't hit the bottle, she would succeed in rebuilding.

Even more concerning to Jackie was her mother's current mental state. Most days, Lovie seemed normal. But Jackie had been warning her sisters for years that her condition would change, that their mother would slip into a state of confusion and never return. They'd done nothing to prepare for that eventuality. Her sisters had been furious when, several years back, Jackie had taken Lovie to visit the Hermitage Retirement Community in Charleston. She'd even offered to make the deposit required for placement on the waiting list. If they'd followed through then, Lovie would now be tucked away in a nice apartment in independent living with a straight and narrow path across the property to assisted living or the memory care unit when the time came. But her sisters had been adamant that Charleston was too far away for everyday visits. At the time the only retirement facility in Prospect had been a nursing home with none of the amenities the Hermitage offered.

She'd arranged her summer schedule to spend two days of the workweek in Charleston as opposed to the usual five. Although cutting back her hours troubled her, the additional time would give her the opportunity to help her sisters assess their mother's mental state and make decisions regarding her future. She'd already planned to do the same for her son, but for very different reasons. So much for empty nesting. This was not the life of freedom she'd anticipated when she'd shipped her twin boys off for their freshman year in college.

Cooper was thriving at Virginia Commonwealth University. He was fully engaged in his studies, and his grades reflected his enthusiasm. He planned to stay in Richmond for the summer to work as an intern at a boutique marketing agency. While one twin seemed on track for a career in graphic design, the other was floundering at the University of Georgia. At least as far as academics were concerned. Sean was plenty successful in his frat boy social life. Jackie was beginning to think she'd made a mistake in encouraging him to attend her alma mater. In hindsight, a school with a population of nearly thirty thousand, where the students were not held accountable for attending classes, had probably not been the right choice for a small-town boy. He'd dropped one class his first semester and barely passed the other four. She had no idea what to expect of his second semester's grades. After weeks of trying, she'd finally gotten in touch with his adviser late yesterday afternoon.

Professor Paul had spoken frankly with her. "I'll tell you like I told Sean, Mrs. Hart. He will have to perform miracles on all of his exams to pass any of his courses this semester. Prepare yourself. In all likelihood your son will not be invited back next term."

Jackie had known things were bad, but not this bad. "You mean he's going to flunk out?"

"That's precisely what I mean."

Jackie had hung up and immediately called Sean. She'd threatened him with everything she could think of, including taking away his car and making him reimburse them for the wasted tuition, but based on his hostile tone, it was already too late. She would whip him back into shape in no time. He needed some direction in his life, and she aimed to help him find it. The sooner the better in order for her to continue building her career. She loved her family. She'd devoted two decades of her life to raising her sons. But now it was her turn. She resented this intrusion. She was in her prime, hitting her stride professionally, and she had a lot of living left to do.

She changed out of her cashmere bathrobe into a crisp white

blouse, khaki pencil skirt, and wedges—casual attire suited for the work ahead. Her doorbell sounded promptly at nine as she was zipping up her cosmetics bag. She kept her work wardrobe, plus a few outfits appropriate for business dinners, at her house in Charleston and the rest of her clothes at Moss Creek Farm, her waterfront estate in Prospect. After she finished with her installation, she would drive to the farm and cook dinner for her husband. They needed to discuss the consequences of their son's poor academic performance in advance of his arrival home from college the next day.

She dropped her cosmetics bag into her Louis Vuitton tote and hurried down to open the door. Jackie's federal-style home had unofficially been on the market for months. She hadn't bothered to consult her Realtor, and the only marketing she'd done was through word of mouth. She'd received several full-price offers, but had rejected them all. She wanted buyers who appreciated the house's historical significance and could afford the upkeep. She'd purchased the house as a project, never intending to fall in love with it. She'd restored it with the help of her detail-oriented contractor, Hugh Kelley, and then filled it with antiques she'd selected herself. The carriage house had provided the ideal space to launch her fledgling interior design business, while the main house had showcased her work to potential clients she'd entertained with cocktail parties and elaborate sit-down dinners. But the main house had more space than she needed now, and her business had outgrown the carriage house. In search of a solution, she'd found a single house on Church Street that needed a loving touch, and a converted warehouse on Meeting Street that would be ideal for her showroom.

Jackie was surprised at how young the potential buyers appeared, but judging from the size of the diamond on Catherine Doyle's hand, they could afford her asking price. She invited them in and conducted the tour.

"Have a look around," she said when the tour concluded in

the master bedroom. "I'll be downstairs in the kitchen if you have any questions."

She was finishing her coffee thirty minutes later when they sought her out. "We're serious about making an offer," Catherine Doyle said. "How serious are you about selling? We've heard—"

"I'm aware of the gossip," Jackie said. "I told you on the phone, the house isn't officially on the market. With that said, I have a couple of new projects in mind. The time has come for me to move on. If you make me your best offer, I promise to consider it in good faith."

"Would you be interested in selling the furnishings?" Catherine asked.

Jackie lifted her gaze to the ceiling as she thought about it. "Perhaps. There are a few pieces I won't part with. But be aware that would drive the price up significantly. There are some priceless antiques in here."

The couple seemed satisfied with her answer. "We'll be in touch," Hank Doyle said when she showed them out.

Jackie took her time locking up, contemplating which pieces she'd keep as she walked from room to room. On her way to the installation, she drove by the single house for sale on Church Street. Her Realtor had shown her the house on Monday, and she'd driven by it numerous times since then. The house had real potential. She would need to act on it soon before someone else snatched it up. Her stomach churned with excitement over the prospect of starting a new project.

She was surprised and disappointed upon arrival at the installation site on South Battery to find that her client was away. Most of Jackie's clients supervised every last detail of an installation.

"Ellie's gone down to her studio," Liza explained. "She asked us to call her when we're finished. She doesn't want to watch it come together piece by piece. She prefers the wow factor of seeing the finished product all at once."

"*Wow* is definitely the response I'm hoping for," Jackie mumbled.

She walked from room to room, marveling at her choices of fabrics and carpeting and wall coverings. A stunning Turkish Oriental in shades of coral and blue greeted guests at the door in the center hallway, while contemporary furniture in shades of gray set a comfortable yet elegant tone in the living room. But the most dramatic transformation had taken place in the library —Ellie's architect husband's study. An antelope carpet on the floor and neutral fabrics in shades of beige and khaki on the furniture and drapes accented the wood paneling and transitioned the room from the dark dungeon it had once been to a bright and inviting space.

Jackie, though eager to get on the road to Prospect, refused to leave until Ellie got there. The expression on her face when Ellie saw her new rooms was worth the wait.

"I must admit, I've been nervous about your reaction," Jackie said. "I typically have more input from clients when decorating their homes."

Ellie Hagood nodded her pretty auburn head. "I had reason to give you carte blanche. You're the expert. As an artist, I wouldn't want anyone telling me what or how to paint. I decided to give you a blank canvas and let you do your thing."

Jackie agreed with her logic. "I'm just glad you like the result. We'd be having a very different conversation if you hadn't." She pressed her cheek against Ellie's in parting and hurried out to her SUV.

She navigated the midday traffic downtown and was crossing the Ashley River Bridge when her phone lit up with a call from Sean. His sobs filled the line when she answered, causing her heart to race.

"Sean! What is it, son?"

"I've been arrested, Mom. I need you to come bail me out."

FOUR

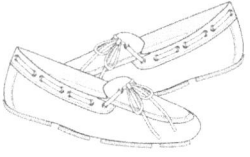

SAM

Sam and Eli's bungalow was small but charming, with views of the inlet from every room. The first floor featured a master suite, upscale kitchen, and main room with an area for lounging by one of two stone fireplaces and a section designated for dining by a wall of windows overlooking the water. Two small bedrooms and a shared bath occupied the upstairs, where Jamie slept when he was home. Even though they would be tripping all over one another in the cramped space, Sam was looking forward to having her only child home for the summer. The days of Jamie living under her roof were numbered. When he graduated in December, he would move out of the house for good and into an apartment of his own. Whether he would have a job to pay for that apartment had yet to be determined.

Sam had never considered her son's living anywhere else. He'd always been determined to return to Prospect. And she'd never discouraged him. Since he was a tiny boy, she'd dreamed of having him by her side at Sweeney's. Had she done the wrong thing by not encouraging him to spread his wings? He was too young to understand what he was missing out on. This was his one chance to explore the world and discover something of himself in the process. His course was his own to chart. If he never came home again, she'd deal with it. Best case scenario, he'd move to Charleston. With historic inns and five-star dining, Charleston was the heart of tourism in the Lowcountry. And it was only forty-five minutes up the road.

She paced the heart pine floorboards from one room to the next. She was worried about her mother, who wasn't answering her calls. Sam was distressed about the fire and knew she would go stark raving mad without a way to fill her days. Maybe she'd take up a sport. Tennis, perhaps. Wouldn't Eli love to see her legs in one of those little skirts? Although golf was probably a better choice. Golf required more time—four hours for eighteen holes. She mentally slapped herself. Who was she kidding? She wouldn't be happy if she wasn't earning money. And too much idle time was risky for a recovering alcoholic. She was resourceful, organized, and creative. She could do something entirely different. At nearly fifty-one, was she too old to start over? If her sister could launch a new career at this stage in her life, why couldn't she?

Faith was not fooling anyone. She claimed to be retiring from the market in order to spend more time at home with her daughter and husband. But Bitsy, Faith's nine-year-old daughter, was in school all day, and Mike, an emergency room physician, worked long hours at the hospital. Sam had known for some time that her sister wasn't happy at Sweeney's, and sensed Faith was searching for a way to fill an emptiness inside herself. She had never fully recovered from her abusive marriage, and having more children didn't appear to be in the cards. Sam believed her sister might discover her passion by working with abused women, but Faith needed to come to that conclusion on her own.

Why not start a new business? I could do something out of my home, Sam thought. What about catering? Takeout catering had occupied a huge segment of the market's business in recent years. And her kitchen was her best asset, with its commercial-grade appliances and miles of granite countertops. The wheels in her head began to spin. If Annie and Heidi could be successful at catering, so could she. But she would first need to find her mother's secret recipes.

As she started for the door, she caught a glimpse of herself in the mirror. Her eyes were red rimmed and bloodshot from smoke and fatigue, and she had yet to change out of her pajamas. She dropped her bag on the floor by the door and went to her room to shower. She left the house fifteen minutes later, face shiny and hair still wet, dressed in a pair of denim shorts and a moss-green Captain Sweeney's polo.

As she headed up Creekside Drive, she placed a call to Roberto, the middle-aged Mexican man in charge of Sweeney's kitchen. They talked briefly about the fire, and he offered to help her any way he could in rebuilding.

"Honestly, Roberto, I haven't decided whether to rebuild or not. There are a lot of obstacles to consider, one being Mom's recipes. I know you had her box out yesterday afternoon when you were looking for her conch salad recipe. Do you remember whether you put it back in the safe?"

Silence filled the line. "There's a good chance that I didn't, although I'm not absolutely positive. I'm so sorry, Sam."

Sam sighed. "I don't want you to worry about this, Roberto. You had no way of knowing the place was going to burn down."

The police had taped off what remained of the building and the adjacent parking lot. Sam parked at the marina and jogged across the street. She stood at the tape and stared into the black hole of burned debris. The acrid stench of smoke hung in the air. The brass ship's clock that had hung over the front door, marking the decades since 1959, lay half-melted in a pile of ash. This time yesterday, she had been opening the front door to the line of customers waiting patiently outside. Twenty-four hours later, she no longer had a door to open or merchandise to sell.

She thought about the customers she'd served over the years, folks from all over the state who'd shopped with them year after year on their annual pilgrimage to the beach and locals who stopped in several times a week to share a tidbit of gossip while they purchased a salad for lunch or a pound of crabmeat for dinner. She was too lost in the past to hear someone calling her name until Donna Bennett appeared in front of her. A young reporter with a microphone stood behind Donna.

"I'm not buying whatever you're selling," Sam said and returned her attention to the rubble.

Several years ago, Donna had published a scalding review in her family's tabloid newspaper, *Prospect Weekly*, that referred to the recent renovations at Sweeney's as "Too Uptown for Small Town." The article had brought a screeching halt to their business a week after their grand reopening. Fortunately, Eli had arranged an interview with a friend of his at *Lowcountry Living*, a monthly magazine out of Charleston that carried more influence with a larger readership. Janie Jasper's glowing review saved Captain Sweeney's from bankruptcy.

"No need to be rude, Samantha. I'll only take a moment of your time. As you know, I pride myself on being fair. I'd like to give you a chance to comment on the rumors circulating around town. My sources tell me that you are responsible for starting the fire."

Sam's head jerked up. "Are you out of your mind?"

The young woman shoved the microphone at her.

"Get that thing out of my face!" Sam snarled.

Donna shooed the reporter away. "Give us a minute, please, Janice."

Janice, who was wearing a red cocktail dress despite the early hour, teetered away on black strappy heels.

"Now, where were we?" Donna tugged her too-tight blouse down over her muffin top. "Are you denying these allegations?"

"What allegations?" Sam leered at her archenemy. She'd known Donna since they were children. For whatever reason, her sister Jackie had chosen Donna as one of her close friends. The mousy little brat had grown into a vindictive bitch. The hate was etched in deep lines around Donna's mouth and eyes, wrinkles no amount of Botox could soften. "Your imagination is working overtime again, Donna. Why on earth would I destroy my family's livelihood on purpose?"

Donna removed a notepad from her gaudy Chanel tote. "Sources say your business is in trouble," she said, reading from the pad. "That you burned the place down in order to get the insurance money so you can retire."

"Read your insurance policy, Donna. Standard provisions exclude fires caused by arson when the person who set the fire is a beneficiary of the policy." Sam's tone matched her flaring temper. "I fully expect the investigation will prove that lightning caused the fire. Now get off of my property."

Donna glanced down at her feet. "The city owns the sidewalk, Samantha. I have every right to be here."

A fire department SUV with Jared at the wheel turned into Sweeney's parking lot. He'd changed out of his fireman's uniform into navy chinos and a gray knit shirt with his fireman's shield pinned to his chest. He clunked over to them in his size-twelve work boots. "Is there a problem here, ladies?"

"Yes, as a matter of fact there is," Sam said, fists clinched at her sides. "Tabloid Tracey here is looking for a story. She's got it in her deranged mind that arson was involved, that I'm the one who started the fire."

"If not you, maybe your loony tunes mother is responsible," Donna said. "Rumor has it she's gone off her rocker again."

Sam looked at Jared for help. "Will you please set her straight?"

"Unfortunately, I'm not able to discuss an ongoing investigation," Jared said. "Out of respect for the Sweeney family, I'll ask you not to print anything in your paper or spread gossip around town until we report our findings."

Heat rushed to Sam's face. Jared had done little to dispel

Donna's accusations. Last night he'd seemed convinced that lightning had started the fire.

"Will you hold a press conference when you conclude your investigation?" Donna asked.

"This is a small town, Donna," Jared said, a smile of amusement on his thin lips. "We don't hold press conferences in Prospect."

Donna pressed him. "When can I expect a statement from your department?"

"Whenever we have one." He tipped his hat to her. "Good day now."

Donna stuffed her notebook back in her bag and stormed off in a huff.

Jared turned his lanky frame to Sam. "Did you get any sleep?"

"I didn't even try." She nodded at the three-drawer fire safe, the lone tower among the ruins. "It's a good thing we purchased the heavy-duty safe. Can you help me get some things out of it?"

"Technically, since this is a crime scene, I'm not supposed to. What is it that you need?"

"My mother's wooden recipe box is the most important thing. You'll know it when you see it. It should be near the front of the bottom drawer. I also need a file labeled 'Insurance' and the black checkbook binder. You'll find those in the middle drawer."

"The Insurance file is the only thing I can see that would be a problem. And since the Insurance company has copies of the policy . . . Let me get my gloves out of the truck."

While he went to his SUV for his gloves, she ducked under the yellow tape and wandered over to her mother's car. The metal was scorched, the tires flat, and all the windows blown out.

Jared joined her a minute later, tugging on his gloves. "I'm sorry, Sam. The car's a goner."

"Whatever. We've been looking for an excuse to get Mom off the road."

He held his gloved hand out to her. "Do you have the key to the safe?"

She flipped through her ring until she found a medium-size square silver key.

He eyed her boat shoes. "You'll have to wait here."

Stepping through the debris, he unlocked the safe and searched through the drawers. He returned with the insurance file and checkbook.

"You didn't see the recipe box?"

He shook his head. "I'm sorry. I imagine those recipes are vital to your business."

Her eyes frantically searched the rubble. "Do you mind looking around on the ground on the other side of the building near the back? The box was wooden and the cards paper. I'm sure it was destroyed, but just in case by some miracle . . ."

"Of course."

She watched as he kicked through the debris in and around the kitchen area. He gave up after ten minutes. "I'm sorry, Sam. I don't see any signs of it."

She felt sick to her stomach. Lovie knew most of her recipes by heart. The question was whether she could remember them in her current state of mind. "Thanks for trying."

"I can have some of the guys bring the safe to your house this afternoon," Jared said.

"That would be great. They can put it in the garage. I'll leave the side door open for them."

Sam held the file and checkbook to her chest as they walked together toward the front of the lot.

"I'm glad I ran into you, Sam. I was going to call you this afternoon. We've turned the investigation over to the police. For obvious reasons, I didn't want to say this in front of Donna, but we're almost certain arson was involved. We found two containers of gasoline in the dumpster." He waved his hand at the big green dumpster beside her mother's car. "Heavy duty or not, I'm surprised your safe survived. It appears that area is where the fire started."

Sam collapsed against his SUV. "I don't understand why someone would do something like that." She thought about her encounter with Donna. "Unless someone did it out of vengeance, like Donna Bennett. She's had it in for my family for a long time."

He removed an index card from his pocket and scribbled Donna's name on it. "I'll look into it. But you should know your mother is our primary suspect."

Sam's mouth fell open. "That's absurd! Captain Sweeney's means more to her than her own children. What motive could she possibly have to destroy it?"

"I can't answer that. But we can't ignore the fact that she was already at the scene when we arrived. She was talking out of her head. Some are suggesting that she was confused and didn't realize what she was doing."

Jared's cell phone rang, and he removed it from the clip on his belt. "Rhodes." He listened for a minute and said, "I understand," and hung up. He returned the phone to his belt clip. "That was the chief. The police are on the way to question your mother now. Have you spoken with her this morning?"

Sam stared at him wide-eyed. "She's not answering her phone."

He squeezed her elbow. "You should probably get over there. Whatever you do, don't let them question her if she's confused like she was last night."

As she hustled across the street to her car, Sam called Faith and explained the situation.

"I'll meet you there," Faith said. "Mike came home from the hospital for lunch. I'll bring him with me to gauge Mom's mental stability."

Sam hung up with her sister and tapped Eli's number.

"I've just been made aware of the situation," he said. "Because of my relationship with your mother, I've recused myself from the case. But I promise to make sure we handle it by the book. I won't lie, honey. It doesn't look good for her."

"The whole thing is ridiculous, Eli. She has no motive."

"She was not in her right mind last night. You saw it. I saw it. The whole fire department and half of my coworkers saw it."

"Regardless of her state of mind, no little old lady is capable of filling two containers with gasoline and setting fire to a building." Sam made a right-hand turn into her mother's complex and saw patrol cars parked haphazardly in front of Lovie's town house. "Get over here, Eli." She counted the cars. "There are five units here."

"I'm a mile away. Wait for me out front."

"Like hell I will," Sam said, and hurled her phone to the passenger side floorboard. She slammed her car in park in the middle of the lot and jumped out of her Jeep. She stomped up the front steps and through the town house to the sunroom out back. Her mother was cowering on the sofa, surrounded by a half-dozen policemen. She wore the same dirty nightgown as the night before, and her face was still smeared with soot. Sam barged through the uniforms. "Leave her alone! Can't you see you're scaring her? What are you thinking, badgering an old woman like this?"

A rookie officer Sam had never seen before stepped forward. "She's our primary suspect in an arson case, ma'am. We have no choice but to question her."

"Who the hell are you?" she asked, staring him down. She felt certain he had a pea brain to match his tiny head.

"Officer Goodall, ma'am," he said with a salute. "And who the hell are you?"

Eli entered the room. "She's my wife. That's who the hell she is."

Officer Goodall gulped, causing his Adam's apple to bulge. "Sorry, Detective."

"You damn well better be," Eli said. "Where is Detective Brunson? He's the one assigned to the case, and the only one who should be questioning Mrs. Sweeney right now."

One of the officers sitting beside her mother stood to face Eli. "Brunson sent us here to bring her in."

Eli pointed at the door. "Well, I'm ordering all of you to get out of here right now."

The five of them departed the room in a single file.

Eli called after them, "Tell Detective Brunson, if he wants to question Mrs. Sweeney, he may do so in her home. And only when I'm present."

Sam and Eli sat down on the sofa on either side of Lovie. "Are you okay, Mom?"

Eli drew his mother-in-law close. "I'm so sorry, Lovie. I'll make sure that doesn't happen again."

Lovie's teeth chattered and her body trembled and her words were incoherent when they tumbled out of her mouth.

"Shh." Sam stroked her mother's leg through her nightgown. "It's all right now." She removed the wool afghan from the back of the sofa and draped it around her shoulders.

By the time Faith and Mike arrived, ten minutes later, Lovie's breathing had evened out.

Mike sat down on the edge of the coffee table in front of Lovie. "Hey there, sweetheart," he said, placing his hands on her knees. "We're having a tough day, aren't we?"

She stared back at him, but no words came out of her mouth.

"Can you tell me what happened last night before the fire?"

She shook her head.

"Do you remember anything at all about the fire?"

She shook her head again.

"Can you tell me your name?"

"Louvenia Spencer Sweeney," she mumbled.

"And who's the president of the United States?"

"The man with the funny hair," Lovie said, patting herself on the head. "Donald Trump."

They all giggled and let out a collective sigh of relief.

Mike straightened. "She should definitely not be talking to the police right now. And I don't recommend her staying here alone until she feels more like herself."

"She can stay with me," Sam and Faith said at the same time.

"Why don't y'all talk about this in the other room?" Mike said, cutting his eyes at Lovie.

The sisters went to the kitchen, where, after several minutes of intense discussion, Faith won, arguing that it made the most sense for Lovie to stay where Mike could observe her behavior. Sam was secretly relieved. In addition to the challenges her small house presented, her mother, in her current mental state, would need full-time supervision. Sam had tried to be everything to everybody once. As a result she'd lost her way and found herself in a bottle of booze. She would not let that happen again.

FIVE

FAITH

Mike went with Eli to pick up sandwiches while Sam and Faith helped their mother pack some of her things and clean out the refrigerator. Sam then went ahead in her Jeep, and Faith followed with their mother. As Faith pulled away from Lovie's town house, she saw a single tear slide down her mother's cheek. Lovie knew without having to be told—her days of independent living were over.

Faith tried to carry on a conversation on their way back to town, but when it became clear that it would be one-sided, she allowed her thoughts to wander. She didn't mind Lovie staying with them for a while. Taking care of her loved ones made her feel needed. She'd always wanted a big family, but she was never able to have more children after a difficult pregnancy and delivery with Bitsy. Not that she'd have cared to have any more of Curtis's children. Protecting one child from an abusive father was enough. She and Mike had talked about adoption. They were even working with an agency. But the wait was long, and their chances seemed smaller and smaller with each passing day. She would turn forty-five next month. No adoption agency in its right mind would give her a baby. Mike remained hopeful that he'd come across a situation in the emergency room—a pregnant teenager interested in finding a good home for her baby—but Faith considered that a long shot.

Faith watched for her mother's reaction to the burned-out building when they drove past the market. With her eyes glued to the windshield and her expression impassive, Lovie neither flinched nor cried nor uttered a word. Faith wondered what thoughts were running through her mother's mind.

As much as she liked working at the market, Faith didn't love it the way her mother, sister, and nephew loved it. Which was why she'd decided to let Jamie take over her duties. After graduating from high school, she'd taken a few accounting classes at the local community college. She'd learned enough to manage the finances at the market, but not enough to get a job in an accounting firm. She was good at it, but bookkeeping wasn't her passion. Whatever that was had thus far eluded her. She yearned to make a difference in the world. She'd thought about becoming a nurse but been intimidated by the entrance requirements for study. She'd tried writing a romance novel but had trouble organizing her thoughts. She continued to explore her options, hoping that something or someone would inspire her.

When they arrived home, Sam unloaded the suitcases from the car while Faith helped her mother out of her soiled gown and into the shower. Once the guys arrived, Sam joined them in the kitchen to help prepare lunch. Faith was arranging her mother's things in the chest of drawers and closet when Lovie emerged from the bathroom in her robe. She went straight to the bed and turned down the covers.

"I know you're tired, Mom, but you'll sleep better if you eat something first."

"I'm not hungry," Lovie mumbled as she slipped between the sheets.

"I'll bring you a sandwich anyway, in case you change your mind." When Faith came back with the lunch tray five minutes later, her mother was sound asleep, snoring softly with her mouth wide open. She left the tray on the nightstand, closed the blinds, and turned out the light.

Faith returned to the kitchen for a pitcher of sweet tea and four glasses before joining the others at the table on the screened porch. "Mom is zonked. She'll probably sleep all afternoon."

She relaxed in her chair and drew in a deep breath of salty air. The sun shone bright in the periwinkle sky, its rays glistening off the water. The weather was perfect for taking a long walk or working in her yard. Tomorrow morning she would take her mother to the garden center and purchase some annuals for her containers.

Faith never tired of looking at the marsh, not after years of living with Curtis in a ramshackle trailer in the woods. Their house on the inlet was nothing fancy. Built ten years earlier, with gray HardiePlank siding, black shutters, and a red front door, the craftsman-style home was set off Creekside Drive on a wooded lot, offering privacy from their neighbors on either side. A center hallway split the single-story home, with three bedrooms on one side, and family room, dining room, kitchen, and breakfast room on the other. The porch stretched across the back of the house above a walkout basement that provided storage space for Mike's fishing and hunting gear.

She removed a pastrami and Swiss on rye from the tray. "Do the police really have a case against Mom?"

"It looks that way," Eli said, spreading Dijon mustard on his ham and cheese. "The first responders confirmed that she was already at the market when they arrived. It would help our case if you can prove the market was in good financial standing."

"The desktop computer was destroyed in the fire," Sam said.

Faith pointed her sandwich at Sam. "But the files are backed up to the cloud. I can access them from any computer."

"Great," Eli said. "Print a copy for me so I'll have them if I need them."

"You need to bring Donna Bennett in for questioning," Sam said. "If anyone in this town would do something like this, it's Donna. She hates our family."

"She hates you, Sam, not our family," Faith said and popped a chip into her mouth.

Mike furrowed his sandy brow. "Who is Donna Bennett?"

Sam set her vegetarian sandwich down on her plate. "Remember Christmas before last, when Jamie brought that awful girl, Sophia, home for the holidays, and you had to make a house call when she got drunk out of her mind?"

"I remember," Mike said. "That was right before your wedding. But what does this Donna Bennett person have to do with that?"

"Donna went to New York that week and left her children at home alone. Her daughter, Rachel, was Sophia's sorority sister at USC. They had a raging party in her mother's absence, hence the reason for your house call."

Mike nodded. "Go on."

"A couple of nights later, Donna's younger child overdosed on cocaine supplied by Sophia and Rachel. The poor kid nearly died. Donna blames Jamie, even though he wasn't at the party that night."

"Didn't Donna make some sort of threat to you?" Faith asked.

"It was more of a confrontation than a threat," Sam said. "Bottom line—she holds me responsible for what happened to her son."

"We'll check her alibi for last night," Eli said. "But it's going to be difficult to make a case against her based on a personal vendetta. This thing with Sophia happened eighteen months ago. It makes no sense that she'd wait until now to threaten you."

"It makes more sense than these allegations against Mom," Sam said. "She would never do something like this, Eli. The market was her life. Your buddies on the force shop with us. They know my mother."

"I realize that, Sammie. But they saw for themselves that she wasn't in her right mind last night."

"She may have set the fire without realizing what she was doing." Mike reached for Faith's hand. "You told me earlier that your mother claims Oscar Sweeney visited her in a dream, warning her there was trouble at the market. What concerns me is that she referred to him by his first and last name, not as your father or her husband. For all we know, it was a hallucination and not a dream. And who's to say this apparition didn't tell her to start the trouble at the market instead of warning her about it?"

Faith yanked her hand free of Mike's. "Whose side are you on?"

"I'm on Lovie's side, of course. I'm simply playing devil's advocate. I love your mother dearly. But I'm a physician, and I've seen normal people exhibit strange behavior during times of confusion. What if it turns out she started the fire? Correct me if I'm wrong, Eli. But she won't be held accountable based on her mental instability, will she?"

Eli wiped his mouth with a napkin. "The family would face a complicated court battle with their insurance company, but no judge is going to send an eighty-five-year-old demented woman to jail."

Faith tossed up her hands. "So now she has dementia."

"Calm down, honey," Mike said, resting his arm on the back of her chair. "You shouldn't be surprised by any of this. We've seen this coming for some time. I'm glad she's staying here with us so I can keep an eye on her, but I think we need to schedule an appointment for her to see a neurologist as soon as possible."

"I can do that," Sam said, raising her hand. "I'll see if I can get her in with the same doctor she saw before."

After a similar spell several years ago, they'd taken their mother to see a neurologist at the Medical University of South

Carolina in Charleston. She'd passed all his tests at the time, but he'd warned Faith and her sisters to expect more of the same behavior down the road.

Faith stared out across the water. "What if she has Alzheimer's?" she asked in a soft voice.

"We'll deal with it," Sam said. "Let's just take it one step at a time."

Faith nodded, unable to speak past the lump in her throat.

Sam lifted the top slice of bread off her sandwich. "I know the Island Bakery is the best place to buy gourmet sandwiches in town, but the bread's stale, the lettuce is slimy, and the avocado is brown."

Faith looked at the untouched sandwich on her own plate. How could her sister be thinking about food at a time like this?

The three of them offered to help her clean up, but Faith insisted they get on with their day. She wanted time alone with her mother. They needed a quiet afternoon to recover after being awake half the night. Faith hoped that doing ordinary things like shopping for groceries and cooking beef stew for dinner would snap her mother out of her confused state of mind.

After tidying up the kitchen, Faith sat down at the breakfast room table with her laptop computer. She accessed the files she needed in her Dropbox account and printed all the documents necessary to prove the market had been in good financial standing. As an afterthought she printed copies for Sam as well, in case she needed to borrow money from the bank.

She waited as long as she dared, but at two thirty she finally woke her mother. She did not argue when Lovie paired a plaid cotton blouse with seersucker slacks. She'd been dressing that way for years. The sisters viewed their mother's odd attire as her way of expressing her quirky personality.

As she drove the short distance to Bitsy's school, Faith asked her mother a series of questions to test her stability—simple things about their family to which she should know the answers.

But Lovie, her face pinched in confusion, shook her head in response to every one.

Bitsy was thrilled to see her grandmother. On the way home, she chatted about the invitation she'd received for a sleepover on Saturday night. Instead of quizzing her granddaughter about the party, Lovie sat slouched over in her seat, staring straight ahead at the road in front of her. Faith watched her daughter through the rearview mirror, her dejection at her grandmother's disinterest becoming more pronounced with each passing mile.

Bitsy was starving when they got home. Faith sat her mother and daughter down at the kitchen table and served them peanut butter crackers, apple wedges, and carrots with ranch dressing. When Lovie refused to eat, Bitsy gobbled up everything on both their plates, and then played with Snowflake, their miniature cockapoo, for a few minutes before running off to do her homework.

Faith was placing their plates in the dishwasher when the house phone rang. She never answered her landline anymore, as telemarketers were the only people who ever called it. Thinking someone might be calling about the fire, she lifted the receiver, but she was not surprised when Heather greeted her in a cheerful voice with a special offer to win a vacation in paradise. Faith hung up the phone and lifted the receiver again. The stuttering dial tone prompted her to access waiting voice mail. When she punched in the code for her mailbox, the automated voice informed her that she had two missed messages. The first was a reminder from the pediatrician's office of Bitsy's checkup the following Tuesday. But the second voice message caused Faith to break out in a cold sweat. On Tuesday at 4:34 in the afternoon, nearly forty-eight hours ago, Bernard Fox, the warden at Broad River Correctional Institution in Columbia, had called to alert Faith that her ex-husband was being released on parole that very afternoon.

"I apologize for any inconvenience this may cause your family," Warden Fox said in a tone that didn't sound apologetic at all. "Curtis has exhibited exemplary behavior during his incarceration. Our prisons are overcrowded, and we can no longer accommodate him. Instead of keeping him locked up, our goal is to rehabilitate him into an honest, hard-working citizen. He will be required to live in a halfway house, find a job, and report regularly to his parole officer. If you have any questions or concerns, please do not hesitate to call me."

Faith slammed down the receiver. *Questions or concerns?* Her husband had beaten her face to a bloody pulp, tormented her sister and their family for weeks on end, and they were turning him loose after serving only a fraction of his sentence. Fear crawled up her spine, and she fell into the nearest chair.

"Is something wrong, dear?" Lovie asked, the first words out of her mouth all afternoon.

Faith stared at her mother in disbelief. Lovie's eyes were alert, and she wore an expression of concern.

She grabbed hold of her mother's hand. "Tell me the truth, Mama. I promise you won't get in trouble. Did you set the fire at the market?"

"Not me," Lovie said, digging her thumb into her chest. "Your husband started the fire. I saw him with my own eyes."

Faith frowned. "I don't understand. Why on earth would Mike set the fire?"

Lovie's face clouded over once again. "Who's Mike?"

Faith pressed a hand against her belly, willing her lunch to stay down. "You know who Mike is, Mama. He's my husband."

"I don't know who you're talking about. Curtis is the one I saw running away from the fire."

SIX

JACKIE

Jackie pulled off the highway into a vacant parking lot while she spoke to her son by phone. It took her ten minutes to get him calmed down enough to tell her what had happened. He'd gotten caught using a fake ID at a local hangout in Athens. When he tried to argue his way out of a minor-in-possession charge, the officer arrested him. Sean was carrying a small amount of marijuana and two bars of Xanax. The police dropped the resisting-arrest charge, but the possession charges carried steep penalties—the possibility of jail time and a mandatory suspension of his driver's license.

After hanging up, instead of taking a left toward Prospect, Jackie headed in the opposite direction, toward Athens, Georgia. She waited until she was clear of heavy traffic before calling her husband. Bill got in touch with their attorney, who reached out to one of his associates in Athens, who agreed to counsel their son through the arraignment. By the time Jackie arrived in Athens four and a half hours later, Sean had been released on bail.

Furious with her son and terrified to let him out of her sight lest he get into more trouble, she booked a room at the Holiday Inn and insisted he stay the night with her. Over dinner at the

Last Resort Grill, Sean confirmed he would not be returning to Georgia in the fall. He'd failed every one of his second-semester classes.

"That's just great, Sean. You wasted a year of your life and a hell of a lot of our money."

She helped him move his things out of his dorm the following morning and paid one of his friends, a freshman girl from Charleston who didn't have a car on campus, fifty dollars to drive his 4Runner to Prospect. Jackie and Sean arrived home late Friday afternoon. She ordered her son not to leave the property, went to her room, closed the door, and stretched out on the bed with a cold washcloth on her forehead.

Bill sought her out thirty minutes later when he arrived home from work. He sat down on the bed beside her. "I know you're upset, Jack. But you need to settle down so we can handle this situation like rational parents. I'm sure I don't need to remind you what happened the last time one of our boys was in trouble."

Of course you don't, Jackie thought. When Cooper had gotten his girlfriend—Jamie's half sister, Annie—pregnant the winter before last, Jackie had torn her extended family apart by being insensitive and demanding. She was used to running her design business with an iron fist, holding her employees accountable when they made mistakes, because their mistakes cost her money and tarnished her reputation. But when it came to her boys, she wasn't as efficient or as effective, and her emotions ran high. She felt like an utter failure as a parent.

She snatched the cloth off her head. "Why do you think I'm hiding out in here? The truth is, I'm protecting our son from me. I'm so angry at him I could inflict God only knows what kind of bodily harm on him." She propped herself up on her elbows. "Since you're the voice of calm and reason, how do you suggest we handle the situation?"

Her husband's even temper infuriated her at times like these, when she felt so out of control. She reminded herself that he was a cardiovascular surgeon. His patients' lives depended on his tranquility.

"I suggest we call Moses." Bill showed her the phone in his hand. He was ready to make the call.

Jackie fell back against the pillows. "You're a genius. Why didn't I think of that? Big Mo is just the man we need."

"I'm glad you agree. Let me see if I can reach him," Bill said, scrolling through his contacts.

The tension drained from her body when she heard Moses's deep voice through the phone when he answered Bill's call. Even though he was trained as an adolescent psychiatrist, Dr. Moses Ingram had counseled several adult members of the Sweeney family over the years, including Faith after her divorce from Curtis and Sam when her drinking spiraled out of control. While Jackie and Bill had never sought his professional guidance, they considered him a friend. As did Cooper and Sean.

After exchanging pleasantries with Moses, Bill explained the situation and then listened for a minute before ending the call. "He's on his way." Bill stood up and pocketed his phone. "He'll be here in a few minutes."

Jackie swung her feet over the side of the bed. "I need to fix my face. I must look a mess." Placing her hands on his shoulders, she pressed her lips to his. "Thank you."

"You're welcome." Bill brushed her dark hair back from her face. "But remember, sweetheart, we must keep our minds open. He can't help us if we aren't willing to accept his advice."

She gave a firm nod. "Point taken."

Moss Creek Farm was a six-acre estate located five miles from the outskirts of Prospect. Live oak trees with Spanish moss dangling from their rambling branches bowed low over the gravel driveway and dotted the expansive lawn. With massive columns and a wide two-story porch, the old Georgian was set on a hill overlooking the marshy inlet. The main living space, including the kitchen and master bedroom, was located on the second floor, with a game room for the boys occupying the ground level and three bedrooms on the third floor. The age of the property made it a maintenance nightmare, but Jackie took meticulous care of the buildings and grounds.

Jackie and Bill were waiting for Moses on the back terrace when he drove up in his little red sports car. She'd never understood how this gigantic black man could cram his enormous body into such a tiny space. Big Mo engulfed Jackie in a bear hug, his strong arms offering reassurance that everything would be okay.

Bill extended his hand to Moses. "Thank you for coming to our rescue on such short notice. Especially on a Friday afternoon. I'm sure you have other plans."

"Not at all. My patients, or in your case my friends, are my priority. I'm sorry to hear Sean is having some trouble." His eyes traveled to the solitary figure on the dock—lanky body and auburn head bent over a fishing rod. "Do you have another rod? I'd like to chat with him first before I sit down with the two of you."

"Fine by us. Let me get you a rod." Bill disappeared into the garage and returned less than a minute later. "Here you go." He handed Moses the rod. "This one is already rigged for flounder."

Jackie and Bill watched as he tromped across the lawn and out onto the dock. When Sean looked up at Moses and smiled, Jackie said, "I feel better already."

Bill rested his hand on the small of her back. "He's good at what he does. Probably the best around. But he's not a miracle worker. Xanax is a highly addictive antianxiety medication. I'm worried Sean may have already crossed the line from recreational use to addiction. This may be only the beginning of our problems."

Jackie, no stranger to Xanax, took it during times of stress or on nights when she couldn't sleep. But since learning of her son's arrest, she'd taken way more than *as needed*. Did that make her a hypocrite? She didn't think so. After all, her dosage was small and her usage carefully monitored by her internist.

Moses spoke with Sean for more than an hour. Jackie was slicing vegetables to roast for their dinner when he came back up to the house. She wiped her hands on her apron and slipped it over her head. "How'd it go?"

"We had an open and frank discussion. We're off to a good start, but only time will tell how deep-seated his problems really are."

"Let's sit down." She motioned him toward the adjoining family room. "Can I offer you some sweet tea or something stronger, perhaps? It is six o'clock on Friday night."

He held his big palm out to her, declining her offer. "I'm fine. I'm meeting my wife at a cookout later."

"And we're making you late. I'm sorry. Let me get Bill." She called out to her husband, who was down the hall in his study.

Once they were seated, Bill and Jackie on the sofa and the therapist next to them in a tufted armchair, Moses said, "I don't need to tell you that your son has had a difficult year at Georgia. Not everyone is cut out for big SEC party schools. For the first time in his life, Sean was forced to face the world without his twin by his side. Plain and simple, he's suffering from an identity crisis."

"But Sean has always been the more confident and assertive of the two," Jackie said.

Moses nodded. "Because he's always had Cooper's quiet strength guiding him. Joining a fraternity can be a good thing at a school the size of Georgia. But in Sean's case, he became a follower instead of the leader he was in high school. And he followed some of his pledge brothers into some very bad habits like skipping class and experimenting with drugs."

"Did you get a feel for the extent of this experimentation?" Bill asked.

"Unfortunately, no. He seemed reluctant to go into detail."

Tears stung Jackie's eyes. Bill was right. Moses could not offer them a quick fix. "I was selfish in wanting him to go to my alma mater. I never stopped to think about the social challenges a boy from a small town would face."

Moses leaned in close to her. "You can't blame yourself, Jackie. Some kids thrive on large campuses. But I definitely wouldn't send him back there, even if it is an option, which it doesn't sound like it is."

"Maybe he should take some time off from school," Bill suggested.

"If you do that, you'll run the risk that he'll never go back. He needs to be in school, somewhere smaller, with more structure in his life. I mentioned the College of Charleston to him. He seemed to like the idea. I have a friend in the admissions office who might be able to help if you're interested. I would not let him join a fraternity, though, and I would think twice about allowing him to live on campus. Every college in this country has its share of drug problems right now."

Jackie considered the logistics. "He could stay with me in my house on Lamboll during the week and come here on the weekends." Her nest would not be empty, but the arrangement would allow her to focus on her career while keeping tabs on her son.

"Talk it over amongst yourselves. If you decide to proceed, I recommend getting his application in right away." Moses clasped his hands. "Now, with that said, my bigger concern is for his immediate future. Sean tells me he'd planned to work at the market this summer. I get the impression he doesn't know about the fire. And I didn't mention it to him. It's probably better for him to hear the news from you."

"Darn it." Jackie squeezed her eyes tight. "I totally forgot about the fire in all the confusion with his arrest."

"Understandably so," Moses said. "I'm sorry, by the way, about the fire. I know how much Captain Sweeney's meant to your family. I plan to give Sam a call this weekend."

"I'm sure she'll appreciate that." Jackie made a mental note to check in with Sam. She prayed her mother had returned to reality. The last thing she needed was another crisis.

"Sean will have to find another job," Bill said. "I'm going to insist he help pay for his legal expenses. He needs to be held accountable for his actions."

Moses's lips turned up into a gentle smile. "I'm glad to hear you say that. When considering a job for the summer, remember that physical activity is a good choice for a boy his age. One thing I've always admired about Cooper and Sean is their love for the outdoors. Maybe he can work on one of the fishing boats."

Jackie wrinkled her nose. "My father was a fisherman, Moses. It's a hard life. Forgive me for wanting something better for my son."

"I understand your point, but the seafood business has served your family well."

Bill stroked her knee. "Not everyone can be a doctor or a lawyer, Jack. Maybe we should have Cooper talk to him. He seems to have his future all planned out."

Skepticism crossed Big Mo's face. "I'm not sure I'd do that just yet. I got the impression that Sean is intimidated by his brother's success. Look." Moses planted his elbows on his beefy thighs. "Sean needs to figure out what he's good at and how to translate it into a career. We all know the most successful people are the ones who make careers out of the things they love to do. Jackie, you're a perfect example of that.

"Let me tell you, that kid knows his way around a fishing rod. He's got a cooler full of flounder out on that dock, and I didn't catch a single one of them. The College of Charleston has a hospitality and tourism management program similar to the one Jamie is studying at Carolina. I'm not saying he has to be a fisherman, but there are any number of careers he might find interesting." With a glance at his watch, he stood to go. "I need to get to my cookout before my wife comes looking for me."

Jackie and Bill followed him to the stairs.

"Sean is a good kid," Moses said. "He's gonna be just fine. I'd like to continue working with him if that's something you're interested in."

Jackie shot a questioning look at Bill, who nodded in return. "That goes without saying. We are in over our heads here, Moses."

"In that case, I'll have my receptionist call you on Monday to set up some appointments. In the meantime, keep a close eye on him. Depending on how much and how often he was using Xanax, he may exhibit sudden and severe withdrawal symptoms. You're a cardiologist, Bill. I'm sure you're aware of this. We can't rule out the possibility of rehab."

They walked in a single file down the stairs to the game room. Moses turned to them as he opened the door. "You have my number. Call me anytime, day or night."

Sean was waiting beside Moses's car with a gallon-size ziplock bag full of flounder fillets. Big Mo's face lit up. "Are those for me?"

Sean nodded and hung his head.

"You're a good man." Moses offered him a fist bump as he took the bag of fish. "These will get me out of the doghouse with my wife." Placing a hand on Sean's shoulder, Moses drew him in close and whispered something Jackie couldn't hear that brought a smile to her son's face.

Moses got in his car and drove off.

"We have a lot to talk about," Bill said once his car was out of sight.

Noticing the tears in her son's eyes, Jackie said, "Let's wait until after dinner." She watched Sean's dash across the yard and down the hill to the dock. "I feel like I might throw up," she said as she leaned against her husband.

"Tell me about it." Bill wrapped his arm around her.

"I'll never sleep again for worrying about him. He'll be married with children before I'm comfortable letting him out of my sight."

He chuckled. "That might make it difficult for him to have those children."

They stood on the terrace and watched their son reel in a small flounder. He removed the hook from its mouth and tossed it back into the water.

Jackie closed her eyes and tilted her head to the sky. "I stink at crisis management when it comes to the boys. After the way I treated Cooper, I'm grateful he's even speaking to me. But Cooper is his own person. He had the guts to stand up to me, to defend Annie when I was so hard on her about the pregnancy. Sean is more volatile, though, more pigheaded like me. I'm worried I'll say the wrong thing and drive him away. Which is why I've hardly said anything to him since all this happened."

"You're not alone in this, Jack. If you get angry, go to your room for a few minutes like you did this afternoon. Think about what you want to say instead of flying off the handle. We'll work through this together. Sean needs us to be strong for him right now. It's our job to help him find his own way, not force him down the path we want him to travel. Regardless of what career he chooses, living a clean and healthy life is what really matters."

"But clean and healthy doesn't always pay the bills," Jackie mumbled, more to herself than her husband.

Bill tilted his face to the breeze blowing in off the water. "I hate to waste this nice evening. Sean isn't in any hurry to eat dinner. Why don't you start the fire while I fix us some adult refreshments?"

"Sounds perfect." Jackie clicked on the gas logs and settled into one of four lounge chairs arranged around the fire pit on the terrace. Bill returned with two glasses of rosé and a plate of aged Gouda and water crackers. He handed her one of the glasses, sank into the lounge chair next to her, and set the cheese on the table between them. He held his glass out to hers for a toast. "To the summer's first rosé."

Jackie clinked his glass, and then a second time. "To surviving the summer."

"We're going to survive, honey. Sean is a good boy with a good head on his shoulders. He just needs a little guidance."

"A job is what he needs. And the sooner the better. He's coming off a semester-long bender. His party is over." Jackie sipped her wine while she considered his options. "What about construction? That would give him plenty of outdoor physical activity. He'd have to get up early, which means he wouldn't be able to stay out late at night. The skills he learns will serve him well in whatever career he chooses. Besides, every husband should know how to fix a leaky faucet."

"I wouldn't start making demands about his summer job, Jack." Bill cut a hunk of Gouda and popped it into his mouth. "It's going to be a big blow for him when he learns about the fire at the market. We should tell him tonight before he hears about it from someone else. I'm worried how he might respond. I think you underestimate how much your family's business means to him."

Jackie realized she was being selfish, but she couldn't stop obsessing about how all this would affect her work schedule. She'd planned to take some time off to spend with her son, but she couldn't afford to take the whole summer off. "All the more reason for him to start looking for a job right away. He needs structure. He's liable to find his way into trouble if he has too much time on his hands."

On the dock Sean landed a doormat-size flounder. He looked up at the house to see if anyone was watching and held the fish up for them to see.

Jackie couldn't help but smile. She gave him a thumbs-up. "Maybe working on one of the fishing boats isn't such a bad idea after all. He certainly can't get in trouble out on the ocean. Communing with nature might help him do some much-needed soul searching." Getting up before dawn and spending the day on the ocean would leave little time for much else. Which meant she wouldn't have to sit on him like a mama wren sitting on her eggs. "Whatever we do, I think we should strongly suggest he stay away from restaurant work. The restaurant scene, with its late hours and alcohol consumption, might be too tempting."

Bill set down his wineglass. "Speaking of alcohol consumption, I've been wondering . . . Do you think maybe we've set a bad example for the boys, that we're responsible for Sean's addiction problems by the lifestyle we lead? We have wine most nights and sometimes during lunch on the weekends."

"But we never have more than one or two glasses, except on the occasional holiday," Jackie said. "We taught our children how to tie their shoes and drive a car. It's our job to teach them how to be responsible about drinking alcohol."

"I feel guilty for letting them drink scotch with me on Christmas Eve."

"Come on, Bill. That's more about male bonding. You never give them more than a sip." Jackie twirled her wine around in her glass. "You'd think Sean would have learned something from watching Sam struggle with her addiction."

"Maybe we should have Sam and Eli talk to him. I admire the way they cope with their addictions. They might be able to offer him some valuable insight."

"Over my dead body." Jackie nearly came out of her chair. "I refuse to involve my family in my son's problems."

"Don't get so upset. I'll leave it up to you whether to tell them or not." Bill pulled her back down to her chair. "I'm just making the point that families are supposed to support one another at times like these. You should know that better than anyone. Your family has certainly had its fair share of trouble."

"And we nearly killed one another over Annie's pregnancy crisis. I mean it, Bill. Not one word of this to my sisters. Sam will try to drag Sean to the drug user's equivalent of Alcoholics Anonymous, and I won't have my son standing up in front of a roomful of people and proclaiming himself a drug addict."

Bill cut his eyes at her. "Why not, Jack? Are you afraid to admit your precious child is anything less than perfect?"

SEVEN

SAM

Sam stopped by Faith's house on the way to the grocery store midafternoon on Saturday. She had market business to discuss with her sister, and she wanted to see if their mother had come around. Faith's car was in the driveway, but the front door was locked, and no one answered when she rang the doorbell and hammered the knocker. She walked around to the backyard and spotted her mother and sister out on the dock with her niece. Bitsy was fishing for crabs with a chicken neck attached to a spool of string while Lovie and Faith watched from nearby wooden Adirondack chairs. Neither mother nor daughter heard Sam calling their names until she was standing in front of them on the dock.

"Dang it, Sam!" Faith's head jerked back and her hand flew to her chest. "You scared the bejesus out of me." She clambered out of the Adirondack chair. "You can't go sneaking up on people like that."

Sam lifted her Ray-Bans and inspected her sister's face. Her pale skin was pulled tight over her cheekbones. Had those crow's-feet been there two days ago? Was she upset about the fire, or had the situation with their mother taken its toll that quickly? "I didn't sneak up on you, Faith. I called your name three times."

She knelt down beside her mother's chair. "Hi, Mom. How're you feeling today?"

"I'd be better if everyone would stop fussing over me."

"In that case, I'm happy to oblige. I like it when you're feisty." She walked to the end of the dock and sat down beside her niece, dangling her legs over the side. "How's it going, squirt?"

With a toothy grin, Bitsy pointed at the five-gallon bucket beside her.

Sam peeked inside the bucket. "Holy smokes! You got yourself a whole mess of crabs here, young lady. Is Mike going to steam them for you?"

Her perky brown ponytail bounced up and down as she bobbed her head. "For dinner! Tonight."

Faith left her mother and migrated to the railing beside Sam. "Why didn't you call first to tell me you were coming?"

"Since when do I need to call first? I was on my way to the grocery store, and I thought I'd stop in to see if you needed anything. Jamie got home from school yesterday, and he's already munched his way through all the snacks in the pantry."

Faith slumped against the railing. "We don't need anything, but thanks for checking. I guess I'm a little on edge with the fire and having Mom here."

Sam glanced over at Lovie, who was picking at the frayed hem on her rainbow-striped plissé housecoat. "How's she doing, by the way?"

"About the same. She has a few lucid moments, but not many." Faith watched their mother for a moment before directing her gaze to something up at the house.

Sam brought her knees to her chest and leaned back against a piling. "The first available appointment with the neurologist is a week from Monday. Why don't I plan to take her?"

"I think we should both go to the appointment. Jackie too, if she's free," Faith said, her attention still focused on her house.

Sam's eyes roamed across the green span of lawn. "Are you waiting for someone?"

Redness crept up her neck to her face. "What makes you say that?"

"Because you're watching your house like you're expecting someone."

"I was just looking at my house, Sam. Can't a person admire their home? It wasn't so long ago that I lived in a trailer."

"Geez, Faith. You need to take a chill pill. I thought maybe Mike was on his way home from the hospital or something." Sam got to her feet and stood beside her sister at the railing. "You're really jumpy. Are you having some kind of delayed reaction to the fire?"

"I don't know. Maybe." Faith lowered her voice. "Someone set fire to our business, and there's a chance that that someone is living in my house with me. So what if I'm a little unglued? You would be too."

"I know who started that fire, and it's not Mom."

Sam felt her sister's body go rigid beside her. "Who, then?"

"Donna Bennett. She's guilty, whether she had an alibi or not."

"How do you know she has an alibi?" Faith asked.

"Eli questioned her. She claims she was home alone in bed asleep the night of the fire, which no one can dispute since she's divorced and her children are away at school."

"Did Eli say whether they found any fingerprints on the containers of gasoline?" Faith asked, her eyes closed as though she was bracing herself for bad news.

What is up with her odd behavior? Sam wondered. "Nope. There were no fingerprints. You and I talked about installing security cameras. If only we'd followed through . . ."

Faith pushed off the railing and spun around to face Sam. "So you're blaming *me* now, since I dropped the ball on getting a price for the cameras."

"I'm not blaming anyone, Faith. I'm simply suggesting we install a state-of-the-art security system, including surveillance cameras, in the new market." As the words crossed her lips, Sam realized there'd never been any doubt about Sweeney's future.

"I thought you were undecided about rebuilding?"

"I was. Until now. Jamie and I stayed up late last night discussing the pros and cons. I need to work, Faith. My livelihood and my mental stability depend on it. I considered trying something different, but with Jamie graduating, it makes sense to continue the family tradition."

Faith crossed her arms over her chest. "Well, leave me out of it. I'm done with Sweeney's."

"I figured as much." She looked over at Lovie, who was snoozing peacefully with a smile on her face. "I think Mom's working days are over as well."

"Where will you get the money if the insurance company won't settle?"

"I'll use Mack's money if I have to."

Sam had always thought of her father's best friend as Uncle Mack. With no children of his own, Mack had doted on Oscar's three daughters. When he died two summers earlier, he'd left his vast estate to the three Sweeney sisters and their mother.

Sam had been saving what she referred to as her rainy day mad money for her retirement. She often joked about buying a luxury trawler and cruising around the world, but secretly the money gave her peace of mind about some unforeseen tragedy falling upon her family. A month shy of turning fifty-one, she was mentally and physically years away from being ready to retire. And Lovie, who'd worked hard from the time she was a new bride at twenty-five until she turned eighty-five, had been her inspiration. Sam felt confident risking the investment. She and Jamie would make the new Captain Sweeney's Seafood a success. Their income would be greater with only Sam's and Jamie's families to support.

"Didn't you already use Mack's money to decorate your house?"

"I only bought a few pieces of furniture, Faith. I gave the rest to a broker to invest. He's grown my portfolio considerably. Hopefully, I won't have to use much of my money. The bank should approve a loan based on our P&L's from the past few years."

"Speaking of which, I printed those documents for Eli. I made copies for you as well. They're inside on the kitchen counter."

"Look, Mama!" Bitsy cried, dangling her empty line in the air.

"I see, sweetie. Looks like you need some more bait." Faith nudged Sam. "Keep an eye on these two while I run up to the house for another chicken neck."

"Grab those documents while you're up there," Sam called after her sister.

She moved to the empty Adirondack chair beside her mother. Lovie had woken up and was watching a butterfly dance around her head. "You know what I've been craving, Mom?"

"Hmm . . . What's that?"

"Your banana pudding. Do you by any chance remember the recipe off the top of your head?"

Banana pudding was a good test of her mother's memory. It wasn't one of the items they sold at the market, but Lovie had served it to them at least once a week when they were growing up. Even now, she often brought it to family potluck get-togethers.

"Of course I remember the recipe. One box of vanilla wafers, three cups of milk, three or four bananas, four eggs, and a half cup of ketchup." She giggled like a schoolgirl.

"Ketchup? That's not funny, Mom. That's gross." The thought of ketchup mixed with bananas made Sam feel nauseous. "Be serious for a minute. What else is in the recipe?" She knew the answer was somewhere in Lovie's rattled brain. If only she could regurgitate it.

"I have no idea, Samantha Lynn. You'll have to look in my recipe box. It's in the cabinet to the right of the stove up at the house." Lovie flicked her wrist in the direction of Faith's house.

Her mother hadn't called her Samantha Lynn since she was a little girl. And why would her recipe box be in Faith's kitchen? Was Lovie referring to the cabinet to the right of the stove in the cottage where she and her sisters had grown up?

Sam gripped the arms of her chair. "What about vanilla extract? I bet you put some of that in your banana pudding."

Lovie's eyes clouded over, and a painful expression crossed her face. "Stop pestering me with all these questions I can't answer. Now run along and play."

Run along and play? Her mother's prior bouts of confusion had been fleeting moments of disorientation and memory loss. This current spell was altogether different. Based on this conversation, her mother had slipped back in time four decades. This created a whole new host of challenges for Sam and her sisters. Faith wouldn't be able to take care of their mother for long. They would have to find a caretaker or a memory care unit. Although they'd known for some time that this was possible, Sam had been unprepared for the swift decline. She'd thought they'd have more time.

And what about the lost recipes? Not to seem callous, but the success of the market depended on them.

The answer came to her during the Lord's Prayer at church the following morning. Eager to share her light-bulb moment with her sister, she reached for Faith's hand, and then remembered that Faith had skipped church that morning. And Sam had given Jamie permission to play hooky, as he was recovering from exam week and needed to rest up before starting his new job as a bartender at the Roost the following day.

"Can we stop by Staples on the way home?" Sam asked Eli as they walked to the parking lot after the service.

"What for?" He took her keys from her. Even though she had a perfect record, he teased her about her driving; Sam suspected that driving her Wrangler made him feel like a boy again.

"Office supplies. Duh." She grabbed his arm and dragged him to the Jeep. "I'm just kidding. I'll explain on the way."

Eli thought her idea brilliant and pushed the cart for her while she shopped for the items she needed—a dry-erase board and markers, a notebook binder, a box of plastic sleeves, notepads, pens, and index cards.

Jamie was in the kitchen eating a bowl of cereal despite the lunchtime hour when she got home. "What's all this?" he asked when he saw the shopping bags. "And where's Eli? I was hoping he'd go fishing with me."

"Eli's in the bedroom changing. I'm sure he'd love to go fishing with you. This"—she dropped the bags on the floor—"is a solution to our problem." She propped the dry-erase board on the counter against the cabinets and scribbled "*Test Kitchen*' across the top in green marker. "Lovie doesn't remember her recipes, which means we have to create our own. We're both good cooks, Jamie, you more so than me because you instinctively know what ingredients go best together. Can I count on you to help me?"

"Heck yeah!" Jamie offered her a high five. "I take it this means you've decided to rebuild?"

"That's exactly what this means." Sam slid onto the bar stool beside him. "I see this as an opportunity to reinvent ourselves. We'll continue to offer fresh-from-the-ocean seafood, with friendly tips on how to prepare it, and our traditional prepackaged meals that everyone loves. We added wine and fresh produce after the last renovation. This time we'll hire a butcher and incorporate a cheese counter. We'll give our customers products that are organic, grass fed, locally sourced, and sustainably harvested. And we'll feature a new line of prepared foods. We'll reinterpret the southern classics by using healthy ingredients and modern cooking methods." When Sam paused to breathe, she noticed her son eyeing her and listening intently. "Of course, the fun part will be the testing and the tasting. We'll start with the tried and true. We have our work cut out for us getting our recipes as close to Lovie's as possible. We'll make up the rest as we go."

She hopped off her bar stool and went around the counter. She removed her iPad from her junk drawer and placed it on the counter before continuing. "One thing I've learned from this experience—we need a backup. I have an app that I use for organizing recipes. And it automatically backs up to iCloud." She removed the notebook and plastic sleeves she'd purchased from the Staples bags. "Just in case, we'll print hard copies and put them in this binder." She snapped her fingers. "Darn, I forgot to buy a printer."

"I brought one home from school," Jamie said, his dark eyes gleaming with excitement. "Printed recipes in a binder will be much easier to read than Lovie's chicken scratch on those tiny index cards."

"I think so too." Sam rested against the counter, spent.

"You're brilliant, Mom. I'm proud of you."

"Don't say that yet. A lot of things need to fall into place before you can be proud of me."

EIGHT

FAITH

Faith white knuckled the steering wheel on the way home from dropping Bitsy at school on Monday morning. Her mother sat in the passenger seat beside her, ripping a tissue into tiny shreds. Only the Lord knew what thoughts were crossing Lovie's mind. Faith had spent the weekend in her own private hell. She didn't know what to think or what to do, where to go or whom to turn to for advice. Eli would be the obvious choice, but she couldn't, she wouldn't, drag her family into this insanity again. Curtis's last rampage had driven Sam to become an alcoholic. She would not put her loved ones in harm's way again. Then again, hadn't her silence already put her family at risk if he was somehow responsible for starting the fire at the market?

She'd combed through her in-box and found among the plethora of advertisements in her spam file an email from the parole board dated three months earlier, alerting her to her ex-husband's upcoming parole hearing. She'd gotten slack. She'd become so comfortable in her new life with Mike she'd ignored the potential threat. The authorities had warned her from the beginning that good behavior could earn Curtis a chance for early parole.

She'd contacted the warden and Curtis's parole officer over the weekend. Both had expressed confidence that her ex-husband had not left the city limits of Columbia since his release on Tuesday.

"I assure you, we are watching him closely," Emmett Reyes, the parole officer, had said. "We have a system in place, and that system has proven effective time and again."

"I hope you realize who you're dealing with, Mr. Reyes. My ex-husband is a slimy snake capable of slithering through the narrowest of cracks."

Faith wanted to believe that her mother had started the fire, however screwed up it was to wish your demented mother had burned down your family's business. To an outsider Lovie was the obvious guilty party. She had been on the scene when the fire trucks arrived, and she hadn't been in her right mind since. But no matter how much Faith tried to convince herself otherwise, or how much the evidence stacked up against her mother, she knew Lovie would never destroy her beloved market regardless of her mental stability.

Curtis was somehow involved. She felt it deep down in her core. The situation reeked of him. That the fire had happened the night after he was released from prison sent a message loud and clear—he was free, and he was coming for her. He was a sneaky little shit with no moral compass and friends every bit as mean as he. Considering the two-and-a-half-hour drive from Columbia to Prospect, he could have slipped out of his halfway house and conned some poor unsuspecting person into giving him a ride. And if he'd managed to elude their *system* once, he would do it a second and third time. Until he got the revenge he wanted on her family. Faith refused to be victimized again. She had her daughter to think of. And her mother as well. Her mother had also been a victim of Curtis's last rampage. He'd broken into her house, held her at gunpoint, and robbed her of $500.

She sneaked a glance at Lovie beside her. Her mother wore an expression of innocence, riding alongside Faith without a care in the world. What decade was she reliving in her mind today? The late eighties, Faith's teenage years, when they'd lived in the waterfront cottage next to Moss Creek Farm? Or the forties, when Lovie had been a young girl living with her parents on their family's hog farm?

Faith vowed to take whatever measures necessary to protect her family. She considered hiring a hit man. Someone like Earl Sessions, one of Curtis's low-life buddies who had made more than one pass at her when she was married to Curtis. She would offer him a blow job as payment for killing her husband. She pounded the steering wheel with the palm of her hand. *What the hell are you thinking, Faith? Are you losing your mind now too? Providing sexual favors to deadbeat scum is going too far.*

"Is something the matter, dear?" Lovie asked.

"No, Mom. Everything's fine."

Faith didn't need Earl or Eli or Emmett Reyes. She had a plan. She would take care of Curtis herself.

Faith took her mother home, fixed her a cup of hot tea, and planted her in front of the TV. The TV Land channel was hosting a *Golden Girls* marathon that lasted until noon, which should buy her enough time.

"I'll be back soon, Mom." Faith kissed the top of Lovie's head. "Maybe we'll grab a bite of lunch somewhere and make that trip to the garden center. You can help me pick out some annuals for my planters."

"That sounds nice, dear," Lovie said, already engrossed in the show.

Faith double-checked all the doors to make certain they were locked before she left. She drove to the west side of town to Guns and Reels, a locally owned sporting goods store where the men in her family shopped for fishing and hunting gear. At nine thirty on a Monday morning, she was the only customer in the store.

"I'd like to purchase a handgun," she announced to the fat redneck at the gun counter in the back.

His lips parted into a smile, revealing a half-inch gap between his front teeth. "What does a pretty little thing like you need with a gun?"

"That's none of your business, now is it?"

He snickered. "I've got a little pink number you might be interested in."

"I don't want a pink handgun, mister, any more than I want your attitude. Is there someone else in the store who can help me? Preferably a female."

He spread his flabby arms wide at the empty store. "Sorry, but you're stuck with me."

"In that case, I'd like to see a Smith & Wesson Bodyguard and a Ruger LC9s if you have them in stock." She'd stayed up half the night researching guns online. She was torn between a revolver and a single-stack magazine.

"Whoa now. You're talking about a lot of gun for a little lady. Do you even know how to shoot it?"

"My father taught me how to shoot, thank you very much. Rifles and shotguns and pistols. I could take you out in a single shot from a mile away."

He winked one of his beady brown eyes at her. "Feisty little thing, now ain't you?"

Faith felt a surge of anger. She knew his type. She'd been married to his type. She planted her palms on the counter. "You are wasting my time. I came here to make a purchase. Are you going to help me, or should I take my business elsewhere?"

He dropped his smile and straightened. "Nah, no need to go anywhere else. Let me fetch those guns for you outta the back. We have both in stock." He disappeared through a swinging door and returned with the two handguns. Much to her relief, he discussed the pros and cons of each in a professional manner.

Deciding on the Ruger, she also purchased two boxes of

ammo and a gun safe big enough to house the gun but manageable enough to carry in her bag. He gave her the names of several instructors she could call for the training necessary to apply for the concealed weapons permit. The application process could take up to ninety days, but she felt comfort in knowing she could at least protect herself in her home until then.

Faith left the sporting goods store and drove three miles farther west to the shooting range the redneck had recommended. She was grateful to find a young woman behind the counter who didn't sneer or leer at her. Faith filled out the paperwork and paid the fee for the membership.

"I'm a bit rusty," Faith admitted. "I haven't shot a gun in years. Is there someone here who can give me instruction?"

She'd expected to be told to come back later in the week, but the woman said, "Sure. Mondays are slow. Ronnie's in the back." She motioned Faith to the inside range.

To her surprise her aim wasn't as bad as she'd anticipated. Ronnie complimented her on her form and agreed to give her another lesson on Wednesday. She drove home feeling proud of herself for taking matters into her own hands and feeling confident that she could take care of herself. She'd matured a lot since her divorce from Curtis. The old Faith would've dragged her family into her problems. This new Faith, the one she barely recognized, was learning to stand on her own two feet.

When she got home, she headed straight to the master bedroom at the end of the hall and hid the gun pouch in an empty shoebox on the shelf at the top of her closet.

"Mom, I'm home," she called on her way to the family room. She stopped dead in her tracks when she saw the empty chair. Betty White was still babbling on the television, and the cup of tea she'd fixed for her mother before she left remained untouched on the table beside the chair. Faith's heart raced as she frantically searched the house and the yard, but there was no sign of her mother anywhere. She knew it was common for dementia patients to disappear. She should never have left Lovie home alone. She called the neighbors on either side of her, but neither had seen or heard from Lovie. She grabbed her car keys, and for the next thirty minutes, she drove up and down Creekside hoping to spot her mother walking along the side of the road. It was almost noon, and the thermometer on her dash registered eighty-three. Her mother would be parched and hungry. She returned home praying she'd find her mother back in front of the TV. But the chair was still empty, as was her house.

With a heavy heart, she called her sister. "Sam, get over here fast. I lost Mom."

NINE

JAMIE

Annie called Jamie early Monday morning to ask if he could meet earlier for lunch. "Does eleven work for you? I have to be back in Charleston late afternoon for a party I'm catering tonight, and I want to see Faith and your mom while I'm in town. Lovie too, if I have time."

Jamie blinked the film off his eyes. Her call had woken him from a deep, peaceful sleep. It dawned on him through his haze that Annie had failed to include Jackie on her list of family members she wanted to visit. He didn't blame her, considering the way Jackie had treated her. Annie wasn't one to hold grudges, but Jamie suspected his sister would always hold his aunt partially responsible for her losing the baby.

"Eleven is fine," Jamie said. "I have to warn you, though. I went to see Gran yesterday. She's not doing so well. She's been confused since the fire."

"Aw, poor Lovie. I'm sorry to hear that." Annie had worked at Sweeney's during the brief time she lived in Prospect. Despite the age difference, she'd really hit it off with his grandmother.

"I know, right?" Jamie said. "We're all hoping she'll snap out of it."

"By the way, I'm bringing a friend with me," Annie said and hung up before he could interrogate her.

Jamie assumed this so-called friend was a new guy Annie was dating. He'd always hoped their individual journeys of discovery would eventually lead his cousin and his sister back together. But maybe it wasn't meant to be for Cooper and Annie after all. Which was a shame since they were perfectly suited.

When they met outside the Pelican's Roost at eleven sharp, he discovered that Annie's friend wasn't a guy but a serious babe. Lizbet Horne was not hot the way most guys he knew considered a girl hot. She was a classic beauty with reddish-brown hair and petite facial features.

"Lizbet works with us at Tasty Provisions," Annie explained. "She's a whiz in the kitchen. She's been accepted at the culinary institute and will be moving to New York next fall."

His heart sank. He'd only just met this girl. Why did he care if she moved to New York? He was sure she already had a boyfriend anyway. Nice girls like Lizbet were always in serious relationships. "Do you plan to come back to Charleston when you finish?" he asked, feeling the heat rise in his face.

"Without question," Lizbet said. "I'm excited to experience New York, but I'm not a big-city girl at heart. Even Charleston feels too big for me at times."

He flashed her a smile. "You've come to the right place then, if you like small towns."

Lizbet gazed out across the marina. "Even better if the small town is located on a body of water. If we have time, I'd love to walk down on the boardwalk."

The main building at the Inlet View Marina, including the marina store and the restaurant above it, served as the north anchor for the waterfront complex, which featured an ice cream parlor, hot dog hut, and small gift shop. The wooden boardwalk extended another quarter mile to the south, offering plenty of opportunity for development. He wondered why no one was taking advantage of the prime real estate. Prospect was growing at a rapid pace, with young families and retired northerners moving to the area every day.

"We'll make time," Jamie said, holding the door open for them to enter the restaurant.

The Roost was empty of employees and patrons. They stood at the hostess stand, waiting for someone to seat them. He was starting work here tonight, but he'd yet to meet any of the other employees. "Looks like we get to pick our own table," Jamie said finally. "Let's sit by the water."

As he was ushering them to the row of booths overlooking the inlet, a heavyset waitress he'd never seen before waddled toward them from the back. "Sorry, y'all. The waitress in charge of this station is late to work. You'll have to sit on the other side."

Overlooking the market, he thought.

Annie cast him an uncertain glance. "Are you all right with that?"

"It's fine," he lied. He'd driven past the market several times since arriving home, but he couldn't stomach more than a quick glance at the pit of charred rubble.

They settled themselves in the booth with Jamie on one side, opposite the girls. The waitress handed them laminated menus, took their drink orders, and disappeared into the back.

"What are their specialties?" Lizbet's pale-gray eyes narrowed as she studied the menu. "It looks heart unhealthy."

Annie giggled. "I should have warned you. The food is not what you're used to, but it's the best place in town."

Jamie let his menu fall to the table. "What do you mean the best place in town? Since the Main Street Grill closed, it's the *only* place in town. Aside from the Island Bakery, whose bread is as stale as their menu options."

"What happened to the Main Street Grill?" Annie asked. "I loved their burgers."

"The owner died in his sleep of a heart attack six months

ago," Jamie said. "He closed the restaurant on a Thursday night and never showed up for work the next day. He didn't have any family to leave the business to."

Annie crinkled her nose. "That's so sad."

Jamie pointed at an item on Lizbet's menu. "You can't go wrong with the fish and chips."

"Fish and chips it is," Lizbet said, her lips parting to reveal gleaming white teeth.

Jamie shook his head to clear his mind of the image of her succulent lips on his.

All three ordered the fish and chips when the waitress brought their drinks—sweet tea for Jamie and Lizbet and a Diet Coke for Annie. She collected the menus and disappeared into the back.

"It's hard to believe it's gone," Annie said, staring out the window at the burned-out building. "When do you think they'll start construction?"

"Mom's interviewing architects this week. She's hoping to get the rubble cleared by next weekend. Summer's still a month away, but some folks have already started traveling to the beach on the weekends. We'd rather our clients see an empty lot than that mess." Jamie forced himself to look across the street. He'd grown up helping his mother and grandmother at the market. As a child he'd stocked shelves, emptied the trash, and mopped the floors. As he grew older, his passion for experimenting in the kitchen had inspired him to seek a degree in hospitality management. "If we incorporate all the changes Mom is planning, the building will take up the whole lot, including the parking area."

Annie squinted. "I see a sign on that building behind the market. Is it for sale?"

Jamie couldn't see the front of the building from his side of the booth. "What are you talking about? The stationery store?"

Annie accessed the camera app on her phone and zoomed in on the building. She studied the photo before handing him the phone. "Yes, Paper to Pen. The sign says it's for sale. I'm not surprised. No one sends paper invitations or handwritten notes anymore. You should consider buying the property. It would give you more flexibility in the building you design and plenty of room for parking."

"Leave it to you to figure out a solution to our problem." Her resourcefulness was only one of the many things he admired about his half sister.

Annie beamed. "I'm full of advice." She elbowed her friend. "Lizbet gets sick of listening to all my ideas."

Lizbet elbowed her back. "That's not true at all, and you know it."

"Speaking of your amazing creativity . . . Mom has come up with a new concept for the new market. Her goal is to reinterpret traditional southern cuisine. Would you be interested in helping us?"

Annie's brown eyes grew as large as his gran's double-chocolate-chip cookies. "Are you kidding me? I'd love to brainstorm some ideas."

The waitress delivered steaming baskets of fried flounder fillets and round homemade potato chips. Annie and Lizbet followed his lead when Jamie doused his food with vinegar. The women talked about the catering business while they ate, their faces lighting up as they discussed recipes, cooking techniques, and wine pairings. They had a clear understanding of the types of cuisine and level of service food snobs expected in today's highly competitive restaurant and catering industry. Listening to their discussion brought what he'd studied at Carolina to life. Suddenly he could hardly wait to get out in the real world. Construction on the market could take twelve to eighteen months. Maybe he should look for a job in Charleston, if only for a little while.

As though reading his mind, Annie asked, "What're you

doing this summer, Jamie, now that your work plans have changed?"

He took the last bite of fish and pushed his basket away. "Working here, as a matter of fact."

"Here." Annie clicked her fingernail against the table. "As in the Pelican's Roost?"

"Yep." Jamie sat back in the booth. "They hired me to bartend."

"Ha." She tossed her wadded-up napkin at him. "Since when are you a bartender?"

"Since I turned twenty-one last December. I bartend for a couple of caterers in Columbia during the school year. It's a fun way to earn spending money. I'm pretty good at it too."

"Cool!" Lizbet said. "We're always looking for bartenders. You should work for us some this summer."

"That's right." Annie tugged on her lip as she considered this. "In fact, we're still looking for bartenders for the Pickett wedding this weekend. We are short on help because it's Mother's Day and graduation at the college. The bride's parents are hosting the reception at their fab house on Legare Street. Are you interested? You can spend the night with me at Heidi's."

"Sure. Why not?" He managed to sound cool despite the pounding of his heart. He would jump at the chance to spend more time with Lizbet.

"Don't you need to check your work schedule here?" Annie asked.

"I already did. Honestly, I'm not sure how much they're going to need me this summer. They seemed excited about hiring me, but I'm only working three nights this week."

"In that case, we have several other big weddings coming up," Annie said. "I'll text you the dates when I get back to the office. I'm sure Heidi would love to give you the work."

"By the way, how's it going, working and living with Heidi?" Jamie asked.

"Believe it or not, we're getting along great. We don't have time to argue. Our lives are too busy. And she's hardly ever in the store. She's either in her office or meeting with clients. Work is work. She's the boss and I'm the employee when it comes to our professional relationship."

When Lizbet politely excused herself to use the restroom, Annie waited until her friend was out of earshot before she leaned over the table and said in a loud whisper, "I knew the two of you would hit it off!"

"The two of who?" He had to work hard to keep a straight face. If Annie had intentionally set them up, maybe Lizbet didn't have a boyfriend after all.

Annie let out an exaggerated sigh. "Duh. You and Lizbet, silly. You're perfect for each other." She kept her eyes glued to the restroom door while she talked. "You both like spending time outdoors. Family and food are important to you. And she loves small towns. You heard her say so yourself."

"Your imagination is on steroids again. She said that sometimes Charleston seems too big for her. That doesn't mean she's ready to move to Prospect."

"What. Ever," Annie said with an exaggerated eye roll. "I have a special intuition about these things. We'll hang out after the wedding on Saturday night, and see how it goes."

Lizbet's return put an end to their conversation. Annie checked her phone for the time and searched the room for the waitress. "We should get the check. I want to stop by and see Sam and Faith on our way out of town."

Annie's body tensed, and Jamie followed her gaze to the door, to where Sean stood waving at them. "That's Sean, Annie, not Cooper. Cooper's working in Richmond this summer."

"Of course! I knew that." She peered closer. "It's eerie how much alike they look." She motioned Sean over.

Sean flashed her a smile and made his way to the table. She

stood to greet him, and he gave her a hug. "Why didn't you tell me you were coming to town?"

"Because I had no idea you were already home from college." Annie introduced Sean to Lizbet. "We've already eaten. Otherwise I'd ask you to join us. Can you sit with us for a minute while we wait for our check?"

Annie sat back down, and Sean slid onto the bench beside Jamie. "But only for a minute. I have a job interview with the manager, whenever he gets off the phone."

Jamie offered his cousin a high five. "Really, dude? I'm working here too."

"That's cool!" Sean clasped his hands together on the table. "I'm really sorry about the market, cuz. The place means so much to us, I feel like someone in our family died. I was really hoping to work there full-time this summer."

Jamie directed his gaze across the street. Sean was right. Losing the market *was* like having a death in the family. "With any luck we'll be reopened by next summer."

"My mom's gonna kill me," Sean said. "She's forbidden me to get a job at a restaurant. Jackie's gonna freak when she finds out they hired me to bus tables."

Jackie? Jamie tried not to let his surprise show. He'd never heard either of the twins refer to their parents by their first names.

"How funny is that?" Sean talked on. "I got the bottom-of-the-barrel job. What did you get hired for?"

"Bartending," Jamie said.

His blue eyes gleamed with mischief. "That's awesome, cuz. You can sneak me some drinks."

"Sorry, bro, but I can't risk the Roost losing their liquor license."

Sean let out an awkward laugh. "Just kidding, dude."

"I can't believe how long it's been since I've seen you," Annie said. "How's Cooper? We text all the time, but I haven't seen him since . . . Well, you know."

"Cooper is setting the world on fire." Sean punched the air with his fist. "Everything my brother touches turns to gold."

Jamie exchanged a look of concern with Annie. His usually laid-back cousin seemed off, skittish almost.

"Come on, Sean," Annie said. "I'm sure your first year at Georgia was just as successful."

"So successful I'm not going back," Sean said and hung his head.

"Oh." Annie's face fell. "Well, college isn't for everyone. I'm living proof of that."

Sean's head jerked back, and he stared at her with contempt. "You went to culinary school, Annie. You got to pick your own career."

Jamie was relieved to see the waitress heading their way, and he signaled for the check. As he was turning his head back around, he spotted a figure sifting through the rubble at the market. He did a double take. "Is that Lovie over there?"

Four sets of eyes looked out the window at once.

"Damn!" Sean said. "It sure looks like her."

"What on earth is she doing?" Annie asked.

"We'd better get over there." Jamie cast a nervous glance toward the kitchen. "I wish our waitress would hurry up with the check?"

"Go! I'll take care of the check." Lizbet waved them on with a flick of her wrist.

Jamie and Annie dropped cash on the table, and they and Sean raced down the stairs and across the street. Jamie stuck his arms out to stop Annie and Sean when they reached the sidewalk on the other side. "Be careful," he said in a low voice. "We don't want to scare her."

As they inched their way toward Lovie, Jamie motioned for Annie and Sean to stay behind him. "What're you doing, Gran?"

He took a tentative step toward his grandmother. "You're getting all dirty." Lovie's hands, arms, and clothes were black from the soot.

"I'm looking for something," she said without raising her head.

"Whatever you're looking for, I don't think you'll find it in here. Come on." He gently took hold of her arm. "Let me take you home."

She snatched her arm away. "Get your hands off me, young man."

Jamie's blood ran cold. "Gran, it's me, Jamie, your grandson."

Lovie cocked her head to one side. "Whose child are you?"

"I'm Sam's son, Gran."

She looked past him at Annie and Sean. "And who are they?"

Out of the corner of his eye, he saw Sean inch away, his cell phone pressed to his ear.

Annie stepped forward. "I'm Annie. Do you remember me? We used to make up recipes together when I worked at Sweeney's."

Lovie studied Annie's face and shook her head. "I'm sorry. I don't remember you."

Lovie's eyes were damp, and Annie's bottom lip began to quiver. Jamie needed to act quickly before they both fell apart. "I'm taking you home." Wrapping his arm around her shoulders, he drew her in close and held her tight so she couldn't escape. "My truck is parked across the street at the marina."

Shuffling along beside him, she looked up at him with cloudy eyes. "Are we going to see Oscar Sweeney at the marina?"

TEN

JACKIE

Jackie stomped on the gas pedal and sped down Creekside at nearly eighty miles an hour, barely slowing as she made the turn into Faith's driveway. She skidded to a halt in the gravel in front of the house. She marched up the steps, burst through the front door, and stormed down the hall. "Why didn't you tell me Mom was so bad off?" she demanded of Sam, the first person she encountered when she entered the family room.

Sam jumped to her feet and got in her face. "We would have told you, if you'd taken the time to call one of us."

"Well . . . I . . . " Jackie took a step backward. She was guilty as charged. She'd been too preoccupied with Sean all weekend to think about how the rest of her family was coping after the fire. "I guess that's fair. I've had a lot going on."

Sam glared at her. "Haven't we all."

She heard movement to her right and saw four faces staring at her from that hideous blue corduroy sofa. How was it that she shared DNA with her baby sister when their tastes were polar opposites? "I see the gang's all here." Annie, bless her heart, was cowering behind Jamie at the far end of the sofa. Jackie cautioned herself to tread lightly. The poor girl was terrified of her, and making a scene would only make matters worse. She'd last seen Annie in the hospital after Annie had lost the baby. Jackie had apologized for the way she'd treated her, but the hurt in the girl's eyes indicated forgiveness would not soon be forthcoming.

Annie rose from the couch. "We should probably get going. We have an event to prepare for tonight."

The other three kids stood in unison. Sean turned to Jamie. "Do you want to help me put out my crab traps?"

Jamie hunched his shoulders. "Why not? I could use some fresh air."

They stopped in turn to speak to Sam and Jackie as they filed out of the room.

Jackie gave Annie's rigid body a quick hug. "Welcome home. It's nice to see you, although I'm sorry it's under these circumstances."

Annie offered her a smile that fell short of reaching her pretty brown eyes. She would have to work harder to earn her way back into the girl's good graces. As Jamie's half sister, Annie was part of the family, and Jackie had nothing against her as a person. She was undeniably a lovely girl with much to offer some lucky young man. If it worked out in the future between Cooper and Annie, she would throw them the biggest wedding the Lowcountry had ever seen. When the time was right. When an unplanned pregnancy wasn't dictating their future or forcing them to make a commitment they weren't ready for.

She extended her hand to Lizbet when it was her turn. "It's nice to see you down in our neck of the woods." She'd met Lizbet during the dinners and cocktail parties Heidi had catered at her house in Charleston. She'd found her professional and pleasant to work with.

She kissed Jamie's cheek and ruffled Sean's hair. "You boys be careful out on the water today. And don't forget to put on sunscreen."

She waited until she heard the front door click shut before turning to her sister. "Where's Faith?"

"In the bathroom with Mom, helping her get cleaned up." Sam did an about-face and said over her shoulder on her way to the kitchen, "I don't know about you, but I could use some coffee."

Jackie followed Sam into the kitchen. "Are you sure Mom didn't recognize any of the kids?" She plucked a Chai Latte from the variety display of K-Cups and popped it into the Keurig. "Maybe she was just distracted."

"I wasn't there, remember? I'm just telling you what Jamie told me. According to him, she had no clue who any of them were."

"Does she know you?" Jackie asked, one eye on the machine as her latte brewed.

"I haven't seen her today, but she did on Saturday when I last saw her." Sam removed the cream from the refrigerator and the sweetener from the cabinet next to the stove. "She seemed to know who Bitsy was then too, unless she was faking it. I'm worried about how quickly she's losing ground. I wish we could see the neurologist sooner. I wasn't able to get an appointment until next Monday."

Jackie removed her phone from her blazer pocket. "What's the doctor's name? I'll see if Bill can get us in sooner."

"Dr. Jerome Lawson at MUSC."

Bill answered after the third ring, and she quickly explained the situation. "None of this surprises me," he said when she'd finished talking. "Your mother suffered a traumatic ordeal in watching the market burn to the ground. And now, not only has she lost her job of nearly sixty years, she's no longer living in her own home. That's enough to discombobulate anyone that age, but people with dementia have an even harder time adjusting to change. I'll call Lawson's office and see what I can do to get her in sooner, and then I'll text you back if I'm able to change the appointment."

She thanked him and ended the call. "How did this even happen? Where was Faith when Mom slipped away?"

"Running an errand, apparently."

Jackie's dark brows met in the middle. "What kind of errand? Why didn't she take Mom with her?"

"She seemed reluctant to say." Sam leaned back against the counter beside her sister as she sipped her coffee. "I pressed her, but she would never give me a straight answer. If you ask me, she's been acting kinda squirrelly lately too. Maybe it's a delayed reaction to the fire."

"You seem fine." Jackie leaned in close to Sam and sniffed her breath. "You're the one I expected to fall apart."

Sam peered at her over the rim of her coffee mug. "Gee, thanks for the vote of confidence."

Jackie mussed her hair. "Don't get your britches in a wad, little sis. I'm just teasing. I'm proud of you for the way you're managing your addiction."

Faith entered the kitchen and went to the sink for a glass of water. "I'm exhausted." Bracing herself against the counter, she drained the glass in one gulp. "Mom has suddenly become combative. I had to fight with her to get her into the shower."

Several strands of Faith's hair had escaped her ponytail and were plastered against her sweaty face. Her white T-shirt was soiled, and she had black finger smudges on her forearms.

"Where is she now?" Jackie asked.

"Asleep. Thankfully. I need to sit down."

Sam and Jackie trailed their sister to the table in the adjacent breakfast room.

Sam held a chair out for Faith. "You can't do this alone, honey. I'll help as much as I can, but we're eventually going to need a trained nurse."

Jackie's blood pressure shot up to an all-time high. *Eventu-*

ally came and went three years ago. If you'd listened to me then, she would have a nice apartment in independent living at the Hermitage Retirement Community. She'd be playing bridge with all her new friends as we speak, with a plan in place to move her to the memory care unit when the time came."

Sam gave her the stink eye. "We made the right decision for Mom at the time, Jackie. She had three good years, doing what she loves best, which is working at the market."

"Humph." She pressed her lips tight. "She could've gotten ten good years if the two of you hadn't been driving her hard like a workhorse every day."

"Be quiet, Jackie!" Faith cried. "I can't handle this right now. Either help us figure out a solution or leave." She stretched her arm out, pointing at the door.

Jackie stared wide-eyed at Faith. She'd never known her baby sister to get so angry. "I'm just saying that our choices are limited now because we didn't act sooner."

"Watch it, Jackie," Sam warned.

"Fine." Jackie folded her arms over her chest. "I'll keep my mouth shut and let the two of you figure this thing out." Her phone dinged in her hand. She read the text from Bill. "But you might want to know, before I shut my mouth, that Bill was able to move Mom's appointment up to nine o'clock on Thursday. Why don't you let me take her?"

"Why don't we all take her?" Sam said.

Jackie's mind raced ahead to Thursday. The Doyles had been pestering her for another look at her house on Lamboll. If she drove her own car to her mother's appointment, she could arrange to meet them afterward. She was itching for a project, and she couldn't stop thinking about the Church Street property, but she couldn't sell her house on Lamboll until she'd secured a place to move her business. Which meant she would need to make an offer on the Meeting Street warehouse. Sean would be fine unsupervised for one day. He could go fishing with Jamie.

She'd seen no signs of alcohol or drug use since they'd arrived home from Athens. He'd hit a bump in the road, but she felt he was over the worst of it.

"You're right, Sam. We should all go. Three sets of ears are better than one when listening to doctors. I'll meet you there. I have business in Charleston afterward." Jackie stood to go.

"Not so fast, Jackie." Sam yanked her back down to her chair. "We're not finished here. We need to figure out a way to help Faith. It's not fair for her life to be turned upside down like this."

"I'll ask Bill. I'm sure he knows a retired nurse we can hire," Jackie said, eager to leave so she could schedule her appointment with the Doyles.

"Hiring someone isn't what I had in mind," Sam said, her expression one of exasperation. "We need to pitch in, to give Faith a break."

"I can manage until Thursday," Faith said.

Sam squeezed Faith's hand. "I'll help you, honey, since Jackie is obviously too busy. I'll take Mom with me to run errands tomorrow. Maybe we'll go out to lunch afterward if she feels up to it. Or, if you'd rather, I'll stay with her here."

Jackie felt their eyes on her, but she kept her mouth shut. She didn't have time to babysit their mother. She had a business to run.

"Thanks," Faith said to Sam. "Midmorning for a couple of hours would be great. Take her to your house or stay with her here. Either is fine with me."

Jackie spent the rest of the afternoon in a funk. The sooner they found a permanent solution for their mother the better. But that was easier said than done with Sam and Faith involved. They would insist on visiting every retirement facility on the East Coast. They would drag it out for weeks on end, hemming and hawing every step of the way. In the meantime Lovie would continue to live at Faith's, which meant they would have to share the burden of taking care of her. Jackie felt a pang of guilt for not volunteering to help out this week. She reached for her bag and removed the bottle of nerve pills. Between her mother and her son, she was losing control of her life, and as a result her grip on her business was slipping. She needed to stay on top of her game. And she couldn't very well do that from Prospect.

She was having a glass of wine at the counter in the kitchen when Sean got home a few minutes after six that evening. She slid off the stool to face him. "Where have you been?"

"Out on the boat with Jamie."

She studied him closer. His eyes were clear and his breath smelled like mints. "Since when does it take five hours to set the crab traps?"

"We went fishing after we set the traps." Brushing past her, he went to the stove and lifted the lid on the marinara sauce. "What's for dinner?"

"Spaghetti." She peered over his shoulder as he spooned sauce into his mouth. "Did you find a job?"

"Jesus, Mom. Will you back off? Yes, I found a job." He returned the wooden spoon to the spoon rest. "Jamie got me a job at the Roost."

"Are you kidding me?" She grabbed him by the elbow and spun him around to face her. "That's the one place I told you I didn't want you to work. Will you be waiting on tables?"

"They hired me to be a busboy."

Jackie planted her fists on her hips. "You can't be serious. What's Jamie's position?"

"He's a dishwasher." Sean stared past her, refusing to meet her eyes.

"Jamie is graduating from college in December, and the only kind of job he can get is washing dishes?"

"Chillax, Mom. We'll get promoted to waiters once business picks up for the summer," Sean said and started to walk away.

"Wait just a minute, young man. Get back here. Have you started your application for the College of Charleston?"

He stopped in his tracks. "Not yet. I haven't decided if I even want to go there. I'm not sure college is my thing."

"You are too young to know what your *thing* is."

"I know what my *thing* is better than you. I'm not Cooper. I'm not your golden boy. You can't control my life, Mom. The sooner you get that through your thick head the better," he said, storming out of the kitchen.

Jackie hustled to catch up with him. "You are going to college, even if that means the local community college." He mounted the stairs, and she said to his back, "And by the way, I have to be in Charleston on Thursday. I want you to make arrangements to spend the day with Jamie."

"I don't need a babysitter," he said as he ascended the stairs.

"Are you sure about that? Your recent run-in with the Athens police suggests that maybe you do. And don't forget you have an appointment with Moses at two o'clock tomorrow afternoon."

He turned right at the top of the stairs, and seconds later she heard his bedroom door slam.

ELEVEN

SAM

Sam picked up her mother at ten o'clock on Tuesday morning, but instead of running errands, she took Lovie back to her house. She had another plan for extracting the needed recipes from the deep caverns of her mother's memory. *If* the disease eating away at her memory hadn't already gobbled them up.

"I have some things to do at home," Sam explained on the drive over. "If you help me, we can finish early and go to lunch."

"What sort of things do you need me to help with?" Lovie asked in a concerned tone.

"I'm having some friends over for lunch tomorrow. I'm serving shrimp salad and coleslaw. Everyone always raves over your shrimp salad. You have the special touch, Mom. I've tried to make it, but mine doesn't taste the same." During the past few days, Sam had spent hours on the Internet researching dementia and Alzheimer's, including effective ways to interact with people afflicted with those conditions. One of the websites recommended speaking kindly and complimenting them to increase their self-esteem, and giving them accomplishable tasks to help maintain their sense of self-worth. But the website also warned not to expect more than a person was capable of.

Lovie didn't respond. She stared into her lap and fidgeted with her hands the rest of the way.

"Who lives here?" her mother asked when they pulled up in front of Sam's bungalow.

"This is my house, Mom." Sam hurried around to Lovie's side and helped her down from the passenger seat. She unlocked the front door and stepped out of her mother's way so she could enter.

"Your home is lovely, dear," Lovie said, exploring the great room as though she'd never been there. "Allen must be doing well to afford all this."

Allen is dead, Sam thought, but there was no need to tell her that. She wouldn't remember it in five minutes anyway. According to Sam's online research, her mother was incapable of forming new memories.

Ignoring her mother's comment, Sam led her to the kitchen, took her purse from her, and set it down on the breakfast table. Jamie had purchased two pounds of shrimp for her off one of the boats at the marina. Sam had cooked it earlier that morning and organized the other ingredients on the counter, along with measuring cups, mixing bowls, and knives. Placing her hand on the small of her mother's back, she walked her around the counter to the prep side of the kitchen, where she'd set up a cutting board with a Vidalia onion and chopping knife. "Mom, why don't you dice the onion while I peel the shrimp." She hoped the shrimp salad recipe would come naturally to her mother once she got caught up with preparation.

Lovie eyed the shrimp in the colander in the sink. "Did you remember to cook the shrimp with lemon?"

"Lemon, huh? I never knew you did that." She felt like jumping up and down with glee. Her plan was working. "Do you think they'll taste okay without the lemon?" Sam didn't care how they tasted. With or without the lemon, the shrimp salad would be fine for their dinner.

Lovie removed one of the shrimp from the colander, peeled it, and popped it into her mouth. "Next time add the lemon."

Sam snickered. "Yes, ma'am!" she said, and jotted a reminder on the notepad beside her.

She set the pen down and began to peel the shrimp, watching her mother out of the corner of her eye. Lovie picked up the knife and stared curiously at it, as though she'd never seen one before and wasn't sure what to do with it. She set the knife back down on the cutting board, abandoning the cooking project, and rounded the counter to the bank of windows. "You have a lovely view. What did you say Allen did again?"

Ignore it, Sam. Remember, that website on dementia said it's better to play along with her than to correct her. "He works on one of the fishing boats."

While her mother stared out across the marsh, Sam finished preparing the shrimp salad, tasting and making notes as she added a little bit of each ingredient. Before the fire, Sam and Lovie had worked together every day. Maybe that explained why she hadn't noticed the changes in her mother. But now, looking back over the past year, she was able to see the signs. In addition to the strange combinations of clothes she wore, as she'd been doing for years, Sam categorized her appearance of late as unkempt. Her hair was not always clean, and oftentimes she wore no makeup. It wasn't just her physical appearance but her demeanor as well. She talked to herself all the time, and got frustrated when she couldn't remember things. She'd been reserved with their customers, even borderline rude on occasion. Out of concern, several had mentioned Lovie's brash behavior to Sam. On some subconscious level, she must have known what was happening to her mother, but she'd been unable to face the idea of losing her. When, in fact, she'd already lost her.

Sam finished with the shrimp salad and moved on to the

coleslaw. "Mom, do you have any ideas on ways to improve the slaw?"

The sound of her voice startled her mother out of her trance. She darted her eyes around the room, as though confused about where she was, and was visibly relieved when she set her eyes on Sam. She staggered over to the nearest bar stool. "Did you say something, dear?"

"I asked if you had any ideas on how to improve our coleslaw. Our recipe is the tried-and-true traditional slaw. I'd like to create an alternative that doesn't have mayonnaise."

Lovie stared straight at her and responded, "When can I go home?"

Sam let out a soft sigh, wondering which home her mother had in mind. Surely not Faith's house. Maybe her town house, but Sam suspected the home she was referring to was the cottage on the inlet where Sam had grown up. "We're going to lunch when I finish this. I'll take you home after that."

Lovie watched her slice and dice the cabbage, but after a few minutes she grew bored. "Where's your powder room, dear?"

Sam pointed at the doorway. "Across the main room, through the master bedroom. Do you need me to show you the way?"

"Don't be ridiculous, Samantha. I'm not an invalid, you know." But as she shuffled out of the room, Sam thought her mother looked exactly like an invalid.

Sam became so engrossed in experimenting with her cabbage, she forgot all about her mother until she realized, some fifteen minutes later, she hadn't returned. She washed her hands and hurried to her bedroom, where, much to her relief, she found her mother fast asleep in her bed. The odor greeted her as she entered the room. Her mother had wet herself, the urine soaking through her elastic-waist denim jeans and saturating Sam's white down comforter.

She planted her face in her palm. It eventually happened to everyone, and now it was happening to them. Parent and child had switched roles. Grabbing a stack of old beach towels from the linen closet, she took them out to her car and draped them over the passenger seat. She went to the kitchen and quickly put away the food and cleaned up her mess before returning to the bedroom.

"Wake up, Mom." She gently shook Lovie awake.

Lovie blinked her eyes open. "Where am I?"

"You're at my house, remember? You took a little nap while I was finishing in the kitchen. I don't know about you, but I'm hungry. Let's go grab some lunch."

Lovie sat up and swung her legs over the side of the bed, seemingly oblivious to her wet clothes or the stain on the comforter. Sam linked her arm with her mother's as she walked her to the car.

Sam held her breath against the odor as she drove down her driveway. "Why don't I swing by home so you can change? I'm taking you someplace nice. You should probably put on some slacks."

"Have I ever been to this restaurant?"

"Many times. We're going to the Pelican's Roost." *Definitely not nice,* Sam thought, *but there's no other place in town for lunch.*

"Never heard of it. Where is it?"

"It's the restaurant at the Inlet View Marina."

"Oh, I see. You're talking about the Inlet Bar and Grill," Lovie said, referring to the original name of the restaurant. New owners had changed the name when they purchased the marina in the early seventies. "Since when do I need to dress up to go there?"

"Since it's not the Inlet Bar and Grill anymore," Sam said. During the rest of the short drive, she ignored her mother's endless string of questions.

"Let's hurry. We don't want to miss our reservation," Sam said when they arrived at Faith's house. She dragged her mother out of the car and into the house without giving her a chance to challenge or complain. She helped her out of her soppy jeans and into a pair of dry navy slacks, leaving the soiled clothing on the bathroom floor. She would start a load of laundry when they got back.

Sam requested a booth with a view of the water. Having to look at the burned remains of Captain Sweeney's Seafood might upset her mother. Fortunately for them, the hostess was able to accommodate the request. If the nearly empty restaurant was any indication, Jamie would be looking for another job before summer even started.

"What do I usually get here?" Lovie asked the waitress when she handed them menus.

Sam smiled a knowing smile at Raquel, the gray-headed waitress who had worked there forever.

"I'll give you a few minutes to decide," Raquel said and scurried away.

Be patient, Sam, she reminded herself. "You usually have the fried flounder sandwich with sweet potato fries, Mom."

Lovie set the menu down. "Then that's what I'll have." But by the time the waitress returned, Lovie had forgotten about the fried flounder sandwich and copied Sam by ordering a chicken Caesar salad.

Lunch was a torturous affair. Her mother asked one question after another. The *same* questions over and over. None of them were of any importance. Most pertained to the logistics of her going home. Whichever home was on her mind. When Sam finally stopped answering her questions altogether, Lovie didn't seem to mind or notice. She babbled on and on about the la-la land where she was currently residing. The best Sam could make out, her mother had ventured back in time to when she and her sisters were young adults and their father was still alive. Jackie was living and working in Charleston, and Sam and Faith had just started full-time at the market. They had not yet married, and none of the grandchildren had been born. Sam first felt sorry for her mother and then wanted to wrap her fingers around her neck and choke the life out of her. One thing she knew for certain—Faith would go batshit crazy if they didn't put her in a home.

By the time she got her mother back to her sister's house and down for her nap, Sam was craving vodka, but she would have to settle for sweet tea. She gathered her mother's soiled laundry and started a load of wash. When she went to the kitchen, she was surprised to find Mike eating a sandwich at the counter.

"I didn't know you were here," Sam said, pouring herself a glass of tea from the pitcher in the refrigerator.

"I heard you getting Lovie settled, and I didn't want to disturb you." He held his sandwich up. "I'm working a double shift. Just came home for a quick shower and a bite to eat."

She sat down next to him at the counter. "Surely you know some nurses who are either retired or need extra work. Mom needs professional help. Faith can't do this alone."

"I've already given Faith a list. I offered to interview them, but she insisted she'd handle it. As far as I know, she hasn't called any of them yet." He set his sandwich down and wiped his mouth with a paper napkin. "We brought Lovie here to live with us so that I could assess her condition. In my professional opinion, she is ready for full-time care. Faith is against putting her in a retirement home. With the right help, I don't see why we couldn't manage Lovie's care here."

Sam considered this. "That would totally disrupt your life. We could move her to Jackie's guest cottage and set her up with a staff of nurses out there."

"Or you could move her back to her town house."

"True. Except that Bill would be able to keep an eye on her at the farm. Having a family member around would keep the nurses in line." Sam considered the financial implications. "That would work in the short term, but a long-term arrangement with round-the-clock nurses would eat through her savings in no time. Don't misunderstand me. I'm not concerned about inheritance. We need to make certain she has enough for her health care if she lives another ten years."

He offered her a sympathetic smile. "I think you and I both know that's not likely to happen. Then again, you can never predict these things." He checked his watch and stood to leave. "I need to get back to the hospital, but don't worry, Sammie"—he gave her shoulder a squeeze—"it'll work itself out in due time."

TWELVE

JAMIE

Jamie was willing to bet his first paycheck that his cousin had been smoking weed before he picked Jamie up to go fishing on Thursday morning. Sean was wearing sunglasses despite the early hour, and he laughed hysterically when he rammed his boat into the dock upon arrival. Sean, who'd handled boats since he was old enough to sit on his father's lap and grip the steering wheel, could dock a boat in his sleep. He usually took excellent care of his family's fleet, particularly this fiberglass skiff their father had bought for the twins on their sixteenth birthday.

Jamie loved his cousin like a brother. He'd been keeping an eye on Sean at work, concerned about the crowd he was hanging out with in the kitchen. The kitchen staff at the Roost was a rough bunch, but one in particular, the dishwasher, seemed worse than the rest. Night before last, Jamie had spotted Sean smoking with Julius out behind the dumpster. At the time he'd thought they were smoking a cigarette, but it could have been weed. Sean, claiming his car was in the shop, had bummed a ride home after work on Tuesday night, but when Jamie dropped him off at the farm, his cousin's 4Runner was parked in the garage. Sean had always been mischievous, more of a prankster than a trouble-maker, but Jamie had never known him to tell a bold-faced lie. When Jamie questioned him about it, Sean had blown it off by saying his mother must have picked up his car. Jamie would've believed him if not for his sheepish grin.

Stoned or not, Sean knew where to find the fish. When they grew tired of reeling them in, Sean drove the boat to a nearby deserted island and anchored close to the beach. They swam for a while before stretching out flat in the sand. Jamie was surprised when Sean removed a plastic flask from his pocket and took a swig of the clear liquid.

"Want some?"

Jamie shook his head at the offered flask. "We have to be at work at six, you know."

"So? That's hours from now. Come on, bro." He pressed the mouth of the flask to Jamie's arm. "You're in college. Don't you ever day-drink?"

"I don't drink much at all, actually, aside from an occasional beer. Watching my mother struggle with her addiction has shed new light on our drinking culture."

"Too bad for you, dude." Sean took another gulp and put the flask away.

Jamie closed his eyes and basked in the warm sun. He was dozing off when Sean asked, "When did you decide to make a career out of the seafood business?"

He opened his right eye. His cousin had rolled over on his side and was staring at him expectantly. "That's hard to say, cuz. I've never really considered doing anything else. Sweeney's is in my blood."

"Sweeney's is in my blood too. How come nobody ever gave me a chance to work there?"

"What're you talking about?" Jamie said, tossing a handful of sand at Sean. "You've been supplying us with seafood for the past three summers."

Sean sat up and drew his knees to his chest. "That's not a real job, though, like working in the kitchen or taking care of the customers."

"Believe me, your role is vital to our success. But I understand what you're saying." Jamie paused for a minute, thinking. "I was exposed at an early age because Mom was a single parent and I had nowhere else to go during the summers. Let's face it, dude, your mom is not the biggest fan of the seafood business."

"You've got that right," Sean said, rolling his eyes. "Have you ever thought about living somewhere other than Prospect?"

Sensing his cousin had a lot on his mind, Jamie scrambled into a sitting position so he could make eye contact with him. "A lot of my friends at school can't wait to explore the world. They envision themselves living in exotic places like Hawaii and Australia. I don't have the wanderlust gene. Sometimes I wonder what it'd be like to live in Charleston or maybe Wilmington. But I like the South and I want to live on the water.

"I have a feeling that Prospect is going to explode in the next few years. It's a charming little coastal town with a lot to offer young people who are looking for a safe place to raise their families. The world is getting smaller, Sean. It won't be long before we're considered a suburb of Charleston. Think of what it'd mean for our economy if we landed a large company like Boeing."

"That's true," Sean said. "I hadn't thought about it."

"What're you thinking?" Jamie shoulder-bumped his cousin. "Are you trying to decide what you want to be when you grow up?"

"Something like that." Sean rested his chin on his knees. "I can see myself in the restaurant business. Not as a dishwasher. And not as a chef. But maybe in management."

"I can totally see you working in the restaurant business. As long as that restaurant is on the waterfront. But don't sell yourself short. Think bigger than management. Think ownership. Your parents have the means to back you."

"My mother would sell her shoe collection before she gave me money to open a restaurant." Sean picked up a nearby piece of driftwood and drew the outline of a crab in the sand. "Are you glad you majored in restaurant management? They have a similar program at the College of Charleston. I'm thinking of applying."

"That would be perfect for you. What're you waiting for?"

Sean lifted a shoulder. "I'm not sure. I guess I'm afraid I might screw up again."

Jamie wasn't sure if by *"screwing up"* his cousin meant flunking out of college or if there was something more. "If you work hard, you won't screw up. You'll find your classes easy if you enjoy what you're learning."

Jamie's words seemed to strike the right chord with Sean. His face lit up and his eyes glistened. "Maybe I'll give it a shot." He got to his feet and brushed the sand off his butt. "I'm starving. Let's go get some dogs."

They purchased three hot dogs apiece from the HotDog Hut at the marina and sat down to eat on a nearby bench on the boardwalk. Back in their grandfather's day, commercial fishing boats had been the only boats that docked at the marina. But over the years a string of different owners had added several more docks. They still held a fair number of fishing vessels, but plenty of leisure yachts rented year-round slips as well.

"How do you like working at the restaurant?" Jamie couldn't let the day go by without warning his cousin about the unsavory employees who worked there.

Sean cut his eyes at him. "What do you think? I'm busing tables. I'd much rather be bartending."

"Bartending isn't much of a job when you don't have any customers. I hope business picks up after Memorial Day. From what I've seen of the kitchen, I don't know why the health department hasn't shut the place down. There are some questionable-looking dudes working back there."

"They're not so bad." Sean stuffed the last of his first dog in his mouth.

"Are you kidding me? Julius looks like he came straight out of prison. Whatever you do, don't invite him home to dinner."

"Chill, cuz. You sound just like Jackie."

They watched the boats coming and going as they finished their hot dogs in silence. The gentle salty breeze made Jamie feel lazy. He stretched his legs out in front of him and propped his hands behind his head, lifting his face to the sun.

Sean wadded up his hot dog wrappers and tossed them into a nearby trash can. "Is it bad that I don't have higher aspirations for myself like Cooper?"

"Not at all, bro. You are your own person. I know Cooper is your twin. Your identities are connected on some level I will never understand. But I totally get how different the two of you are. I don't think of you as 'the twins.' I think of you as Cooper and Sean."

"Really?" A wide grin spread across Sean's face, pushing his freckles closer together.

"Truly," Jamie said, punctuating his proclamation with a firm nod.

Sean jumped up off the bench. "In that case, you won't think my idea is stupid. Come on." He pulled Jamie to his feet.

"Where are we going?" Jamie asked, lengthening his stride to match Sean's pace on the way back to the boat.

"You'll see," Sean said as he untied the rope from the cleat.

He started the boat and took off down the creek toward his house. They were almost to his dock when Sean changed course and headed down a winding marsh creek. "I need to check my crab traps," he hollered over the whine of the motor. They meandered through the marsh creeks before he slowed the engine. He idled to the first of five red-and-white floats and put the boat in neutral.

Jamie looked around, disoriented. "Is this the same spot where we came the other day?" he asked, envying the twins' knowledge of the inlet.

"Nah, I pulled those traps in the other day. The bait goes bad if you leave the traps out for more than twenty-four hours." Sean tugged on the yellow rope and lifted the trap into the boat. The wire cage was filled with large blue crabs trying to claw their way out.

Jamie's jaw dropped. "Damn! There's dozens of crabs in there. That's a fortune at forty bucks a dozen."

"Exactly!" Sean returned to the wheel and putt-putted over to the next trap. With Jamie's help, he had all three traps in the boat in no time.

"I have an idea how we can make money off of selling crabs," Sean said. "I'll tell you about my plan if you come with me to my house and help me steam these."

Jamie, a pro at steaming crabs, gave him a thumbs-up. The twins had always delivered the crabs live to the market for Jamie and Roberto, Sweeney's full-time chef, to steam.

Sean put the boat in forward, and as they sped toward the farm, Jamie grew excited about the opportunity to cook in his uncle's fancy outdoor kitchen.

Jamie and Sean set two large pots on the gas burners, put two cups of water and a splash of vinegar in each, and placed the steamer racks inside the pots.

"What did you do with the crabs you got the other day?" Jamie asked while they were waiting for the water to boil.

"My dad took them to the other doctors in his practice. You can take some of these home to Sam and Eli, if you want."

They worked diligently for the next hour as they cooked the crabs in batches. Sean eyeballed their haul once the crabs were spread out on newspaper to cool. "I'd say we have at least twelve dozen crabs here. If we sold them for forty dollars a dozen, we would make four hundred eighty dollars, which is two hundred forty dollars apiece. Not bad for an afternoon's work."

Jamie pursed his lips. "Yeah, but who's gonna buy them?"

"Our customers, who else?"

Jamie looked at his cousin as if he were crazy.

"No! Listen, man. Our customers are in the habit of stopping by Sweeney's on Saturdays on their way to the beach. We can sell our crabs out of coolers from the parking lot. Word about the fire has spread on social media. People will slow down as they drive by to look at the damage and they'll see us in the parking lot with our 'Crabs for Sale' sign." He picked up a pair of tongs and began tonging the crabs into paper bags. "It's how Lovie got started all those years ago."

Jamie leaned back against the stainless-steel counter, rubbing his chin in thought. "If it worked for her, I don't see why it wouldn't for us. The human-interest angle alone could earn us some press. Mom hired a construction crew to clear the lot. They promised to be finished by tomorrow afternoon."

"I'm telling you, bro." Sean jabbed the tongs at Jamie. "We stand to make a fortune."

"You're a genius, cuz. Let's do it!" Jamie grabbed his cousin in a bear hug and swung him around until Sean belly laughed.

THIRTEEN

JACKIE

Jackie was late meeting her prospective buyers for their scheduled appointment at eleven thirty on Thursday morning. Upon entering the kitchen, she was appalled to find a trail of mouse droppings on the kitchen counter. She should've thought to have Liza or Cecilia freshen up the house, as no one had been inside since she left for Prospect a week ago. Fortunately the Doyles, completely enamored with the craftsmanship of her cabinetry, took no notice when she ripped off a paper towel and quickly wiped up the droppings.

"Please make yourselves at home," Jackie said to Hank and Catherine. "I have a family medical emergency and need to make a few calls. I'll be on the piazza if you need me." She aimed her phone at the glass door leading to the side porch.

The Doyles thanked her and ventured off to explore their potential new home.

Settling into the wicker chaise lounge on her piazza, Jackie placed the call to her husband. She burst into tears when he answered.

"What's wrong, Jack?" Bill asked in an alarmed tone. "Have you been in an accident?"

"My mother has Alzheimer's!"

His voice fell flat. "Oh. Is that all?"

"What do you mean, is that all? Isn't that enough?"

"Yes . . . Of course . . . That's more than enough. I'm sorry, honey. I didn't mean to be insensitive. I'm just surprised that you're surprised by the diagnosis. I thought that's what we expected."

Jackie squeezed her eyes shut, holding back the tears. "No, you're right. That *is* what we expected." She inhaled a shaky breath. "Her doctor is an insensitive ass, by the way. He pronounced the diagnosis right in front of Mom. Hearing him say the word out loud—*Alzheimer's*—took away any hope that Mom might be having another one of her spells. The woman who raised me, the mother I love so much, is never coming back. This horrible disease will eat away her mind and turn her into somebody we won't recognize. It's so degrading for her."

"It is degrading, sweetheart, but more so for you and your sisters than for Lovie. She doesn't understand what's happening to her. You might find it easier to cope if you keep that in mind."

"You're right about that. She doesn't have a clue." Jackie stared up at the porch's haint blue ceiling. "She didn't seem to understand, or even care, about what the doctor was saying."

"What exactly did Lawson say?"

"He ordered an MRI and a battery of other tests to confirm his diagnosis, but he explained that vascular dementia can coexist with Alzheimer's, and he thinks she has both. He thinks she may have had a stroke that caused this sudden decline."

Bill sighed. "That's what I was worried about."

Jackie heard the Doyles' voices in the kitchen. "I need to run, honey," she said, swinging her legs over the side of the chaise. "I'm meeting with some clients."

"I didn't realize you were staying in Charleston. I thought you were coming home after your mother's appointment. Who's looking after Sean?"

"Sean went fishing with Jamie. He's twenty years old. He doesn't need a babysitter."

What Sean really needs is someone to whip him into shape, she thought after she hung up. *A personal trainer, life coach, and prison guard all combined. And I'm not qualified for the job.*

Jackie had been nagging and fighting with Sean all week and had accomplished absolutely nothing. She'd given him a list of family friends to contact about a respectable summer job, and he'd gone out and gotten hired as a busboy. And he'd missed his appointment with Moses on Tuesday. Big Mo had been gracious about it, but Jackie knew he wouldn't be as understanding if it happened again. At least her son wasn't doing drugs. Of that much she was sure.

The Doyles emerged from the house. "Do you mind if we take a look at the carriage house?"

Jackie got to her feet. "By all means. Have a peek at the garden and pool area too while you're out here." She swept her arm in the direction of the backyard.

She watched Catherine and Hank stroll hand in hand toward the carriage house. They seemed like such a nice couple, the kind of people who would take care of her home. Jackie left the porch and went inside to the kitchen. She filled a glass of water from the refrigerator dispenser, drained it, and set it down on the counter. She ran her hand over the smooth Carrara marble. She'd personally chosen every surface, paint color, and wall covering with extra care. She loved this house. She should probably talk to Bill before she accepted an offer, but three years ago, when she had her mini midlife crisis, she'd realized that having the freedom to make her own choices about her professional life was vital to her happiness.

She glanced at the clock on the oven. She was due to meet her Realtor and contractor at the house on Church Street in twenty minutes. In addition to four bedrooms—the smallest of which she planned to convert into a home office—the Church

Street house had a living room, dining room, and family room adjacent to the kitchen. Stylistically, she was aiming for contemporary cozy, way less formal than Lamboll but more upscale than the farm.

She moved to the back window and watched the Doyles make their way through the garden to the pool. They sat down at the umbrellaed table, and for the next ten minutes talked with their heads close together. Jackie was thumbing a text to her Realtor, to let her know she'd be late to meet her, when the couple finally stood up and headed toward the house. She greeted them at the porch door.

"We've made a decision," Hank said. "We'd like to make an offer on the house. Fully furnished, of course."

Jackie worked hard to keep a straight face when he told her they were willing to pay her asking price plus a handsome amount triple the cost of the furnishings.

"We know you've turned down offers in the past," Catherine said. "We're willing to negotiate."

If she didn't accept this beyond-generous offer, word would spread around town, and she'd never be able to sell the house. But she had yet to consider the logistics of moving. "When would you want to close?"

Catherine shot her husband a glance of uncertainty. "The sooner the better for us," she said. "But obviously that's up to you."

If not for Sean, she could manage a few months of commuting daily from Prospect. If it did work out for him to attend the College of Charleston, they would need someplace to live while the Church Street house was being renovated. And what about her business? She was banking on moving her workroom to the Meeting Street warehouse. If for some reason that didn't work out, she would be stuck up a creek at low tide.

"I'll need some time to get my new place ready, and to move my business out of the carriage house. I can probably swing early

November, which would give you time to get settled before the holidays."

Disappointment crossed Catherine's face, but she quickly recovered. "We'll make that work. Whatever it takes."

A frown creased Jackie's forehead. "I hadn't really thought through to the next step, the paperwork and inspections. I want to make certain everything is taken care of properly. Do you mind if I involve my Realtor in the transaction?"

"As long as you don't mind if I involve mine," Hank said. "I'm a bond trader. I have no idea how to write a contract to purchase a home."

"Deal." They shook on the unofficial offer, and Jackie led them to the front door. "I'm supposed to meet my Realtor in five minutes. Her name is Midge Calhoun. Shall I have her call your Realtor?"

Catherine giggled. "That would be great. I'm sure she has his number. We've been working with her husband, Bennett."

Jackie smiled. "All the better. This might just be the most hospitable real estate closing in history."

Midge and Hugh Kelley were waiting for Jackie on the sidewalk in front of the Church Street house.

Hugh kissed Jackie's cheek. "It's good to see you."

He'd done a meticulous job on the Lamboll Street project, and she was looking forward to working with him again. His attention to detail had prevented her from making a bad decision on more than one occasion. Never mind that he was handsome in a rugged boots-and-blue-jeans kind of way. He'd been in a relationship with Heidi now for several years. A perfect match for sure. Jackie felt certain they'd eventually marry, most likely when they could find the time off from their demanding careers to tie the knot.

Jackie and Midge wandered through the house from room to room while Hugh examined the mechanics—the plumbing and electrical. When they paused to enjoy the warm sunshine and light breeze on the second-floor piazza, Jackie explained about the Doyles' offer on her house on Lamboll Street. "I just earned you a handsome commission and you didn't have to lift a finger."

"Yippee!" Midge clapped her hands like a kindergartner. "I'm taking you to lunch at the Charleston Place to celebrate."

Jackie hesitated. Hugh had yet to inspect the Meeting Street warehouse, and she needed to get home to Sean as soon as possible. But she had to eat lunch at some point. "Sounds lovely."

"I can't wait to tell Bennett," Midge said, removing her phone from her bag.

As Midge paraded back and forth on the piazza, phone pressed to her ear, Jackie admired her black Theory shift and Christian Louboutin patent pumps. Her Realtor had great style in clothes, with a fun-loving personality to match. She wasn't flashy, nor did Jackie consider her a classic beauty. She was the pretty girl with pert nose and hot body that all the boys lusted over in high school.

They had moved to the sidewalk in front of the house when Hugh emerged from the basement fifteen minutes later. "The electrical needs upgrading," he said, rubbing his grimy hands on his jeans. "As does the plumbing. Gutting the kitchen and bathrooms, like you mentioned on the phone, will take care of most of your major issues."

"How long do you think it'll take to finish the renovations? I just agreed to be out of my house on Lamboll by November first."

Hugh whipped out his phone and examined his calendar. "That depends on when I can start."

Jackie had long since worked out how she would pay for this house and the warehouse without the equity from her old house.

She looked at Midge. "How soon do you think we can close a no-strings-attached deal?"

"The house has been empty for some time, which means we should be able to work a deal. I'd say in thirty days, if you've already worked out your financing."

"If that's the case," Hugh said, "I can make November one happen. But only for you, Jackie."

"Thank you, Hugh. You can count on a handsome bonus for finishing on time."

It took Hugh even less time to inspect the warehouse than it had to inspect the house on Church Street. "Heating and air have been updated and are in pristine condition," he reported after his thorough inspection. "Go ahead and make your offer. But do it fast before someone beats you to it."

Aside from installing computer and phone systems, painting the wall that separated the showroom from the workroom was the only improvement she planned to make.

She hugged Hugh goodbye, despite his filthy clothing, on the sidewalk in front of the building and promised to be in touch as soon as the deals were finalized. She and Midge opted to walk to the Charleston Place to take advantage of the mild weather before the oppressive heat and humidity set in for the summer.

They both ordered the crab salad, and Midge surprised her by requesting a bottle of Prosecco.

"We shouldn't jinx ourselves by celebrating before we've written the offers," Jackie said.

"Then we'd better get busy." She removed her computer from her leather laptop bag.

They sipped Prosecco and nibbled on crab salad while Midge crafted the contracts. An hour and a half later, Jackie was more than a little buzzed when Midge finally shut her laptop. "Now we wait," she said, signaling the waiter. "I'm sorry, but I've got to run. I have another appointment."

Jackie's words slurred off her tongue when she said, "You can't meet a client in your condition."

"What condition?" she asked with a wicked grin on her face. "You drank most of the bottle. I only had a teensy-weensy sip."

Jackie fell back in her chair. No wonder she felt drunk. "You are bad, Midge."

"How else was I going to keep you occupied while I wrote the contracts?" She signed the credit card slip and handed the black folder to the waiter. "Come on. I'll order us an Uber."

"I'm gonna be in so much trouble with my husband. Do you think the Uber driver will take me to Prospect?" Jackie asked as she tripped through the hotel lobby after Midge.

"Take a nap, hon. You'll be fine in a couple of hours."

But Jackie slept hard for four hours. She woke a few minutes before six. When she retrieved her phone from the bedside table to call her husband, she saw she had five missed calls from Midge. She tapped the Realtor's number.

Midge answered on the first ring. "Finally! I was getting worried about you. I have great news. The owners of both properties accepted your offers."

"That is great news." Jackie rolled over on her side and slowly sat up. The room spun around her. "Why'd you let me drink so much?"

"As if I could stop you," Midge said with a snicker. "Don't worry about it. We all need to blow off some steam every now and then. I'm so sorry about your mama."

Goose pimples dotted her arms. "How do you know about my mother?"

"You told me all about her diagnosis. Don't you remember?"

Jackie wasn't in the habit of discussing her personal problems with friends. At least she'd had the good sense not to mention Sean. She brought a hand to her aching head. She *hoped* she hadn't mentioned Sean. She was a drunk, no better than her son or her sister. "Thanks for listening," she muttered.

"Do you need me to take you to your car?"

"No, but thanks. The fresh air will do me good," Jackie said and thought, *And sober me up.*

She rinsed her mouth out, used the toilet, and left the house on foot. She called Bill on the short walk over to Meeting Street. "I'm sorry, sweetheart. I got tied up on a project I'm working on. I'm leaving Charleston now."

She was relieved when he didn't sound angry. "And I'm leaving the office. Why don't I stop by the store and pick up some steaks for dinner?"

"That would be great. I have some exciting news for you. I can't wait to tell you about it when I get home."

"In that case I'll pick up a bottle of bubbly."

Her stomach lurched at the thought of more alcohol, but Jackie managed to say, "That'd be lovely."

FOURTEEN

JAMIE

Sean was visibly hungover when Jamie picked him up from the farm on Saturday morning a few minutes after seven. They'd exchanged words the night before at work. Jamie had witnessed Sean nipping from his flask and called him out on it. "What're you doing, bro? If the manager catches you, he'll fire you."

"Don't worry about it!" Sean tried to walk away, but Jamie grabbed his arm. "Where did you get the liquor?" Sean averted his eyes, and Jamie pressed. "Do you have a fake ID?"

"So what if I do?" Sean yanked his arm free. "Everybody under twenty-one has a fake. You need to back off. You're seriously starting to get on my nerves."

Jamie had been serving drinks to a group of local drunks when Sean left work. Now, based on his bloodshot eyes and the odor of alcohol exuding from his pores, he had gotten drunk somewhere. Jamie hoped it was in the safety of his home, after he got there from work. Sean had bummed rides to and from work all week from Jamie, even though his 4Runner remained parked in his driveway. Jamie suspected his cousin might have lost his license.

"How'd you get home from work last night?" Jamie asked casually on the way to the market lot.

"Julius gave me a ride." Sean stared him down. "I know what you're gonna say, but save the lecture, dude. You were busy when I left, and I was tired and ready to go home."

Jamie decided to let it go for now. They had a busy day ahead of them.

The cousins set up a seafood kiosk that rivaled the umbrella stand where their grandmother had originally started Captain Sweeney's Seafood Market nearly sixty years ago. They'd borrowed the red pop-up tent Sean's parents used for tailgate parties at Georgia football games, and they installed it in the Sweeney's parking lot. Jamie backed his pickup truck under the edge of the tent and use the tailgate as a checkout counter. At Sean's suggestion they filleted the flounder they'd caught on Thursday and sold it by the pound, packaged in Styrofoam containers and secured with plastic wrap. They sold the flounder and crabs out of YETI coolers from the bed of Jamie's truck. Eli borrowed two orange traffic cones from the police department and used them to prop up the metal sign Sam had rescued from the rubble. The sign, with 'Seafood' painted in red in a retro style, had hung on the walls at the market for as long as anyone could remember.

Sam, after a day of baking in her test kitchen, donated the products of her experiments to the cause—blueberry crumb coffee cake, cheddar cheese muffins, and angel food cakes. The most popular item from the selection was her pistachio pound cake. She'd made two batches of cake mix that yielded six loaves, all of which sold within the first hour. Jackie contributed a banquet table and blue gingham tablecloth to display the baked goods and a cooler full of bottled water for the patrons to drink while they shopped.

The Sweeney clan showed up in shifts. Bill came first on his way to his eight thirty tee time. Mike brought Bitsy by on their way home from brunch at the Island Bakery, and Jackie stopped in for a few minutes around ten. Faith was the only family member who couldn't make it. For fear of upsetting her, they'd all agreed to keep Lovie away.

Sam had insisted they operate in a professional manner by running the money through the market account. She'd purchased a cash box and a credit card reader from the office supply store. The line of customers was already backed up when she arrived around eight. She took over the transactions while the boys filled their customers' orders.

During a lull in business around noon, Jamie pulled his mother over to the edge of the lot near the stationery store. "Did you realize Pen to Paper is for sale?"

"Of course, honey. Anita closed down in March. Her business has been way off for the past two years. I hate to see her go. She's been a good neighbor."

He took Sam by the arm and led her to the front door of the store. "Annie suggested we buy it," he said as he peeked inside the window of the stationery store. "And I think it's something to consider. With the expansion plans you have for the new market, we're going to need more space than we had in our old store. A bigger building will leave very little room for parking. We could design an L-shaped building sited on the corner and have parking lots on either side."

Sam's eyes darted back and forth between the stationery store and their lot. "I love the idea, honey. But we can't consider a plan like that until we settle with the insurance company. *If* we settle with the insurance company. As it stands right now, we'll have to file a lawsuit, which means a long, drawn-out court battle."

Jamie shook his head. "I don't understand. Why?"

Sam exhaled a deep breath. "I haven't wanted to worry you with this, but the insurance company is trying to pin the fire on Lovie, and there's a provision in our policy that excludes arson. You and I both know Lovie would never do something like that, regardless of her state of mind, but we're having a difficult time proving it based on the evidence."

"Does that mean we might not get *any* money from the insurance company?"

"Unfortunately, there's a chance we won't get a dime." She cupped his chin in her hand. "But don't you worry about a thing, my boy. One way or another, we'll figure out how to reopen the market. I still have my share of Mack's money. Combined with the documentation that proves the market was on solid financial ground, we'll be able to build a similar setup to what we had."

Jamie hung his head. "So buying the stationery store is out of the question."

She nodded. "Unless we receive an unexpected windfall."

By two o'clock that afternoon, they'd sold every crab, flounder fillet, and baked item on the lot. Farmer Fred Firestone, a local supplier of produce to Captain Sweeney's, stopped in as they were packing up.

"Good to see ya, son." He gave Jamie's hand a firm shake. They reminisced for a few minutes about old times at Sweeney's. "If you're planning to host your farmers' market again, I'd love to get in on the action. I'll pay you a fee, of course."

Jamie liked the idea of a Saturday farmer's market. Why not include other locals with goods to sell?

"Sean and I were just talking about whether to do it again next week," Jamie said, and introduced the farmer to his cousin.

"I've expanded my crops this year," Farmer Fred said. "I have some newfangled vegetables your customers will like. My field is full of different kinds of peppers. My son says I need these varieties to make my garden current. Whatever that means." He chuckled. "Evan's a foodie, you understand. A banker by day and *Top Chef* wannabe by night. I have the tried-and-true vegetables as well. Best sweet corn I've grown in years. I have my own cart on wheels. I promise to stay out of your way. I'll set up wherever works best for you."

"We'll figure that out when we get here on Saturday," Jamie said. "Is seven too early?"

"Heck no! I'm a farmer. I get up when the rooster crows." Fred started to walk off and turned back around. "Oh, and my wife has started a real purdy wildflower garden. I'll have her bundle some up."

Jamie flashed him a smile. "The ladies will love that."

They watched the old man climb into his old beat-up pickup truck and drive away. Sean turned to Jamie. "Seriously, cuz. We made a killing today, and it's not even two o'clock. We could've sold ten times more crabs. If only we had a place to store them. They won't fit in our refrigerator."

Jamie thought about it while they took down the tent. "Maybe the marina store will rent us some space in their walk-in refrigerator. I had to get some ice from them yesterday afternoon when the ice machine broke at the restaurant. Their cooler was practically empty."

"That would be perfect," Sean said, his blue eyes bright with excitement. "We can keep the crabs cold that way, and bring them across the street as we need them."

"We'll need more time next Friday to prepare for the market," Jamie said. "I know that Friday night is the busiest night at the Roost, but we should ask off anyway. I just hope they'll let us have it."

"So what if they don't, bro?" Sean said as he climbed into the passenger side of Jamie's pickup. "We can make way more money selling crabs than pouring drinks and busing tables."

Jamie thought Heidi Butler was a knockout for a woman who

dressed like a teenager and wore her hair in a messy pile on top of her head. He'd found her fun to be around and full of creative ideas when she catered his mother's wedding reception at the bungalow December before last. But that was prior to Annie's discovery that Heidi was her real mother. He did not approve of the way she had abandoned Annie as a baby, but if Annie could forgive her mother, then so could he.

By the end of the Picketts' wedding reception that night, Heidi had totally won him over. Not only was she a talented chef and an efficient coordinator, she treated her employees with a fair but firm hand. She expected perfection from them, and she paid them well accordingly.

"You're a hard worker, Jamie, a welcome addition to my staff," she told him as they were loading her van after the last guest had left. "Make yourself at home tonight. I'm sorry I don't have a guest room, but there's an air mattress in the hall closet. Annie can show you where it is."

"I'll be fine," Jamie said. "Thanks for letting me crash."

Heidi drove off in the van, leaving Jamie with Annie and Lizbet on the sidewalk in front of the Picketts' home, where the wedding reception had been held.

"I know it's late," Annie said. "But I'm wound too tight to sleep. Do y'all want to hang out for a while?"

"If we can go to my house," Lizbet said. "My sister's bored. She's begging me to come home." She held her phone up for them to see the long string of texts from her sister.

Jamie shrugged. "I'm fine with whatever." He would walk on hot coals to Antarctica and back if it meant spending time with Lizbet.

"I live just a few blocks over," Lizbet said as they headed off down the street. "My sister's partner, Sawyer, is doing her residency at MUSC. She works all the time. I feel sorry for Brooke. That's my sister. She gets lonely a lot."

"You'll like Brooke," Annie said. "She's fun and funky. Very artsy." She grabbed Jamie's hand and dragged him down the street. "Let's hurry. I'm thirsty for a beer."

Brooke was waiting for them on the front porch with a cooler of beer and Adele singing at low volume from a wireless speaker. Jamie was speechless at the sight of her. She was smoking hot, with wicked green eyes and her blonde hair in a sassy cut. She wore a tiny diamond stud in her nose and a loose-fitting white sundress that outlined her nipples. Most of the girls Jamie knew wore bras.

Annie introduced them, and Brooke stood on her tiptoes to kiss his cheek. "Welcome, Jamie Sweeney," she whispered in his ear, rubbing her breasts against his arm.

"Get down, you slut puppy," Lizbet said, pulling her sister off him. "She's an incorrigible flirt. She's also crazy in love with her *girl*friend."

"Can't a girl have a little fun?" Brooke said, plopping down on the bench swing. "The cooler's full. Help yourselves. I'm going nuts here without anyone to talk to."

Annie grabbed a beer from the cooler and sat down on the swing beside Brooke, leaving the small wicker sofa for Jamie and Lizbet. He was sure she'd planned it that way.

Annie tucked her foot under her leg, angling her body toward Brooke. "Why don't you work some parties for us, on the nights when Sawyer is at the hospital? That way you won't get so bored and lonely."

Brooke chewed on her lower lip as she considered her suggestion. "That's not a bad idea, as long as I can dictate my schedule. I wouldn't mind making a little extra spending money. Sawyer and I are saving for a trip to Belize, if she ever gets any vacation time."

"I'll text you some dates and you can check both your calendars," Annie said.

"I'm being nosy," Jamie said. "But are you renting this house or do you live here with your parents?" The rent in downtown

Charleston was crazy expensive. He could understand why Lizbet might still be living at home with their parents. But not Brooke, at her age, with her gay lover.

The cheerful mood on the porch tanked, and the color drained from his face. "Did I say something wrong?"

"It's complicated." Lizbet took a pull from her beer bottle and set it down on the arm of the sofa with a clang.

"Our mother died last summer from brain cancer," Brooke said, staring down into her lap.

"I'm so sorry. I didn't know." Jamie glared at Annie. Why hadn't she warned him?

"Of course you didn't," Lizbet said with damp eyelashes. "It's been a difficult year, but my sister and I are closer because of it."

"Our father couldn't stand to live here without our mother," Brooke explained. "When he moved into a waterfront condo last winter, he turned the house over to us."

"Which is why we're always looking for fun people like you to visit us!" Brooke said, and increased the volume on her speaker when an upbeat Brad Paisley song began to play.

The mood instantly improved, and the conversation turned to Jamie. Brooke quizzed him about the fire at the market and his summer plans.

"I'm not getting enough hours at the Roost," Jamie said. "I'm thinking about quitting that job and working as many parties as Heidi needs me."

"Cool!" Annie said. "We're booked most nights for the rest of the summer and some daytime events as well. We'd love to have you."

"I would need a place to stay, if y'all know of anyone looking for a roommate."

"You can stay here with us," Brooke offered. "We have two extra bedrooms. One even has its own bath."

Sleeping in a comfortable bed down the hall from Lizbet appealed to him much more than camping out on an air mattress on Heidi's floor. "That could work, depending on how much you'd charge me for rent."

"Duh. You can live here for free," Brooke said.

Jamie shook his head. "I wouldn't feel right living here without paying something."

Brooke sat up straight in the swing. "In that case you can work off your rent. We're always looking for a strong arm to help us around here. Lizbet's Dr. Dreamy is the only man who ever comes here, but all he's good for is bandaging a knife cut."

Who is Dr. Dreamy? Jamie wondered as his heart plunged.

FIFTEEN

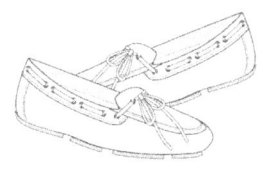

SAM

Sam took a leisurely walk on Sunday afternoon to clear her head before the four o'clock meeting with her sisters to discuss their mother's future. Before she realized where she was headed, she found herself standing in front of the stationery store. Sam would miss Anita. She'd known the woman since she was a child. She used to visit her in her store on days when the market was busy and Sam was under her mother's feet at the market. Anita kept a bag of Tootsie Pops in her desk drawer just for Sam. When she'd come into the market two weeks ago to notify Sam that she was going out of business, she confided what Sam had already suspected. Her invitation business was failing because of culture changes. Folks weren't entertaining the way they once had, with big elaborate affairs. And for the few events they hosted, they sent electronic invitations instead of decorative cards hand-delivered by the mailman.

"Everyone is so casual these days," Anita said. "I don't understand this new modern era of anything goes."

"I know what you mean," Sam responded. "Everything is changing all the time. I can hardly keep up."

But Sam was determined to keep up as best she could for as

long as she could. "Keep on keeping on," her mother always said. "Plant a smile on your face every morning and take advantage of every minute of every day. You won't succeed in all your endeavors, but you can be proud of yourself for giving it your best shot."

Sam had interviewed three architects in the past week, and one she liked hands down better than the other two. They'd scheduled a meeting for the coming week to begin planning the design. Contrary to her son's opinion, Sam thought they could make the expansions she envisioned by adding a few square feet to what they'd had before. Keeping the building small would maintain the cozy feeling folks appreciated at Sweeney's.

She snapped a photograph of the agent's name on the sign, in case she changed her mind about the size of the building or the insurance company came through for her, and walked at a brisk pace on the way home. Jamie had returned from Charleston when she got there. He was out on the dock watching Eli fiddle with his boat motor. They grew quiet when she walked up.

"Uh-oh. Clearly I interrupted something. What's wrong?"

Jamie hopped to his feet and presented her with a bouquet of wilted daisies. "We were discussing what to cook for you on the grill tonight in honor of Mother's Day."

"Aren't you sweet. Thank you, son." She took the flowers from him and kissed his cheek. "Well . . . don't keep me in suspense. What did you decide? What're we having for dinner?"

Eli looked up from his motor and winked at her. "You'll have to wait and see."

Jamie and Sam sat down on the bench together. "How was last night? Did you enjoy working for Heidi?"

"Yep." Jamie stretched his legs out in front of him. "Looks like I'll be working a lot for them this summer. Heidi pays better and they can give me more hours than the Roost."

"Where will you live? It's not right for you to impose on Heidi and Annie indefinitely."

"I need to confirm it, but I may have another place to stay."

He told her about the Horne sisters and how they were willing to give him a room in exchange for his helping them around the house.

"That sounds like an ideal setup. You might end up loving Charleston and decide to move there."

An expression crossed her son's face that she couldn't read. He shook his head as he dismissed the idea. "I can't see that happening."

Sam wanted her son to chart his own course. But when it came to rebuilding the market, his course was her course. She wasn't sure she'd be as eager to go the distance if Jamie weren't on board. She'd have more responsibilities with Lovie and Faith out of the picture, which would mean hiring additional staff. She'd embrace the challenge right now, but in nine years, when she was turning sixty and Eli was retiring from the police department, she might not feel the same way. Then again, her mother had worked until she was eighty-five. They would have the summer to sort out their lives, and their futures, since groundbreaking on the new building wouldn't happen until late August at the earliest.

"So, Mom." Jamie shifted on the bench to face her. "Annie has the most amazing idea. We talked about it over brunch this morning. She thinks we should buy the stationery store and open a sandwich shop adjacent to the market, technically in the same building with a doorway separating the two spaces. Think about the Saturday tourists heading to the beach. We'll be a one-stop shop for them. They can grab a sandwich while waiting for us to process their seafood orders. The locals will be thrilled to have another lunch hangout. And we can have wine tastings and rent the space out for small events."

Sam smiled at her son. He sounded certain of his future at Sweeney's. Time would tell. Prospect certainly needed a new lunch spot, but a sandwich shop sounded like a great big headache. Although, as she thought about it, having a room for wine tastings and small events held some appeal. She admired his youthful enthusiasm, but he lacked experience in the real world. "I told you yesterday, Jamie, I can't afford to buy that building."

"No! You don't understand. Annie wants to invest in the sandwich shop. Or, if we don't want the hassle of operating a restaurant, she will lease the space from us and run it herself."

Sam hesitated. "What does Heidi think of all this?"

"Annie hasn't talked to her about this specific project yet, but they're looking for ways to expand. Annie likes the catering business, but ultimately wants to open her own restaurant. Even though she didn't share specific numbers with me, I get the impression they're making enough money at Tasty Provisions to open ten restaurants."

Sam looked away from her son's eager face. She hated to disappoint him. "Let me think about it, Jamie. I'm not sure how I feel about having nonfamily members as partners."

"But Annie *is* family."

"That's true. And I do love her like my own. But doing business with family and friends is usually not a good idea. I would hate it if something happened to ruin our relationship."

"Happy Mother's Day," Sam said, giving each of her sisters a hug when they arrived a few minutes after four. They usually celebrated Mother's Day by going to church together and then out to Jackie's farm for brunch afterward. This year was different. None of the sisters felt eager to celebrate when their mother didn't know her own grandchildren. "How's Mom doing today? I feel bad I didn't get over to see her today."

"Honestly, it's a good thing you didn't," Faith said. "She's having an off day. Mike and Bitsy have taken her for a ride in the pontoon boat, hoping to calm her down. She seems so agitated all the time now, like she needs something but she doesn't know what she wants or how to ask for it."

Sam felt guilty for obsessing over her business when her sister was coping with their mother's dementia.

"She'll enjoy the boat ride with the high tide and warm sunshine," Sam said. "Besides, she always responds well to Mike."

"Don't we all," Jackie said with a rare, sincere smile. No one in the family ever said a bad word about Mike.

"Let's sit down." Sam gestured to the farm table, where she'd set out a fresh pitcher of sweet tea and three glasses.

Jackie sat at the head of the table, the self-appointed president of the Sweeney board of directors, with Faith and Sam on either side. They pulled out their laptops, notepads, and pens, ready to get to work.

Jackie said, "Bill informed me that Creekside Manor has opened a brand-new, state-of-the-art memory care facility. It's the obvious first choice, since it's right here in Prospect. But in order to get a fair comparison, we should visit several different retirement homes. I'm happy to take the lead on the ones in and around Charleston."

"I've already created a list." Sam handed each of them copies of the list she'd made from her Google search.

Faith's face flushed red. "Visiting those other facilities is a waste of time. Why wouldn't we go with Creekside Manor if we like it?"

"It's a process," Jackie said. "To determine which facility can offer Mom the best care at the right price."

Faith stared openmouthed at their older sister. "Would you listen to yourself, Jackie? You sound like a used car salesman."

Sam smiled at Faith. "We're making an important decision, honey, akin to buying a new car. It would be irresponsible of us not to consider the cost."

"I have a big problem with this whole scenario." Faith stood abruptly and walked over to the window, placing her back to them. "Mom is fine staying with me. I don't see the need to put her in a home at all."

Sam glanced over at Jackie, who nodded for Sam to respond. "Because having Mom live with you is a short-term solution to what could end up being a long-term problem."

"As her condition worsens, Mom will become more difficult to manage," Jackie said. "Eventually the situation will take its toll, not only on you but on your family."

"Think about your daughter," Sam said. "Bitsy loves her grandmother. How will it impact her to watch Lovie decline right before her eyes?"

Faith's shoulders began to tremble, and Sam suspected her sister was crying. She left the table and went to stand beside Faith at the window. "I know this is hard, Faith. It's hard for all of us." She squeezed her sister in a half hug. "Let's take it one slow step at a time."

"Okay." Faith sniffled and wiped her nose with the back of her hand. She allowed Sam to lead her back to the table.

Once they were seated again, Sam planted her palms on the table. "Now. Why don't we start with Creekside Manor? Let's figure out a day we can all go for a tour." She flipped her laptop open and accessed her calendar. "I'm flexible."

"Mike is working days through Wednesday," Faith said, consulting her day planner. "Does Thursday work for y'all? I can get Mike to stay with Mom."

Jackie thumbed the calendar on her phone. "That works for me. I have to be in Charleston on Monday and Tuesday. While I'm there, I'll tour one or two other facilities so we'll have something to compare with Creekside Manor."

"Fine, for the purpose of comparison," Faith said. "As long as you know I'll never agree to putting her somewhere so far away."

Jackie glared at Faith. "Point noted."

"Mom is wearing the same clothes over and over again," Faith said. "Can one of you get some of her things from her town house? I don't think it's a good idea for her to go back there."

"I'll do it," Sam said. "I'll get some boxes and have Jamie help me. Mom will want some of her things with her when she moves to the nursing home anyway."

A discussion of their mother's prized possessions led to a debate over selling her town house. Jackie lobbied for putting it on the market right away, while Faith argued to wait until Lovie was settled wherever she was going.

Sam studied her sisters as they talked. Jackie was polished and sophisticated, while Faith was a simple, pure-hearted soul. Both had faced challenges in recent years. Jackie with her marital problems and her professional crisis, and Faith having left a piece of herself in that gruesome trailer in the woods where she'd lived with her abusive ex-husband. She hoped both her sisters would one day find the happiness they deserved.

"Let me know how it goes in Charleston," Sam said to Jackie when she walked her sisters to the door. "I thought you were taking the summer off from work."

"I am for the most part. But a couple of unexpected projects have fallen into my lap. My assistants, Liza and Cecilia, will handle the majority of the work. I'm meeting with them tomorrow to give them some direction."

Who is she kidding? Sam thought. Her sister was too much of a control freak to turn her pet projects over to her assistants. Whenever she took on a new challenge, she became obsessed and focused on the project to the exclusion of everything else in her life.

SIXTEEN

FAITH

By the time Thursday morning rolled around, Faith was more than ready to pack her mother off to a nursing home. As Jackie had warned, Lovie was becoming increasingly difficult to manage as her condition worsened. She tested Faith at every turn, like a two-year-old. She'd even thrown a full-blown temper tantrum when Faith refused to let her have a Coca-Cola at bedtime. Giving Lovie caffeine anytime was a bad idea. And past dinnertime guaranteed that no one in the house would get any sleep.

When she toured Creekside Manor that afternoon, Faith found the facilities adequate, the staff knowledgeable, and the fees affordable. But the thought of locking her mother away made her sick to her stomach.

"It just doesn't seem right when I'm perfectly capable of taking care of her myself," she said to her sisters in the parking lot afterward.

Jackie peered at her over the frames of her Gucci sunglasses. "I've spoken with the administrators at four different facilities this week, and they have all told me the same thing. There will come a time when you can no longer take care of Mom. She will destroy your home and ruin your marriage."

Faith knew Mike loved her enough to agree with whatever decision she made, but it wasn't fair to turn their lives upside down by keeping her mother in their home. There was also Bitsy to consider. She'd become withdrawn and, since the weekend, had been spending more and more time in her room. The long-term effects for a child her age of having to watch her grandmother's downward spiral could be catastrophic.

"Maybe you're right," she said, forcing the words past the lump in her throat.

Jackie placed a hand on Faith's shoulder. "I've done the research, and I'm here to tell you, we got lucky. This place is as good as, if not better than, the ones I looked at in Charleston. And it's right here in Prospect."

"A lot of good that is." Faith rummaged through her bag for her car keys. "You heard the administrator. Irene Davidson said we can't even visit her."

"That's only for the first week, honey." Sam grabbed her hand. "I know it seems cruel, but her disease is cruel. If she had terminal cancer, we'd be making arrangements with hospice. We have to keep telling ourselves this is all in Mom's best interest."

"I can tell myself that all day long, but I'm never gonna believe it." Faith pointed her key fob at her SUV and pressed the unlock button. "Make the arrangements and let me know the date. In the meantime I'll talk to the doctor about putting Mom on some antianxiety meds, like Irene suggested."

She got in her car and drove toward home. Taking care of her mother had given her a sense of purpose. How would she fill her days with no job and her mother in a nursing home? Bitsy would be out of school for the summer soon. She could spend some quality time with her. They could take day trips to the beach and have her friends over for sleepovers. They could take sailing lessons, as Faith had always dreamed of doing with her daughter.

They could even look into purchasing a Sunfish sailboat. Summer activities would keep her busy for the next three months, but what about all the months and years after that?

Friday proved to be her mother's worst day yet. Lovie had been up at odd hours and roaming around the house on Thursday night, which made her tired and cranky on Friday. Nothing Faith tried seemed to settle her down. She wasn't interested in watching a movie or sitting on the dock. Thinking they could both use some fresh air and exercise, Faith drove her mother out to Moss Creek Farm for a leisurely walk around the property and through Jackie's gardens. But when they got there, Lovie refused to get out of the car.

"I want to go home!" she demanded, pulling the car door shut every time Faith opened it.

Faith finally acquiesced. "Fine, but I have to stop by the store to pick up a few items for dinner, and you're going with me."

The store was packed with shoppers, mostly young mothers with their children, loading up for the weekend. Lovie got so disoriented, with the kids screaming and the women frantically grabbing items off the shelves, that Faith was forced to abandon her cart in the middle of the aisle and take her mother home.

"You need a break," Mike said that evening when he came home from work and found Faith in a foul mood. "Why don't you take Bitsy to the farmer's market in the morning, and I'll stay here with Lovie."

Faith started to object but changed her mind when she saw her daughter's face light up at the prospect of spending the morning alone with her. She winked at Bitsy and smiled at her husband. "A little time with my girl is exactly what I need. Thank you, Mike."

The Sweeney's parking lot was so full they had to park across the street at the marina. Bitsy was almost as excited to see Farmer Fred as she was to see her cousins. She knew him well from the market. Her primary job had been to stock the produce cart with the items Fred provided. She rushed to his side and hugged him around the waist. He plucked a pink zinnia from one of his bouquets and tucked it behind her ear.

Faith waved to Sean and Jamie before taking a seat next to Sam at the bakery table. "Looks like business is booming."

"And everybody in town wants a piece of the action." Sam placed her hand on the legal pad in front of her. "We have a list of people who want to join in the fun next Saturday. We are now officially a farmer's market. Saturdays at Sweeney's. Has a nice ring to it, don't you think?"

"Saturdays at Sweeney's," Faith repeated. "I like it." She picked up the legal pad and read the list out loud. "Virginia's Herb Garden. Bonnie's Berry Farm. The Barbecue Hut. Al's Free-Range Eggs and Grass-Fed Chickens." She set the pad back down. "Wow. Will you have enough room for all these vendors? The lot is overflowing as it is."

"The customers will park across the street from now on, which will leave the Sweeney's lot for vendor setups. I've already cleared it with the marina."

"Sounds like you've thought of everything." Faith kept her eye on Bitsy as the little girl elbowed her way through the sea of people to Jamie's truck. She tugged on his shirttail, and he lifted her onto the tailgate. "Do you need me to handle the finances?"

"Once Mom is situated at Creekside Manor and you have more time, I would love you to *teach* me how to manage the finances. Since you're retiring, I'll eventually need to learn. Might as well be now."

"Let's not talk about this right now, Sam."

Sam's words drove home the realization that she would no longer be needed once Sam took over the books. *Am I making a mistake by retiring before I've figured out what I want to do?*

The boys were so busy, Faith barely got a chance to speak to them except to say hello on her way out. She noticed Sean was not his usual peppy self. He seemed down, as though he'd gotten in a fight with his girlfriend. Did he even have a girlfriend? Faith didn't know. When was the last time they'd had a family get-together? She couldn't remember. She would talk to her sisters and plan something for Memorial Day. After locking their mother away at Creekside Manor on Thursday, they would need something to look forward to, something to get them through the long holiday weekend.

"Sean was mean to me," Bitsy said on the way home in the car.

"I doubt he was mean to you, sweetheart. He probably just has a lot on his mind."

"You mean girls," she said with a giggle.

Faith smiled. Her daughter was growing up too fast.

The rest of Saturday and Sunday went surprisingly smoothly for Lovie. Her new medicine regimen kept her calmer during the day and helped alleviate the symptoms of sundown syndrome, which enabled her to sleep better at night. Faith woke on Monday morning feeling rested and ready to face the week ahead. She'd managed a few mornings at the shooting range during the past couple of weeks, enough time to finish the required course and apply for her license to carry. There'd been no sign of Curtis since the fire, but the proximity of her gun, tucked away in her closet, comforted her just the same.

Faith turned off the burglar alarm and tiptoed past her mother's room on her way to get the newspaper. Mike had yet to come home from his night shift at the hospital, and she relished the thought of a few minutes alone, reading the paper and drinking her coffee, before her mother woke up. She opened the front door and gasped when an overpowering stench assaulted her nose. Lying on the stoop beside the Charleston *Post and Courier* was a decaying fish, a yellowfin tuna covered in maggots with flies swarming about. Tacked to the fish with a rusty nail was her mother's recipe card for tuna salad.

Faith's hand flew to her mouth and nose as she stifled a sob. *Curtis!* Lovie's tuna salad was his favorite of all her recipes.

She glanced down the hall to make sure Bitsy's and Lovie's bedroom doors were still closed. She pulled the front door shut behind her and ran to the garage for a shovel. Stuffing the recipe card in her bathrobe pocket, she scooped up the fish, carried it down to the dock, and dumped it into the water. She rinsed off the shovel and returned it to the garage. When she went back inside the house, she heard her cell phone ringing in her bedroom.

Sam was talking so fast and loud Faith couldn't understand her. "Calm down, Samantha. I have no idea what you're saying."

Sam slowed her speech without lowering the volume. "Donna Bennett left a rotten fish at my front door this morning with Mom's recipe for fish stew attached to it with a nail."

Faith's heart raced as she lowered herself to the bed. Since learning of Curtis's release from prison, she'd waged an internal battle with herself as to whether she should tell her family that he was on the loose. With each day that passed with no word from him, she felt better about her decision to keep his release to herself. If Sam suspected Curtis could've been responsible for the fire, she would go after him like a Labrador retriever chasing a squirrel. And she would get herself hurt. Or worse.

"What kind of fish was it?"

"It was too decomposed to know for sure. I think it might have been a barracuda. What difference does that make anyway?"

It made a lot of difference to Faith. A ferocious predator like a barracuda was exactly the kind of fish Curtis would leave for Sam. His message was clear. He was coming for her. Her sister needed to be aware so she could be alert. But Curtis had driven Sam to drink once. What if that happened again? What if she told Sam about Curtis and it turned out Donna Bennett had left the fish? Sam would start drinking again for no reason. Maybe Donna had done it. She hated Sam enough. Then again, Donna had nothing against Faith, no reason to leave a rotten fish at her front door. It had to be Curtis.

"What does Eli think?" Faith asked.

"He took the recipe card down to the station as evidence," Sam said, her voice considerably calmer. "He says this proves Mom is innocent. Whoever started the fire stole her recipes. And she's too out of her mind to orchestrate this rotten fish thing, even if she wanted to, which she wouldn't because I'm her daughter. Besides, you can verify her whereabouts last night. Did she at any point leave your house?"

"Of course not. Don't be ridiculous."

"See! It has to be Donna. No one else hates me enough to do something like this. Except your ex-husband, and he's in prison."

Now's your opportunity to tell her, Faith thought. But she let the moment pass. She needed time to think.

SEVENTEEN

JACKIE

Unbeknownst to Jackie, her son had canceled his second appointment with Moses, and when he refused to go to this week's session, his third, Jackie went in his place. She called Moses ahead of time to make certain he would see her.

"I'd be happy to meet with you Jackie," Moses said on the phone. "When I counsel a patient, I'm counseling the family."

She took a nerve pill beforehand in preparation. She'd never been for counseling before. She'd never been inside Moses's inner sanctum either, but she'd heard much about it from the members of her family who had been in his care. As soon as she entered, she zeroed in on one wall showcasing his accomplishments as a star linebacker at the University of Georgia. Large framed black-and-white photographs featuring him in action were accompanied by an impressive assortment of brass plaques and silver bowls engraved with his achievements.

Moses stood behind her, peering over her shoulder, as she skimmed the framed article announcing him as a candidate for the Heisman Trophy. "I admit my trophy wall makes me look like a narcissist, but my younger patients, especially the fellas, really get into this stuff. My shrine, as they call it, serves as an icebreaker with my shy patients."

"I can see how it would. I had no idea you were a Heisman Trophy candidate, Moses. That is something to be proud of. You're a shining example to all your patients, young and old." She turned around to face the room. A heavy black-lacquered desk occupied the space to her left, and a pair of contemporary red-leather sofas flanked a custom-made wool rug bearing the Georgia Bulldogs logo. An oversize Lucite coffee table separated the sofas with an array of magazines dedicated to a variety of sports—football, fishing, boating, golf, cycling. In the center of the coffee table sat a large faceted crystal football trophy declaring Moses the most valuable player of the Sugar Bowl in 2003. A theater-size flat-screen TV took up most of the opposite wall. She imagined him here on a chilly autumn Saturday afternoon watching college football while catching up on paperwork.

"I'd like for Sean to see all this," Jackie said, her arms akimbo as she turned in a circle, taking it all in one last time. "If only I can convince him to show up for an appointment."

"Sean will come when he's ready, Jackie." Moses motioned her toward the leather sofas. "Let's sit down. I want to hear how he's doing."

They made themselves comfortable facing each other on opposite sofas. "I'll be honest with you, Moses, I'm at my wits' end. No matter what I do, I can't seem to reach him. He's withdrawn and surly, not at all the same kid I sent away to college nine months ago. I want my happy-go-lucky boy back. With the old Sean, I always knew where I stood. I have no idea what's going on inside this Sean's mind."

"What tactics are you using to get through to him?"

"None that are working, obviously." Jackie picked a piece of lint off her black skinny jeans. "We are in a pattern—I nag and he ignores. I scream at him and he goes into his room and slams the door. I realize that badgering him isn't helping anything, but I can't control myself. He refuses to discuss his future. He dismisses me as if I'm insignificant, and it infuriates me. I can't get him to fill out the application for the College of Charleston. I realize they won't accept him without your endorsement. Not after he flunked out of Georgia. And you have your reputation to consider. I understand completely why you wouldn't go out on a limb for him."

"I appreciate you saying that. And you're right, I wouldn't feel comfortable making the recommendation until I'm convinced this is what he wants. And that he's stopped using drugs."

"I don't think he's using drugs. I think he's depressed. He seems so lost. When he's not fishing or working, he's zoned out in front of the TV. I'm not even sure he's paying attention to whatever show he's watching half the time. He used to play those silly video games for hours, but he hasn't played Xbox once since he got home."

"Okay, let's back up a minute. Where is he working?"

"He's a busboy at the Pelican's Roost. Don't say it!" She held her palm out in front of her. "I realize working in a restaurant isn't the greatest choice for him. But Jamie is working there as a dishwasher. The manager promised to promote both of them to waiters when their summer business picks up."

Moses knitted his black eyebrows together. "I ran into Jamie at the gas station yesterday afternoon. He was on his way to Charleston to work an event for Heidi. He quit his job at the Roost last week because they weren't giving him enough hours. He wasn't washing dishes for them, Jackie. He was bartending."

She stared at him, mouth agape. Anger flushed through her body and sweat trickled down her back. What was worse than Sean's lying to her was her believing him. "How could I be so gullible? I feel like such a fool."

He offered her a sympathetic smile. "Don't be so hard on yourself. Every parent wants to be able to trust their child." He steepled his fingers. "Let me ask you this. What kind of condition is he typically in when he comes home from work at night?"

"Sober, I assume, although I can't say for certain. He's home most nights by eleven. I'm usually in bed reading when he comes in. I never felt like I needed to check on him. After all, he's been at work, not out partying."

"I wouldn't assume anything where your son is concerned," Moses said. "Not in his current state."

"Well . . . like I said earlier, I'm convinced this *state* is depression. I have no reason to suspect he's using drugs. I understand why he lied to me about the job. He knew I am against him working in a restaurant. He and Jamie also have a crab business going. They're doing quite well."

"Jamie told me. Sounds like they're making a lot of money. It's good for Sean to help pay for his legal fees."

Jackie's body grew rigid. "That's the plan."

"But you haven't collected any money from him yet?"

She sighed. "Honestly, I don't know. Bill's handling the legal matter. I've been preoccupied with finding a nursing home for Mom, and I have a new project in Charleston that is requiring more attention than I anticipated."

"I was sorry to hear from Jamie about your mother. She's a lovely lady. Alzheimer's is an ugly disease. Look, Jackie," Moses said, his giant hands splayed out on his gray dress slacks. "I have no way of knowing for sure what is going on with Sean. We had a productive talk the night I visited the farm, but there's a reason he refuses to come see me at my office. My gut tells me his guilty conscience has something to do with it. Your son is in a precarious position for someone with a drug habit. Which is a real thing, as evidenced by his arrest. He's working in the restaurant environment, where drugs are readily available, and he has plenty of money at his disposal to purchase them. Sean needs to be your priority right now. Yours and Bill's both."

Jackie felt the beginning of a headache at the base of her

skull. "Sean is my priority! I'm here, aren't I? What else am I supposed to do?"

"Drug test him. Search his room. Wait up for him to come home at night," Moses began, ticking off each suggestion with his fingers. "Get in his face. Smell his breath and check his pupils. Insist he find a more suitable job. Manage his finances. You have the upper hand here. He's in a lot of trouble with the law. Hold him accountable."

Her cheeks burned. "I feel like an absolute failure. I was so proud of myself for being on top of the situation, but all I've been doing is yelling at him."

"Maybe so, but you've taken a step in the right direction by coming here. I hope I'm wrong about this. For a boy his age, dealing with depression can be much easier than dealing with addiction. Approach with caution. Plan some family time together. Share some laughs. Reconnect. Let him know he can talk to you, that he can trust you. You've been focused on the big picture, and understandably so; you're worried about his future. But I wouldn't push the college issue just yet."

"What're your thoughts on a summer job for him?"

"He might benefit from working with underprivileged kids. He has a lot to offer. Being around children less fortunate than he is might help him realign his priorities. The YMCA is hosting several weeks of camp. I think Sean would make a great counselor."

"I like that idea. Thank you so much, Big Mo." Jackie stood to leave. "Clearly Bill and I have our work cut out for us."

"You'll do great," Big Mo said and leaned over to kiss her cheek.

When Jackie learned her son had Tuesday night off from work, she scheduled a family dinner. After her appointment with Big

Mo, she was eager to try out her new strategies. Bill came home early from the office, so they could discuss how best to get through to their son.

"I'm telling you, he's depressed." Jackie stood at her second-story window looking down on her son, who'd been on the dock staring out at the water for the past hour while she and Bill were talking in their bedroom. "Can't say I blame him. I'd be depressed too if I thought I might have to go to jail."

"I have no intention of letting Sean go to jail. I'll talk to him about the case over dinner. Maybe that will set him at ease."

She left the window and walked into his outstretched arms. Holding tight to her husband, she had a sinking feeling that things would get a lot worse before they got better. "I'll set the table on the terrace," she said when she finally drew away from him. "Our nature boy is always more comfortable being outdoors."

"Good thinking," Bill said as he pressed his lips to hers. "Keep the faith, Jack. Everything is going to be okay."

Two hours later, they gathered at one end of the teak dining table and offered the same blessing they'd been reciting since the boys were old enough to say, "God is great." Bill carved the flank steak while Jackie loaded their plates with Caesar salad and roasted potatoes. They talked while they ate, discussing Sean's crab business and how they wanted to spend the Fourth of July week when Cooper came home for vacation. Sean seemed subdued throughout dinner, and he didn't have much of an appetite, but he spoke without slurring his words, and his thoughts were coherent. He gave her no reason to question his sobriety.

"I talked to Faith about our weekend plans today," Jackie said as they were taking their last bites. "We've decided to have our Memorial Day cookout here again this year. Can I count on the two of you to help me get ready?"

Sean said, "Whatever."

Bill cut his eyes at Sean. "We will both pitch in. It'll be fun for everyone to get together."

She cleared the table, took the dishes to the kitchen, and brought out a strawberry shortcake.

"Son, we need to talk about your court case. I've decided to hire a criminal defense attorney. It'll cost more." Bill paused as he forked off a chunk of cake. "A lot more, actually. But he'll be able to better represent you. There's a slim chance he can get the charges dropped completely. If not, you'll have to pay a fine, take a drug course, and perform community service. But you won't have to do any jail time."

"Does that mean I can have my car back?"

Jackie's jaw slackened. That was not at all the response she'd anticipated. She locked eyes with her husband, who shook his head, signaling her to let him respond.

"That depends on a number of things," Bill said. "Just because the district attorney is dropping the charges doesn't necessarily mean I'm ready to give you your car back. I thought you'd be relieved to hear you won't have to go to jail."

"What d'you mean? I'm already in jail, living in this house with the two of you."

Bill smoothed out the little bit of hair he had left on the top of his head. Jackie recognized the gesture. Her husband was stalling while he gathered his composure.

"You're mistaken, son. You've been living in a detention center since you got home from school. Congratulations, your lousy attitude has earned you a transfer to cell block C."

Jackie admired the patient but firm way her husband responded to their son.

"If you'd like to continue living under our roof here at Moss Creek Penitentiary, you will abide by our rules. First of all, you will pay me a percentage of your summer earnings to help cover the legal fees. You will start making those payments immediately. Secondly, you will attend weekly sessions with Moses. And thirdly, you will find a job doing something other than busing tables."

Sean's head jerked back. "Why? I'm earning good money there."

"You're earning minimum wage, less than you make off a dozen crabs," Bill said.

"But I like working at the Roost."

"This is nonnegotiable, son. Your mother and I feel your time would be better spent in a different kind of job, one that will enable you to learn something about yourself or give your life some direction."

The heavy teak chair skidded across the bluestone as Sean pushed back from the table. He jumped to his feet, his fists balled at his sides. "I'm almost twenty-one years old! You can't tell me what to do."

Bill set his fork on his plate and slowly wiped his mouth with his napkin. "As long as you're living under my roof, I most certainly can."

Jackie and Bill watched their son stomp off toward the house and slam the door.

"You handled that well, honey," she said. "I guess this is what they mean by tough love."

"If the attitude we just witnessed is any indication, our love will need to get a hell of a lot tougher if we want to get through to him."

EIGHTEEN

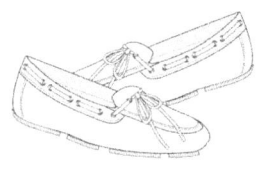

SAM

After a restless night of worrying about her mother and the future of their family's business, at six on Wednesday morning, Sam gave up on trying to sleep and shuffled to the front door for the newspapers. She enjoyed reading the *Post and Courier* for local news and goings-on in and around Charleston, but they subscribed to the *Prospect Weekly* solely for mention of Eli's many successes as a PPD detective. She hated contributing a dime of her hard-earned money to Donna Bennett's tabloid. Every year when she wrote the check to re-up her annual subscription, she considered canceling. But she couldn't do that to Eli. He would never admit it, but he got a kick out of seeing his name in print.

In the kitchen she skimmed the front section of the *Post and Courier* while she brewed coffee and waited for the water to boil for poached eggs. She was spooning two eggs onto toast when Eli stumbled into the kitchen, bare chested, with his cotton pajama bottoms slung low on his hips. He fell onto the banquette and removed the rubber band from the *Prospect Weekly*. He blinked and then rubbed his eyes with his balled fists.

"Uh-oh." He brought his hand to his mouth as his eyes scanned the front page.

"Uh-oh what?" she asked, glancing down at the paper as she slid his breakfast plate in front of him. The headline on the front page of the *Prospect Weekly* read, "Lovie Sweeney Reveals Secret Recipes." Sam snatched up the paper. "What the heck?" Beneath the headline was a photograph of an index card with the recipe for their steamed crab spice blend scrawled across it in Lovie's scratchy handwriting. The article, written by staff journalist Janice Beckman, reported that the fire at Captain Sweeney's Seafood Market had put an end to fifty-nine years of business for the Sweeney family. As a parting gift, Lovie was sharing three of her treasured top-secret recipes. In addition to the spice blend, those recipes were for her cheese grits casserole and pecan pie.

"Ugh!" Sam rolled up the paper and slapped it against the granite countertop as though swatting a fly. "I'm going to kill her! She's not getting away with this."

Sam strode angrily out of the kitchen and across the great room to the master suite. She dug through the laundry basket on the floor for a pair of running shorts and a dry-fit tank. She dressed, brushed her teeth, and slipped her feet into her navy Crocs.

She collided with Eli in the doorway on her way out of the room. "Where are you going?" he asked, stepping aside.

"Where do you think I'm going?" she snapped. "I'm going down to that rag of a newspaper and give Donna a piece of my mind."

"I'm going with you," he called after her. "Give me a minute to dress."

"I'll wait five minutes," she called over her shoulder. "If you're not out by then, you'll have to drive your own car."

Eli hurried out, running shoes in hand, three minutes later. She shifted her Wrangler into gear and took off down the driveway. "She's obviously guilty, Eli. I don't understand why you haven't arrested her."

"I told you, honey," he said, combing his dark, wavy hair into place with his fingers. "We don't have any evidence."

"What do you call that?"

He followed her gaze to the rolled-up newspaper sticking out of her handbag in his floorboard. "A game changer. Donna has some explaining to do. This definitely links her to the rotten fish as well as the fire."

"Although the recipes are important, they aren't the real issue," Sam said. "What matters more is that Donna broadcasted to the entire Lowcountry that Sweeney's is out of business, which is simply not true. When I was a little girl, the *Prospect Weekly*, which was the *Prospect Daily* back then, had a solid reputation for providing unbiased world and local news. Sure, they printed a weekly society column like all newspapers back then. But nothing they ever printed defamed any of our townsfolk. Donna's parents would roll over in their grave if they saw how their daughter has cheapened their paper."

The newspaper's offices had once occupied both floors of a redbrick building at the corner of Main and Maple. The decline in print circulation in recent years had forced the paper to reduce the size of its staff. As a result an attorney's office had taken over the entire second floor.

"We're here to see Donna Bennett," Sam announced to the attractive middle-aged woman behind the counter in the reception area.

The woman peered at them over her tortoiseshell reading glasses. "Who may I say is here?"

"I'm Samantha Sweeney, and this is my husband, *Detective* Eli Marshall." She snapped the paper open in front of the woman's face. "We're here about this."

The color drained from the receptionist's face. "I'll let her know you're here." She punched a number on the desk phone and spoke softly into her headset. "There's a Samantha Sweeney and her husband here to see you." She listened for a minute. "I'll tell her." The woman looked up at them. "Mrs. Bennett is in a meeting right now. Her assistant will be out to speak with you shortly."

"She's not getting rid of me that easy." Sam rounded the desk and burst through the double doors behind the receptionist.

"Wait! You can't go back there."

Sam increased her pace. With Eli on her heels, she marched down the corridor checking the nameplate on each door until she found Donna's office. She barged through the closed door. Donna sat behind her desk with a smug, cat-that-swallowed-the-canary expression on her face.

"Your receptionist said you were in a meeting. Do you pay your employees bonuses to lie for you?" She dropped the paper on Donna's desk. "You have some explaining to do."

Donna sat up straighter in her chair. "I don't have to explain anything to you."

Eli stepped in line beside Sam. "You're under obligation to reveal your sources, if not to Sam, then to me."

Donna pressed her lips tight.

"We can either talk here or down at the station," Eli said. "Your prerogative."

"There's not much to tell," Donna said. "Lovie Sweeney mailed the recipe cards along with a typed letter to one of my reporters."

Sam gawked. "That's not possible! My mother—"

"Sam!" Eli said. "Let me handle this." He jabbed at the paper with his finger. "Did your reporter think to check the credentials of her source?"

"Why would she have any reason to doubt her source?" Donna asked in a nonchalant manner. "We all know that Lovie Sweeney is the sweetest, most honest woman in town."

Sam rolled her eyes at Donna's sugary-sweet tone of voice.

"We need to speak with this reporter. Get her in here." Eli inclined his head at Donna's desk phone. "And ask her to bring her supporting documents."

"Oh, for Christ's sake. Anything to get you to leave my office." She lifted her phone's receiver and summoned Janice Beckman to her office.

Sam recognized Janice as the reporter who had been with Donna at the market the day after the fire. Her snug-fitting denim dress and silver platform heels were only slightly more appropriate than the red-sequined dress she'd worn that day.

Eli held his hand out to her. "I'm Detective Eli Marshall, and this is my wife, Samantha. I'd like to ask you a few questions about the article you wrote for this morning's paper."

"I'll help in whatever way I can, although I don't know much. I received these in the mail." Janice handed him a manila file folder.

"I assume your fingerprints are all over these," Eli said.

Janice's face fell. "I had no reason to question my source."

Eli opened the file. The letter lay on top. Sam read over his shoulder—a three-sentence statement with Lovie's typed signature declaring the fire at Captain Sweeney's Seafood Market had ended the fifty-nine-year business she had started in 1958 and that as a token of her appreciation she was sharing her three most treasured top-secret recipes.

"Anyone could've sent this letter. The message, including the signature, is typed in the default font for Microsoft Word on standard printer paper. Did you think about calling Lovie Sweeney for an interview? Her story could've embellished your feature."

"Am I in some kind of trouble, Detective?" Janice asked.

"No, *you* are not in trouble. Although next time, I caution you to be more thorough in your investigation." He dismissed Janice with a nod. "You may go now."

He waited for Janice to close the door before turning his

attention back to Donna. "You, however, are in a boatload of trouble. I have more reason than ever to believe you may have started the fire at Sweeney's."

Donna scrunched her face up, and Sam thought, *She really should consider a facelift.*

"What did I do?" she asked in a shrill voice.

"You allowed this article to appear in your newspaper, for starters. Sensationalism, I believe they call it. This is not public knowledge, but whoever started the fire at Sweeney's stole her box of recipe cards. And you have three of those recipes in your possession. You saw an opportunity for a front-page story, and you fabricated the letter to make it look as though Lovie Sweeney sent it."

"Someone mailed them to my reporter," Donna snarled. "The envelope is in the file."

Eli thumbed back through the file until he found the envelope. "Right. Typed in the same font and postmarked Prospect. Who's to say you didn't mail the cards to Janice yourself?"

Donna placed her hand on her chest as though offended by his accusations. "Why on earth are you trying to pin the fire on me when everyone knows Sam started it?"

Sam brought her fist down on Donna's desk. "You're a liar, Donna Bennett. And you're not going to get away with this. I'm going to put your rag of a newspaper out of business if it's the last thing I do." Sam spun on her heels and stormed out of Donna's office and out of the building.

Eli caught up with her in the parking lot. "Are you okay, honey?"

"No! I'm not okay! I'm furious." She eyed the folder in his hands. "Are you gonna do something about this or not?"

He slumped against the hood of her Wrangler. "I'll try, sweetheart. But I'm not making any promises. I know she looks guilty, but the evidence has to hold up in court. Your mother's medical condition places us at a disadvantage. We can't put Lovie on the stand to testify that she didn't send the letter or that the recipe box was in the market at the time of the fire in the first place."

"So you're saying she's guilty as sin, but without more proof, you can't arrest her."

Eli hung his head. "Pretty much, yes."

"That means I'll never get my insurance money. I'm going to save my market with or without your help. I'll post a banner at the market so everyone who drives by will see it." Sam tossed her hands in the air in front of her. "It will say, 'Coming Next Spring. Captain Sweeney's Seafood Redo.'"

NINETEEN

JAMIE

Jamie and Lizbet said goodbye to Annie in front of her house and walked along the uneven sidewalks, heading south for one block to Tradd Street and then west for three to the Hornes' house. It was the Wednesday night before Memorial Day weekend, and they'd just finished working a party for a young couple engaged to be married in December.

"I don't feel right living at your house for free," Jamie said, ducking under a low-hanging crape myrtle branch. "We made a deal. You and Brooke need to give me some chores so I can earn my keep."

A slow smile crept onto Lizbet's lips. "Be careful what you wish for. We're having a truckload of mulch delivered on Saturday."

Jamie grinned. "As it happens, I'm an expert at spreading mulch."

Since Jamie had quit his job at the Roost and accepted the Horne sisters' offer of a place to live, on the nights he'd stayed in Charleston, he and Lizbet had gotten into the habit of having a nightcap with Brooke on the porch before turning in. But Brooke was already in bed when they got home.

"I'm not surprised. Brooke was exhausted when I saw her earlier. She's been working around the clock on a big project." Lizbet unlocked the bolt and turned the knob. "Do you want a beer?"

"I probably shouldn't. I have to get up early tomorrow and drive to Prospect. I'm meeting Sean at seven to work the inlet." Jamie walked over to the swing and plopped down. "Let's sit for a minute anyway, since Brooke has vacated her throne. I guess I won't get to tease her this evening for being a swing hog," Jamie said with a laugh.

Butterflies fluttered in his stomach when Lizbet sat down next to him. "It's so nice out tonight." He closed his eyes and rested his head against the back of the swing, feeling the gentle breeze on his face.

Lizbet inhaled deeply. "I smell fresh-cut grass and ligustrum. Summertime is here."

Jamie opened his eyes. "How do you know so much about gardening?"

"My mom taught me. But I still have a lot to learn." She settled back on the bench, tucking one foot under the other leg. "Tell me something about yourself, Jamie, that I don't already know."

"Hmm, let's see." Jamie stared up at the ceiling while he thought about it. "I like blueberries."

"I'm being serious," she said, jabbing him in the side with her elbow. "What's the one thing that has most influenced your life to date?"

Jamie hesitated. That *one* thing was difficult for him to talk about, but he viewed Lizbet's personal question as a sign that she wanted to get to know him better. He willed his voice not to crack. "On New Year's Day of my senior year in high school, I was in an ATV accident with my best friend. Cory was killed on impact, and I suffered a spinal cord injury that left me paralyzed from the waist down. I wasn't sure I'd ever walk again. I was in a wheelchair for six months, the worst six months of my life. I was mourning my best friend and coping with the challenges of my disability. And I lost my baseball scholarship, which at the time was the single most important thing in my life. I wouldn't have made it without my friends and family. Mostly my mom. She never gave up on me."

He finished talking, and silence hung in the air between them. When Lizbet sniffled, he asked, "Are you crying?"

"So what's new? I cry all the time. I thought you already knew that about me." She wiped her nose with the back of her hand. "I'm so sorry you had to go through all that. And I'm sorry about your friend. The death of a loved one changes us in unimaginable ways. Losing my mother is the worst thing that's ever happened to me. I don't know if I could survive losing my best friend."

Jamie lowered his head. "It sucks. Even now. Cory and I had been best friends since kindergarten." Tears blurred his vision as he stared into his lap. "Learning to live with the guilt is the hardest part. I feel obligated to live every day to the fullest to make up for the time Cory lost. I owe him that much." He sucked in a deep breath to steady his voice. "I can't imagine losing my mom, though. How do you cope with that?"

"It gets a little bit easier every day, as I'm sure it did for you after Cory died. I've learned a lot about myself in the past nine months. Mom and I were never that close. Brooke and Mom had more in common, and I always felt like the third wheel around them. But that all changed when she got sick. Mom was a character. She was opinionated, headstrong, and set in her ways. She was staunch in her traditional beliefs, and not very accepting of people different from her. You can imagine how she reacted when Brooke came out of the closet. She eventually accepted Sawyer, but not before she put us all through hell. Mom never had high aspirations for herself. She was happy being a homemaker. I never understood that until I was facing life without her. Then I realized all the little things she did to make our family and our home special." Her voice broke and she couldn't continue.

"Moms are special people," Jamie said, thinking about his own. "I've changed my mind about that beer. Do you want one?" He moved to get up, but she jumped to her feet. "I'll get them. I need to blow my nose anyway."

She went inside and returned five minutes later with a red nose, a handful of tissues, and two opened bottles of COAST HopArt IPA. "I'm sorry for falling apart on you," she said, handing him one of the beers.

"No worries. You can cry on my shoulder anytime," he said, patting his shoulder.

She lowered herself to the swing. "You probably won't believe this after my breakdown just now, but I feel like I've reached a new stage in my grief. After nine months of misery, these tears feel more like bittersweet reminiscence than sadness."

"I remember how much of a relief it is to finally reach that point." He took a swig of beer and licked his lips. "And it's okay. Your Mom would want you to be happy."

"I know that. She even told me that herself." Lizbet picked at the label on her bottle. "I guess it takes a while for your heart to believe it."

"To mending broken hearts." He held his bottle out to hers and they clinked them together.

"Mom taught me a lot, mostly that it's okay for me to just be me." Lizbet swiped at her eyes with the tissue. "I'm more like her than I ever realized. She was happiest when she was puttering around at home. She had her family and her two best friends living next door to her. She despised shopping, and she didn't like to go on trips. I don't have any great yearning to see the world either. Traveling was always Brooke's thing. Although we now know the seven years she lived in California was more about hiding her lifestyle than exploring the world."

"I think I would've liked your mom." Jamie shifted on the

bench toward Lizbet. "I always thought I'd move back to Prospect after I graduate, but ever since the fire, I've been wondering if this is my opportunity to do something different. I like Charleston. There are so many kids our age here, and the food is incredible. I love being able to walk everywhere I need to go. On the one hand, I can see myself here. But on the other, I'm not sure I can give up living on the water. There's a lot to be said for being able to walk out on my dock and go fishing and hunting anytime I want."

"Prospect is a charming little town. I see why you like it so much." Lizbet looked away. "I'm beginning to think that going to New York for culinary school is the wrong decision for me. There are plenty of culinary schools in the South. There's even one right here in Charleston."

"But none are as renowned as the one in New York. Don't shy away from the challenge because you're intimidated by living in a big city. You'll be so preoccupied with your studies, the time will go by quickly. Think of all the like-minded people you'll meet and the amazing restaurants you'll get to try."

Lizbet nodded. "That's what Annie says."

"Are you planning to come back to work for Heidi when you finish?"

"That depends on whether she still needs me. I can't ask her to hold my job for me."

He nudged her with his shoulder. "Sure you can. You know Heidi better than that. She'll make a place for you if you want to come back."

"You're right. But the truth is, I'm not sure my future is in catering. Like Annie, I want to open my own restaurant one day."

"The two of you should consider going into business together. You get along so well, and you're both so talented."

They sat in comfortable silence while they finished their beers. Jamie allowed himself to daydream about being married to Lizbet. She seemed perfect for him. They would have such a nice life together in Prospect with a house on the inlet, two kids, and a yellow Labrador retriever. They would rebuild the seafood market and open at least one restaurant on the waterfront. He felt the warmth of her body beside him. A voice inside his head whispered, *Go for it!*

He set his beer bottle down on the porch floor. "You're an interesting girl, Lizbet Horne. Your Dr. Dreamy is a lucky guy."

Lizbet tensed beside him. "Who is Dr. Dreamy?"

"He's not your boyfriend? Brooke mentioned him the first night I met her. She made it sound like y'all were dating."

Lizbet giggled, and her body relaxed. "You can't listen to my sister. You know how much she likes to stir up trouble. Trevor Pratt is just a friend. He was kind to me when Mom was sick. We went out on a couple of dates, but we didn't have any chemistry. I haven't seen him in months."

"I can't say I'm disappointed to hear that." Jamie wanted to jump off the swing, take her in his arms, and dance her around the porch. He invited her to the Memorial Day party at Moss Creek Farm instead. "It's mostly family plus a few friends. Annie's coming. We invited Heidi too, but she's not sure if she can come yet."

Jamie realized he was being forward, but he didn't care. He'd been suppressing his interest in her since they first met. Now that Dr. Dreamy wasn't in the picture, he planned to stake his claim.

"How are Annie and Heidi going to a party when we're catering an event at noon?"

"Our party doesn't start until five," Jamie said. "The event is at Folly Beach. You could drive to Prospect with me afterward if you want."

"In that case . . ." She grinned as though she was going to accept his offer, but then her face fell. "Wait, Jamie, I can't. I'm sorry. I forgot that Sawyer has to work. I told Brooke I'd spend the evening with her."

"Brooke can come too! My family will love her, especially my mom."

"All moms love Brooke. I hope your mom likes me as well." Her voice was no more than a whisper, and the uncertainty in her gray eyes told him everything he needed to hear. She cared about him. She wanted his mother to like her. He'd cast out his line, and she'd taken the bait.

He rested his arm on the back of the swing behind her head. "You have nothing to worry about."

TWENTY

FAITH

The incessant ringing of her phone was driving Faith out of her mind. She was sick with worry over locking her mother away in a memory care unit and freaking out about keeping her family safe from Curtis. If something didn't give soon, she'd commit herself to a different kind of mental unit. The kind for people who were batshit crazy.

The phone calls had started a short time after she'd discovered the rotten fish on her stoop on Monday morning. The first calls went to her cell phone—one hang-up after another. She'd block the number, and thirty minutes later the calls would begin again from another number with an unknown caller ID. She finally turned her cell phone off altogether, only to have her landline start ringing within the hour. Mike was working days at the hospital. Thankfully, the calls tapered off in the late afternoon, around the time he arrived home, sparing her from having to explain the situation.

Faith's imagination played tricks on her. She felt as if someone was watching her—peeking through her windows and around the aisles at the grocery store—but every time she turned to look, no one was there. She sensed people looking at her in a strange way—the checkout lady at the library and the traffic guard in the carpool line at Bitsy's school—as though they knew she was keeping a deep, dark secret.

Sam called several times a day to rant about Donna Bennett. "I know Donna is guilty! I don't understand why the police can't find any evidence against her."

Faith listened patiently without arguing. Sam would never consider other suspects, namely Curtis, as long as she thought Donna had started the fire.

There was a bright side to her week, a shimmer of sunshine on an otherwise bleak landscape. The anxiety meds the doctor had prescribed for her mother made Lovie more agreeable and less agitated. She seemed happy, giddy even, like a teenager in love. She flirted shamelessly with every man she came into contact with. She was particularly fond of Mike, although she couldn't quite grasp that he was Faith's husband. She was convinced that Faith was still married to Curtis. She asked about him constantly and spotted him everywhere—in the car next to them at the stoplight and behind the window at the dry cleaner's drive-through. It was never her ex-husband, of course, but Faith jumped out of her skin every time her mother exclaimed, "Look, there's Curtis!" As though her ex-husband were someone they'd want to see. As if Faith weren't already skittish enough.

Faith had called the parole officer multiple times. Emmett Reyes insisted that Curtis had not left the Columbia city limits. "It's just not possible, ma'am. We have a network in place that holds him accountable for every minute of his day."

Faith couldn't care less about his network. Emmett didn't know her ex-husband, the little weasel, the way she did. The torture was gnawing at her insides. She couldn't take it anymore. She would tell Eli about Curtis as soon as her mother was tucked safely away at Creekside Manor. She should've confided in him weeks before.

During the past few days, a series of phone conversations

among the three Sweeney sisters and the professionals at Creekside Manor had focused on the best way to transition Lovie to her new environment. Faith was the obvious choice to make the drop-off, as she'd been Lovie's primary care provider since the fire. Jackie and Sam hated being left out of this monumental event in their mother's life, but they agreed that their presence might cause Lovie unnecessary confusion and alarm.

Sam had spent the day before packing up their mother's most valued possessions and the remainder of her clothes from her town house. Jackie had met Sam at the manor late in the afternoon, and together they had organized Lovie's new room.

"Her room is actually pretty nice," Sam had reported when she'd called on her way home. "Jackie added her decorator's touch and arranged Mom's things so the room feels homey without being cramped."

Faith had kept her mother preoccupied with cooking shows on the Food Network that morning while she packed her toiletries and clothes. But when Lovie saw Faith rolling her tattered suitcase out to the car, she started to cry and tried to grab the handle of the suitcase away from Faith. The professionals had given her advice on how to handle such an incident.

"Mike and I are going out of town for a few days, Mom. You will be staying at a hotel with friends who have a lot in common with you. Look at it as an adventure."

This prompted a litany of questions about why she couldn't go with them and when they would be back and why Faith was going on vacation with a man named Mike when Curtis was her husband.

Faith glanced at her watch. She and her mother were expected at Creekside Manor in twenty minutes. "We need to go, Mom. We're going to be late." She took her mother by the elbow and practically dragged her to the car.

The questions started again as soon as she started down the

driveway. "Who is Mike? I don't understand why you're going to California with a man who's not your husband."

Faith swung her head around to look at her mother. *California? Who said anything about going to California?*

"I'm married to Mike now, Mama. I've told you that a dozen times." Arguing with her mother was pointless. Lovie would ask the same question three minutes later anyway. But Faith drew the line at pretending she was still married to Curtis.

She turned up the volume on her country music station and tuned her mother out on the way to Creekside Manor.

Beds of pink and white impatiens greeted them at the front gates of the retirement home, and Lovie grew silent as they drove through the canopy of live oak trees lining the driveway. They passed a small pond on the right where several patients sat on park benches, reading or visiting with their loved ones.

"What is this place again?" Lovie asked.

"A hotel for people your age."

"Will I know anyone here?"

Faith glanced over at her mother. The fear on her face tugged at Faith's heartstrings. "I'm sure you will, Mama. You already know so many people in town. Besides, you make friends so easily. They'll have lots of fun activities for you to do."

Faith parked near the door and helped her mother out of the car. The staff had instructed her to leave her mother's suitcase in the trunk until they got her settled. They entered the building and took the elevator to the second floor. A member of the staff whom Faith had not met but who called Lovie by name greeted them in the reception area. In her late thirties, the woman wore black slacks and a black polo shirt with the Creekside Manor logo on her left breast. Her chocolate eyes were warm and her smile kind.

"My name is Joy Peterson and I'm going to show you to your room and help you get settled. We're so happy to have you stay with us, Mrs. Sweeney. I think you're really going to like it here."

When Joy offered Lovie her arm, her mother cast an uncertain glance at Faith. "It's okay, Mama. I'm coming with you."

Faith followed them down the hall. They paused momentarily in the doorway of the main recreational lounge. The room was divided into separate areas of comfortable seating with potted plants, bookcases, and a large picture window overlooking the landscaped grounds. A group of women were gathered around a table playing cards while another patient sat reading a picture book with a caregiver on one of the sofas.

"These people are old!" Lovie said in a loud voice. "You said there would be people my age here."

"We have all ages here, Mrs. Sweeney," Joy said and kept on walking.

Faith was pleasantly surprised when they entered her mother's room. Jackie had hung her mother's favorite paintings—above the bed a watercolor of a cheerful flower arrangement, and on the opposite wall an oil of the sun rising over the inlet. A yellow-and-white patchwork quilt, taken from Lovie's guest room at the town house, topped the bed, and her favorite butter-colored cashmere throw was draped across the gooseneck rocker she'd had since the girls were babies.

Lovie saw her things and started to back out of the room. "I'm not staying here and you can't make me. Why'd you bring me here, Faith?" She tugged on Faith's shirtsleeve. "You told me we were going to Disney World."

Disney World? Faith forced herself to keep a straight face, but inside she was crumbling. She looked to Joy for help.

"This place is like Disney World in many ways." Joy took Lovie's hands in hers. "We have lots of games you can play and our very own ice cream dispenser for special treats."

"I don't like ice cream." Lovie's lip quivered, and she set her pleading eyes on Faith. "Please don't make me stay here."

Joy gave Faith the nod. The administrator had warned her it could be like this. "When the time comes for you to leave," she'd said, "you may have to make a quick exit. You have to trust that we will take care of her."

Lovie let out a screech when Faith turned to go that made her blood curdle and stopped her in her tracks in the doorway. Two orderlies appeared from nowhere and brushed her out of the way as they entered the room.

When she spun around to face her mother, Lovie whimpered, "Please don't go. Please, Faith. I promise I'll be good from now on."

"I'm sorry, but I can't do this," Faith said to Joy as she rushed to her mother's side. She knew that this decision was just as imprudent as others she'd made in recent weeks, but the look of terror and utter dejection in her mother's face overpowered any resolve Faith had had to leave her there. "Let go of her," she demanded of the orderlies, who held Lovie in their grip.

She put her arm around her mother and escorted her from the room. Joy came running after them. "We understand this is hard. Your mother will be fine within a few days. She will receive excellent care here. This is the best place for her."

"This may be the best place for some people, but not for my mother." They arrived at the elevator. "Please enter the code so we may leave," Faith said, gesturing at the numeric touch pad.

Joy hesitated before entering the code, a look of concern on her face, and Faith gave her mother a gentle shove onto the elevator. As they descended to the first floor, the consequences of her actions weighed on her. How would she justify her decision to her sisters? And to Mike? And to Bitsy?

Lovie's sobbing weakened to a snivel on the drive home. By the time they pulled into the driveway, her eyelids were fluttering as she fought to stay awake.

"We'll both be ready for a nap after lunch. How does a BLT sound?"

Lovie grinned. "That sounds nice."

Faith left Lovie's suitcase in the car. She would get it out after they'd eaten. She disengaged the alarm, and when she opened the front door, she heard Snowflake barking, a yelp that sounded more distressed than her merry yippity-yap.

"What is it, Snowflake?" When she let the little dog out of her crate, Snowflake scampered over to the French doors and began growling at something outside. Faith hurried to her room and retrieved her gun from the closet. She inserted the magazine into the handle and returned to the family room with the gun aimed at the ground. "Stay here, Mom," she said and unlocked the French doors. She stepped across the threshold onto the porch and scanned the yard, including the dock and lower patio, but there was no one in sight. She was stuffing the gun in the waistband of her jeans when she saw the dead pig on the other side of the screen door. Tacked to the pig's forehead, between its empty eye sockets, was Lovie's recipe for pulled pork barbecue.

Faith stifled a scream. Lovie sneaked up behind her and broke into hysterical fits of laughter at the sight of the pig, her painful experience at the nursing home forgotten. Faith raised the gun and held it steady in both hands as she scanned the yard again from left to right. "Get inside, Mom." She backed Lovie into the family room, closed and locked the door, and went to the wall keypad to alarm the security system. She retrieved her bag from the bench in the hall where she'd dropped it when she came in. She dumped the contents on the floor, and with trembling hands she picked up her phone and called Eli.

TWENTY-ONE

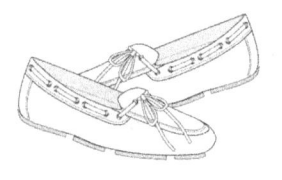

SAM

They arrived simultaneously—he from work and she from home—at her sister's house. "Explain to me why they let Curtis out of prison," Sam said to her husband as they waited for Faith to answer the door. "I felt certain he was locked away for life."

"Our prisons are way overcrowded. Unless convicted of murder, no one serves a full sentence anymore. The bigger question for me is why our department wasn't notified of his release."

They heard the chime of the burglar alarm being disarmed followed by the click of the deadbolt. Faith flung open the door and fell into Sam's arms. "I'm so sorry I didn't tell you sooner. After what happened last time, I was terrified you'd fall apart."

"You don't need to worry about me." Sam smiled a grateful smile at her husband. "I have Eli to hold me together now. Just as you have Mike. I'm guessing you didn't tell him either."

"No!" Faith sobbed. "He's going to be so angry with me."

"Not angry, honey. Disappointed." Sam tightened her hold on her sister's trembling body. "Mike loves you. We all do. None of us want you to go through this alone."

Eli's eyes traveled across the front yard. "Why don't we go

inside." He placed a hand on the small of Sam's back and shepherded them over the threshold, then closed and locked the door behind them.

Faith sobbed uncontrollably, garbling her words as she attempted to tell them her story. Sam massaged her sister's back. "You need to calm down, Faith, honey. We can't understand you."

Faith pulled away from Sam and took several deep breaths. She motioned for them to follow her down the hall and through the family room to the porch. "I received a c-c-calling card from Curtis today," she said, pointing at the dead pig on the top step outside her screen door.

Elbowing her sister out of the way, Sam opened the screen door and stared down at the pig. "That's Mom's recipe for pulled pork barbecue. All this time I blamed Donna Bennett, but it was Curtis who started the fire. He's the one who left the rotten fish and mailed the recipe cards to the newspaper."

"Looks that way, Sammie, but we have to prove it first." Eli removed a pair of tweezers and a plastic bag from his pants pocket. Leaning over, he plucked the recipe card loose and slid it into the bag. "Don't touch the pig, Faith. I'll have one of my men pick it up and take it to the station. We may be able to lift a print from it." He stood to face Faith. "You need to repeat everything you told me on the phone. I could barely understand you."

Faith led them back inside and collapsed in a chair at her pine table. Sam and Eli sat down across from her.

Eli removed a notepad from his shirt pocket. "Start at the beginning."

Faith retrieved a napkin from the basket in the center of the table and blew her nose. "Okay." She inhaled deeply to steady her breath. "I received a message from the warden at Broad River saying that Curtis had been released from prison and that he was in a halfway house and they were watching him closely."

"When did you get this message?" Eli asked.

"He called on Tuesday, the day before the fire, but I didn't listen to the message until Thursday, the day after the fire. I've gotten bad about checking messages on my house line." Faith started to cry again. "If only I'd checked my voice mail earlier, we might have been able to stop him from setting the fire."

Eli said, "I agree the timing is suspicious, but let's not get ahead of ourselves. Remember, the man is innocent until proven guilty."

Sam banged her fist against the table. "That bastard is guilty as sin and you know it! Once we prove it, I'll get my money from the insurance company."

"I'm not as convinced as you are, sweetheart," Eli said. "There are a lot of things that don't add up. I, for one, would like to know how he got all the way down here and back without being missed in Columbia."

"I agree," Faith said with a sniffle. "My guess is one of his goons is acting on his behalf. Although I can't dismiss what Mom told me. She claims she saw Curtis running away from the fire that night. Then again, she's fixated on him for some reason. She keeps having these phantom sightings of him."

Eli looked up from his note taking. "Wait a minute. Back up. When did she tell you she saw him running away from the fire? That night or sometime later?"

"The day after the fire," Faith said.

"Do you have any reason to believe her *sightings* of Curtis could be legitimate?" Eli asked.

"None at all," Faith said, shaking her head. "It's always some random man who doesn't even look like Curtis. She's confused. She thinks I'm still married to Curtis."

"I get it," Sam said, rolling her eyes. "She thinks I'm still married to Allen."

Eli scrunched his face up in confusion. "But you were never married to Allen."

"Exactly," Sam said. "We can't trust anything she says."

"I hesitated even mentioning it to you, but I thought you should know everything." Fresh tears filled her eyes as Faith pressed her fist to her mouth. "I didn't tell you, Sam, but I received a dead fish too. Mine was a yellowfin tuna with the recipe for Mom's tuna salad."

Sam gulped back her response. She wanted to read her sister the riot act for not telling anyone about any of this, for their sakes and for hers. But she could see her sister was suffering enough.

"What'd you do with the card?" Eli asked.

"I kept it." Faith left the table and went to the kitchen. She returned a minute later and handed Eli the card. "My fingerprints are all over it. I wasn't thinking clearly that morning."

Faith lowered herself back down to her chair. "For several days after the fish incident, I received hang-ups on my cell phone and my house line."

Eli's pen flew across his notepad as she told them about blocking the calls and the unknown caller IDs. "I'll get your phone records and we'll see what we can find out."

"I've called the parole officer so many times he's sick of hearing from me," Faith said. "But he swears Curtis hasn't left Columbia."

"Can you give me the parole officer's contact information?" Eli asked, pen poised over the pad.

"That's easy. I know it by heart. His name is Emmett Reyes," Faith said, and recited his phone number.

"I'm interested to see what Mr. Reyes has to say." Eli took his phone and notepad to the kitchen to place his call.

Reaching across the table, Sam placed her hand on top of her sister's. "You poor thing. This has been going on for weeks. I'm sure you were scared out of your mind. I wish you would've told me."

"I was terrified. I am terrified. But having a gun in my closet —just knowing it's there helps." Faith looked away from Sam and stared out the window. "I bought a pistol and took some shooting lessons to brush up on my skills. I've applied for a license to carry. You might want to do the same."

"I'm one step ahead of you." Removing her handbag from the back of the chair, Sam pulled out her holstered handgun and set it on the table. "Eli bought this for me a couple of months after we started dating. He told me I'd find strength in being able to protect myself. And he's right."

Faith set her hazel eyes on Sam. "You mark my words, Sammie, if that bastard breaks into my house, I'll shoot him dead."

"And you would be well within your rights."

Eli came out of the kitchen. "I'm going to Columbia," he said, pocketing his phone. "The parole officer gave me the same runaround he's been giving Faith. I need to see for myself what measures they're taking to keep Curtis in line."

Sam jumped to her feet. "You're not planning to confront Curtis, are you? That man is a deranged lunatic."

The color drained from her sister's face. "I agree, Eli. I don't think that's a good idea."

"Give me some credit here. I'm a detective. I know what I'm doing. I'm going to threaten him the way he's been threatening you." He gave Faith's arm a squeeze. "In the meantime, I want you to keep your doors locked and your security system on."

Faith smiled up at him. "No need to worry about that."

"And I want you to tell your husband everything you just told us," Eli added.

Faith nodded. "I promise."

Eli gave Sam a parting peck on the lips. "Don't worry. I'll be careful."

"You'd better be." She rested her head on his shoulder. "What time do you think you'll—" She stopped short at the sight of her mother shuffling into the room.

"Why didn't somebody tell me we were having a party?" Lovie asked, a wounded expression on her face.

Sam had been too preoccupied to ask how the drop-off at Creekside Manor had gone. "Faith . . . what is Mom doing here?"

Faith rose from the table and came to stand beside Sam. "Things didn't go well this morning. I was waiting until Eli left to tell you about it."

Lovie batted her eyelashes at Eli. "Who are you, handsome?"

Sam gave her sister a questioning look.

"Mike calls this her Lovie-in-Love stage," Faith whispered. "As best we can tell, she thinks she's in her midteens. She flirts with every male she comes into contact with."

Eli tipped his head to her. "I'm Eli Marshall, ma'am."

Lovie giggled. "'Ma'am'? I'm not old enough to be a ma'am."

He winked at her. "I call all southern ladies ma'am, regardless of their age." He turned to Sam. "I really need to get going."

"Are you leaving so soon?" Lovie said, walking her fingers up Eli's arm. "The party's just getting started."

"Not for me. I need to get back to work." He kissed the back of Lovie's hand. "Another time, perhaps."

Sam placed her arm around his waist and led him out of the room before her mother could hit on him again. She turned to her husband when they got to the front door. "Please be careful. And don't forget to call me," she called after him as he walked to his car.

She stood on the front stoop as he drove away, praying they would survive another round of battles with Curtis. She agreed with her sister. If he came near her, she would put a bullet between his beady eyeballs.

She locked the door and returned to the family room. Her mother was watching TV and Faith was frying bacon in the kitchen. "Start talking, sister."

"I couldn't leave her in that horrible place, Sammie." Faith handed her an avocado. "I'm making California BLTs. Do you want one?"

"Sure." She took the avocado from Faith and removed a paring knife from the butcher block beside the stove. "But you're not getting off the hook that easily. We'll talk about this over lunch."

Sam toasted the bread and sliced tomatoes while Faith finished frying bacon. Faith served her mother's lunch on a tray while Sam set two places at the kitchen counter.

Faith pulled up a bar stool next to Sam. "I don't see the point in making Mom suffer at Creekside Manor when she can stay here with me. I can deal with her when she's like this. She doesn't know who I am half the time, but at least she's easy to get along with. Some of the stuff that comes out of her mouth makes me laugh. Even Bitsy thinks she's funny."

Sam took a bite of her sandwich. "What does Mike think of Mom staying here?" she asked with a mouth full of food.

"I haven't told him yet. But he'll go along with whatever I decide." Faith started to take a bite and then set her sandwich back down. "Look, I realize there will come a time when I can no longer handle her here. Nobody knows when that time will be. I think her new meds have really helped with her anxiety. She's night and day from last week. She bounces around in time. At the manor she started crying like a child because I wouldn't take her to Disney World." Her sister shivered and wrapped her arms around herself. "It was awful, Sam, the way she screeched, the look of terror in her eyes."

"I can't imagine it. I'm sorry you had to be the one to go through that."

"Anyway, aside from that horrible incident, for the past few days she's been this flirtatious Lovie in Love that you just witnessed with Eli."

Faith's phone vibrated beside her plate, and the Creekside Manor caller ID appeared on the screen. She accepted the call and listened for a minute. "Sam is here with me, Irene. I'm going to put you on speakerphone." Faith switched the call to speaker and set the phone on the counter between them.

Irene greeted her, "Afternoon, Sam. As I was saying to your sister, this is not the first time one of our families has encountered a traumatic drop-off. I suggest we wait a few days, get through Memorial Day, and then try again. Faith, it might be best if you let one of your sisters try next time."

Faith locked eyes with Sam as she said, "Don't worry. I learned a lot about myself today. My sisters and I will talk about it over the weekend, and one of us will give you a call on Tuesday."

They said goodbye to Irene, and Faith ended the call.

"We'll let Jackie take her next time. She's ruthless enough to handle it." Sam sipped her tea while she considered the situation. "We would have to pay the manor to keep her room set up, if they'll even allow that, but I don't see the harm in letting Mom stay with you for a while. If that's something you truly want to do."

"I wouldn't offer if it wasn't. And her room will be waiting for her whenever the time comes."

"Talk to your husband," Sam said. "He might feel differently when he learns about this Curtis crisis. But if he's on board, we'll discuss it with Jackie over the weekend."

A shriek of laughter came from their mother in the other room. "See!" Faith pointed toward the family room. "I told you she's happy."

"She certainly seems like it." Sam licked her finger and ran it through the crumbs on her plate. "On a more pleasant note, I talked to Jamie this morning, and he's bringing a date to the party on Monday."

"Who? Lizbet?" Faith asked, her sandwich inches from her mouth, poised to take a bite.

Sam's eyes grew big. "How'd you know?"

Faith hunched her shoulders. "I saw the way they looked at each other when they were here the other day. She seems like a nice girl. And pretty too."

"We'll need to get a head count so I'll know how many hamburger patties to make." Sam used her fingers to keep a tally as she listed the party guests. "Lizbet is bringing her sister, so that makes two. Plus ten of us. Jackie invited Moses and his wife. Annie's coming, but Heidi and her boyfriend are maybes. That's a grand total of seventeen including the maybes. It should be a fun party."

Faith dropped her smile. "Unless Curtis shows up. Then it'll be a disaster, Sweeney-family style."

TWENTY-TWO

JACKIE

Jackie took more care than usual preparing for her Memorial Day cookout. She instructed the landscape crew to manicure the lawn and her handyman to power wash the terrace. She spent the day on Friday tending her rose garden and planting her containers with colorful annuals that would tolerate the intense summer heat. Cases of beer, soft drinks, and bottled water were stacked in the garage for Bill and Sean to ice down in tubs on Monday when they set the picnic tables out on the lawn. Her plans for Sunday included making a vat of potato salad and several dozen deviled eggs. Sam was bringing the burgers, hot dogs, and desserts, and Faith was contributing two cold salads—one pasta and one mixed green.

As she orchestrated all the details for the party, other intermittent thoughts kept popping up. She was as annoyed with Faith for botching their mother's drop-off at Creekside Manor as she was with herself for assigning such an important task to her baby sister. She knew Faith was a softie. She herself, on the other hand, was an expert at emotionally detaching from high-stress situations. Except when it came to Sean and Cooper. Once they got through the holiday weekend, she would reschedule the drop-off at Creekside Manor. She would take charge. And she would get the job done. She didn't want her mother locked away in a memory care unit any more than her sisters did. In time Faith and Sam would understand Creekside Manor was the best option for their mother's care. For now they would enjoy their Memorial Day party together. It saddened her to think it might very well be her mother's last.

Since her appointment with Moses on Tuesday, Jackie had been more effective in communicating with Sean. She was taking her nerve pills with more frequency, but they enabled her to remain calm. Sean had yet to quit his job, but he'd created an account on the College of Charleston's website—his first step toward applying. When she stopped by the farmer's market that morning to buy blueberries for the party from Farmer Fred, she was thrilled to see the long line of people waiting to purchase crabs, fish, and the new offering—raw creek shrimp. Sean served his customers with a smile she recognized. One that made his ocean-blue eyes sparkle. One she hadn't seen on his face since he left for college last fall. He was in his element serving customers fresh seafood. There was no denying that Sweeney blood pumped through his veins. Would it be so terrible for him to go into the family business? She'd rather he be a doctor or a lawyer, but she would settle for whatever profession he chose as long as he was happy and healthy. And clean.

Sam and Jamie would be good role models for Sean. Jackie admired her middle sister's determination to rebuild the market. She'd strung a banner across the top corner of the lot, where every car passing through the intersection would see it, announcing the market would reopen the next spring. In front of the vendor area, she'd posted another banner that read "Saturdays at Sweeney's." They'd turned the simple idea of selling steamed crabs to their old customers into a thriving business. When they broke ground on the new building, they would have to either stop hosting the farmer's market or find another location. But for now they were earning a little money while sending an important message to their customers—Captain Sweeney's Seafood was here to stay.

Sean had been zonked out in front of the TV in the game room since he got home around four that afternoon. He was making plenty of money selling seafood. And now that they'd added shrimp to the mix, he was working even harder to prepare for Saturdays, which meant spending much of Wednesdays and all day Thursdays and Fridays on the water. Instead of getting a second job, Bill had suggested that Sean attend summer school to pull up his grades, an idea that Jackie approved. Sean's taking a class or two at the college would enable her to be in Charleston a few days a week to see clients and supervise her construction projects. He would have to act soon, though. The first session started in less than a week. She'd pressed Sean on it several times, but thus far he'd shown no interest.

Bill was on call at the hospital for the weekend, and she was waiting for him to get home to have dinner. She'd purchased a nice piece of salmon from Harris Teeter, and he'd offered to cook it on the grill. She'd begged Sean to join them, but he'd fixed himself a turkey sandwich instead. Despite the nerve pill she'd swallowed an hour earlier, it took every ounce of self-control she could muster not to needle her son. He'd promised to help her get ready for the party, but so far he'd shown no interest in her preparations. As he sat on the sofa exhausted from his day, she wanted to poke at him. She wanted her fun-loving son back, the one so full of energy he could never sit still no matter how tired. More and more, she was convinced he was suffering from depression.

She'd been coming in and out of the room for the past hour as she gathered decorations for the party. The old Sean would have jumped up to help her. This Sean didn't acknowledge her presence.

As she descended the stairs from the kitchen with red

gingham tablecloths draped over both arms, she asked, "Sean, son, can you take a break from your program to help me bring the big hurricane lanterns down from the attic? They're heavy. I can't manage them by myself."

"Can't it wait until tomorrow?" he asked, his eyes glued to his zombie show.

"No." She deposited the cloths in a heap on the floor beside the back door. "I want to bring them down tonight so I can clean them tomorrow."

"All right," he grumbled. "This show will be over in a minute."

She went back to the attic and returned ten minutes later with a cardboard box of cobalt-blue vases she planned to use for the tables. "Minute's up! Let's get moving. I lined the lanterns up at the top of the attic stairs. It will only take us a minute to bring them down."

Sean clicked the power button, turning the TV off, and slammed the remote down on the coffee table. "Jesus, Mom! Can't you give me a break! I'm so sick and tired of you nagging —" He clammed up at the sound of his father's car pulling into the carport.

Jackie stood in place, arms crossed and toe tapping the hardwood floor. As soon as Bill entered the house, he looked back and forth between Jackie and Sean. "What'd I miss?"

"Your son was just telling me how sick and tired he is of me nagging him." She turned on her son. "But guess what, Sean, I'm sick and tired of nagging you. I asked you to help me get ready for the party. That has never been a problem before. I don't understand why it's a problem now."

Bill dropped his keys in the bowl on the chest by the back door and crossed the room to his son. "What's gotten into you? You usually love setting up for family events. Your mother can't do it alone."

"Then you do it." Sean sprang to his feet and stumbled into Bill, who caught him before he fell.

"What did you just say to me?" Bill asked, tightening his grip on Sean's arm.

Sean jerked his arm free. "I said *you* do it!"

Gripping Sean's T-shirt with both hands, Bill backed him against the wall. "What's wrong with you? Have you been drinking?" He sniffed their son's breath. "I don't smell any alcohol." Pinning him against the wall with his left arm, Bill removed his phone from his pocket, accessed his flashlight app, and shone the light in Sean's eyes. "His pupils are dilated. What're you on, Sean? Where'd you get the drugs?"

"None of your damn business." Sean shoved Bill off him and started up the stairs. Bill clambered after him and grabbed his bare foot, pulling him back down. Sean kicked Bill in the face as he scrambled to get away.

"Ow! Damn that hurts!" Bill lifted a hand to his nose.

Jackie dropped to her knees beside her husband. "Are you all right?"

"I think so." Blood trickled from his nose, but he appeared unharmed otherwise.

"I'm going after him." Jackie got to her feet and took the steps two at a time on the way up.

"No, Jack, wait!" Bill yelled. "Let him cool down first."

Jackie kept moving. She had no intention of letting her son cool down. His kicking his father in the face overstepped big-time the bounds of acceptable behavior.

By the time she'd climbed two flights of steps to the third floor, Sean had locked himself in the bathroom. "Open this door right now!" she demanded, banging her fist against the door. She heard the sound of the toilet flushing. "You are way out of line, young man. You kicked your father in the face. I will not allow that kind of aggressive behavior. Either get your act together, or get out of my house."

The toilet flushed again and the door opened. "I didn't mean to kick him, Mom. It was an accident. I'm sorry."

"Save your apology for your father." She pushed past him and stared down into the toilet, where two rectangular tablets lay dissolving at the bottom of the bowl. She stuck her hand into the toilet, removed the pills, and set them on the edge of the sink. "How many pills did you flush?"

Sean stared at the pills as though it was painful for him to watch them dissolve. "I don't know."

Jackie glared at her son. "I take that to mean there were too many to count."

He hung his head.

Bill appeared in the doorway, a bloody dish towel pressed to his nose.

"Oh God, Dad. I'm so sorry. I didn't mean to hurt you."

Bill started to speak and then stopped himself. He studied his son's face for a minute before shaking his head. "I don't even know what to say to you, son. Wasn't getting arrested enough?"

Jackie lifted her son's chin, forcing him to look her in the eye. "Where'd you get the drugs?"

"From a dude at work."

"That's what I figured." She studied her son's face, his coloring and deep-blue eyes so like her father's. Oscar Sweeney would never have tolerated such behavior from his children. He had high expectations of his girls and he held them accountable for their actions. He'd never been unkind, but he'd always been firm. She'd let Sean down. She'd ignored the signs because she had been too preoccupied with her business and her mother and planning their party. Time and again, she'd failed her family by putting her own needs and wants first. But as the three of them stood crammed together in the small space, with the stench of their body odor filling the room, she understood that her son was a drug addict and his life was at stake. His arrest had been a wake-up call they'd chosen to ignore. But she would not let him die. A strength she hadn't known she possessed came from deep inside her. "First thing in the morning, you will call your boss and quit your job."

"But—"

She pinched his chin between her thumb and forefinger as hard as she could. "No buts. If you want to continue living under our roof, you will shut your mouth and do as we say."

His lip quivered as a tear rolled down his cheek. "Yes, ma'am."

TWENTY-THREE

SAM

Sam had a bird's-eye view of the party from the second-floor balcony off Jackie's family room. She needed a moment to collect herself before joining the others. The temptation to drink was greater some days than others. And today was a doozy with her concern over her mother and Curtis on the loose and the fire at the market. Drowning her worries in the pitcher of blueberry mojitos Jackie had concocted for the party would relieve her stress. If only for a brief time. Tomorrow she would wake up with a horrible hangover and an even greater temptation to drink. Abstaining from alcohol seemed to come easier for Eli. He'd been sober longer than she. Then again, he'd been an alcoholic longer than she. Her sister's signature cocktails were always a hit among those family members capable of drinking responsibly. She wouldn't deny them their fun. But she'd stay on the balcony where it was safe as long as she could.

Eli stood on the terrace below with her mother, Jamie, and his friends—a blonde with hair shorter than Sam's on his right and a brunette with hair pulled back in a loose ponytail on his left. Sam wasn't sure which girl was currently holding her son's attention and which was the sister. She'd met Lizbet before, on the day Lovie got lost, but there'd been so much confusion, she hadn't paid her much attention. Even from a distance, Sam could tell the conversation among the group was awkward. The girls smiled politely at Lovie, who was holding court, babbling on about something. She hoped Jamie had remembered to warn his friends about his grandmother's condition. Lovie's outfit alone—cropped red-and-white gingham pants and a white T-shirt with the American flag sequined across it—was enough to make anyone question her sanity.

Eli was eyeballing the grounds as he listened to Lovie with one ear. He'd been on constant alert for signs of Curtis since returning from Columbia. As promised, Eli had confronted Curtis and met with his parole officer. The parole officer had substantiated Curtis's claim of innocence, and the department of corrections had offered an insincere apology and a lame excuse about why the Prospect Police Department hadn't been notified of his release.

"Sometimes these things just slip through the cracks," the director had said in his department's defense.

Eli responded, "And who's to say Curtis didn't slip through the cracks, hail a ride to Prospect, and burn down my wife's business?"

Both men assured him that Curtis was under strict surveillance, but Eli remained unconvinced that Curtis wasn't somehow involved in the fire and strange goings-on relative to Lovie's recipes. But he had no evidence that proved otherwise.

Sam knew it was only a matter of time before Curtis showed his hand. She just hoped it wouldn't be tonight.

Jamie saw her standing on the balcony and motioned for her to come down. With her index finger, she gestured she'd be down in a minute.

The rest of her family was scattered about the grounds. Faith and Mike were on the dock with Bitsy, who was practicing her backflip off the end. Jackie and Bill were stationed in the outdoor kitchen. With aviator sunglasses shielding his eyes, Bill stared, as if in a trance, at the flames licking the grates of his fancy new charcoal grill—a stainless-steel table on wheels large enough to cook oysters for a large crowd. Jackie presented the picture of elegance with the blunt edge of her dark bob brushing the shoulder of her white silk tunic. But Sam could tell by the wringing of her hands and her pacing in circles in her taupe-colored ankle-strap sandals that she was on edge. Both Jackie and Bill had stared at Faith with blank faces, as though they hadn't heard her, when she told them Curtis was on the loose again. Sam wondered if Sean, who was nowhere in sight, was the source of their distraction.

Moses and his wife, Merrill, appeared from beneath the canopy of oaks lining the driveway. Her sister pulled Moses aside, leaving Bill and Merrill in conversation at the grill. Jackie stood in lecture-mode stance with her face tight and chin jutted out. Moses massaged his chin as he listened. *What is that about?* Sam wondered. As far as she knew, her older sister had never sought counseling from Moses. Jackie was hiding something. She feared they would find out what that *thing* was before the night was over.

Eli waved his hand above his head to get Sam's attention. "Help," he mouthed, gesturing for water, and she mouthed back, "Coming."

She went inside, down the stairs, and out onto the terrace, removing two bottles of water from the red plastic drink tub before joining the group. "Here." She handed one of the water bottles to her mother. "Drink this, Mom. It's hot out here. You need to stay hydrated." She turned to the girls and introduced herself. "Call me Sam." She extended her hand to each of them in turn. "I'm glad you could make it to the party."

"Thank you for having us," the girls said in unison.

Lizbet's sister, Brooke, was the more stunning of the two, and, Sam sensed, the more worldly as well. Lizbet was every bit as lovely, but in a softer way, with delicate features, a pert nose, and soft gray eyes.

"There are plenty of drinks in the tub, both alcoholic and the boring kind. Help yourselves." Sam unscrewed the cap from her water bottle and took a swig. "You are kind to offer Jamie a rent-free place to live. Sounds like he's getting the better end of the deal."

Lizbet patted Jamie's arm. "Show your mom your hands."

Jamie held up his hands, showing palms and fingers that were raw and covered in blisters.

"He spread a whole truckload of mulch yesterday," Lizbet said. "He's earned his keep for the week."

Sam smiled. "He's good with a pitchfork and garden rake. He's not bad with a pair of hedge trimmers either."

Jamie gave his mother a half hug. "She should know. She's the slave driver who taught me."

"I also taught him to cook. He's quite proficient in the kitchen. Hint, hint," Sam said, winking at the girls.

Brooke gave Jamie a playful shove. "What's up with that? You've been holding out on us."

"Thanks, Mom! You blew my cover. I've been eating like a Roman god without having to lift a finger." He rested a hand on each of the girls' shoulders. "These two are amazing cooks. So is Sawyer when she's around."

"Ah! But you're the expert on the grill." She pinched her son's cheek. "You should treat them to your barbecue ribs sometime."

"I can attest to that," Moses said as he approached the group with his wife. "Jamie's ribs are the best in the Lowcountry."

Old friends greeted one another, and new friends were introduced. When Sam stood on her tiptoes to kiss his cheek, he wrapped his strong arms around her and lifted her off her feet. "You're looking good, Sammie. Marriage agrees with you."

"I was thinking the same thing about you." Sam was actually thinking that he'd put on a few pounds and lost a little hair since the last time she'd seen him. But he appeared happy just the same, and his eyes twinkled when he smiled at his wife.

Sam had met Moses's wife only once, at their wedding two years earlier. Merrill had a heart-shaped face with high cheekbones and a smile that spread from ear to ear when she looked at him.

They heard squeals of laughter from down on the dock, and all heads turned in time to see Mike shinny up a piling and cannonball into the water.

Jamie gave Sam an expectant look. "Can we join them?"

"You didn't wear your swimsuits for nothing," she said, eyeing Jamie's swim trunks and the girls' bikini straps beneath their cover-ups. "I left a stack of towels down on the dock."

Their three faces lit up like little children's, and they took off running down the hill to the dock.

Eli's gray eyes pleaded. "Does that mean me too?"

Sam laughed out loud. "Yes, that means you too." She could count on her husband to be on the lookout for Curtis even while he was at play. "And take Moses and Merrill with you. Faith will want to see them." She shooed them away. Her mother started to followed them, but she grabbed her by the arm. Lovie had grown quiet during the last few minutes, and her face was set in a scowl. Sam worried she was getting overheated. "Why don't you and I go inside where it's cool."

Bill and Jackie were standing with their heads pressed together beside the grill. "Are you ready for me to bring out the burgers?" Sam asked as they passed by.

Jackie glanced up, a look of surprise on her face. "That'd be great, Sam. Thank you."

Sam turned to her mother once they were inside. "Do you need to use the restroom while I get the burgers from the kitchen?"

Relief washed over Lovie's face. "Will you show me where it

is?" she asked, even though she'd used Jackie's powder room a thousand times before.

Sam wasn't buying into Faith's claim that Lovie was on an upswing. When Eli was around her mother, she caught glimpses of the flirty Lovie in Love her sister had talked about. But Sam was witnessing an increase in confusion and memory loss more than anything. The only notable change was that Lovie didn't seem as anxious or combative.

Sam took the burgers to Jackie and went back inside to wait for her mom, who was taking an inordinate amount of time in the bathroom. When she finally emerged, Sam saw that the toilet was stopped up with toilet paper and on the verge of overflowing.

"Wait for me by the back door," Sam said, aiming a thumb over her shoulder. "I'll be out in a minute."

She located a plumber's friend under the sink and unclogged the toilet. She caught a glimpse of herself in the mirror while she was washing her hands. Beads of sweat dotted her forehead, and her short hair stood on end. *How much is Faith hiding from us?* Sam wondered. *She can't continue to do this indefinitely.*

Grabbing a stack of Jackie's decorator magazines from the coffee table, she took her mother back outside and settled her in a lounge chair on the terrace. She collapsed in the chair next to Lovie, leaned her head back, and closed her eyes. She thought back over the years to the holidays her family had spent together at Moss Creek Farm. Good times and bad. Happy and sad. This was the first holiday she could remember when one of their clan was missing. The party wasn't the same without Cooper. Was he spending the holiday with friends or a special someone in Virginia? Who would be the next in the family to fly the coop? Hopefully not Jamie, although he seemed more and more enamored by Charleston. Maybe Bitsy one day, but that was years away. She had a sinking feeling Lovie would be next to go. Although her mother wouldn't be starting a new life, her old life would be coming to an end.

Loud voices startled her back to the present a few minutes later. She opened her eyes to see Heidi chatting animatedly with Jackie, her mountain of white-blonde hair flopping around on top of her head as she spoke. Annie stood beside her, a white shopping bag in each hand. Heidi's romper was inappropriate for a woman her age, but she rocked it with her long shapely legs and her trim figure. Annie was dressed in raggedy denim shorts and a halter top, not unlike the ones she'd worn when she and Sam first met on the night of Faith's wedding. Had it been only two years ago? It seemed like two decades.

Sam rose to greet them. "Heidi, you look amazing. How is it that you're getting younger when the rest of us are clearly aging?"

Jackie cut her eyes at Sam. "Speak for yourself, little sister."

Laughter broke out among the group.

"I'm sorry Hugh couldn't make it," Heidi said to Jackie. "He has a deadline to finish a project this week."

Jackie cracked the first smile Sam had seen from her sister all day. "Tell him we missed him."

"We brought some leftovers from the last party," Annie said, holding up the bags. "An assortment of salads and some leftover pigs in blankets we thought Jamie and Sean might like."

Jackie's smile dropped at the mention of her son's name. "Speaking of Sean, I should see what's keeping him." She took the bags from Annie and disappeared inside.

Heidi turned to Sam. "I was so sorry to hear about the fire at the market. I understand you're considering expanding when you rebuild."

Sam rolled her eyes at Annie. "I wonder where you got that idea."

"I think that's my cue to leave," Annie said and fled to the dock.

"I'm parched," Heidi said, looking around for refreshments.

Sam showed her to the bar, and Heidi filled a glass with ice and soda water.

"I'd like the idea of having the extra room for wine tastings or to rent out to the locals for small events," Sam said. "But I'm not sure how I feel about opening a sandwich shop. I know absolutely nothing about running a restaurant."

Heidi added a lime wedge to her drink. "You and I have talked about combining forces before. Would you like to revisit the possibility?"

"I have my same reservations as before," Sam said. "I'd hate for business to get in the way of our friendship."

"Things are different now for both of us. Won't you at least consider it?"

Sam hesitated, but only for a few seconds. "I'm willing to consider anything as long as you understand this is a long shot."

Heidi brightened. "Deal."

She studied Heidi more closely. Her complexion glowed and she exuded good health. "I wasn't kidding when I said it earlier. You look damn good. Tell me your secret. Are you on some kind of special diet?"

Heidi leaned in close to Sam. "Shh!" She held her finger to her lips. "Don't tell anyone. I have a sexy man in my bed."

Sam laughed out loud. Over Heidi's shoulder she observed Eli coming up the hill from the dock with a towel wrapped around his waist. His muscular chest and six-pack abs sent a jolt to her nether regions. "I have one too, thank you very much."

Heidi turned around and admired the scenery. "Yes, you do."

"I'm curious to meet your Hugh. I've heard a lot about him from Jackie."

"They have a good working relationship. I'm not sure which of them is more detail oriented. Has she told you about her new project?"

Sam's gaze shifted to her sister, who had returned from inside and was chewing Bill's ear off about something—no doubt that *thing* she was hiding—while he cooked the burgers.

"Nope," Sam said. "She hasn't mentioned it, at least not that I can remember."

Heidi pressed her fingertips to her lips. "Oops. I probably shouldn't have said anything."

"Don't worry about it. My sister always has some sort of project up her sleeve," Sam said, making a mental note to ask Jackie about it.

Heidi guzzled the rest of her soda water. "We should plan dinner together with our men soon. Hugh is a great guy. I'm afraid to admit it for fear something will change. But I finally have everything I've ever wanted. My daughter is back in my life, I'm my own boss, and my business is thriving. Having your kid working alongside you is a thrill. You'll see what I mean when Jamie graduates. I know you've worked together before, but it's different when you share the same career goals. You've done right by him. He has a solid work ethic and he knows how to handle people—both customers and coworkers."

"He enjoys working for you. Thanks for offering him the job."

"Speak of the devil. Here he comes now." Heidi inclined her head to the pack of swimmers straggling up the hill. "He and Lizbet make a nice couple, don't you think?"

"I'm not sure which one he's more smitten with, the girl or the city."

Heidi waved away Sam's concern. "Don't worry about it. He's enjoying his summer in Charleston, but Prospect is his home. I can't see him living anywhere else."

"I hope you're right."

The group of swimmers crowded onto the terrace. Jamie went to the tub of drinks and began passing out SweetWater IPAs to his friends.

"We're starving!" Bitsy announced.

"I guess the grown-ups better get busy then," Sam said.

"Aw, man!" Bitsy said, stomping her tiny bare foot against the bluestone. "You mean it's not ready yet."

"No, squirt. But it won't take but a few minutes to get it on the table." Sam kissed the top of her niece's wet head. "Why don't you go help Uncle Bill and Aunt Jackie with the burgers while your mommy and I bring out the other stuff?"

"Okay," Bitsy said, and trotted off toward the grill.

Everyone pitched in, and within ten minutes they gathered with their plates around the two picnic tables. Sam sat down next to Bill. Upon closer inspection, she noticed dark bruises under both eyes beneath his aviator glasses. Bill offered the blessing, and they were taking their first bites when the back door banged open and Sean tumbled out onto the terrace. Brandishing a bottle of Stoli Blueberi and slurring his words in a loud voice, he wished everyone a happy Fourth of July.

Sam understood what it meant to be drunk. And her nephew was about as drunk as drunk could get.

Jackie stood up and marched over to him. "Son, please! We have company." When he shoved her away, he lost his balance, tripped over his feet, and crashed into the grill. The vodka bottle shattered into pieces and hot coals rolled across the bluestone. Fortunately there was no vodka left in the bottle to catch fire.

Mike raced to Sean's side, but Jackie was already hovering over him. "Oh God, Mike, help him! He's not moving."

"Move over, sweetheart, so I can have a look." Mike knelt down beside him and felt for a pulse. He leaned in close to his ear and called Sean's name, but her nephew remained unresponsive. "Someone call 911."

TWENTY-FOUR

JACKIE

Everyone scattered after Bill left with Sean in the ambulance for the hospital. As desperate as she was about her son's condition, Jackie opted to stay at the farm and let the doctors handle the crisis. She would only be in their way. Two nerve pills helped her appear calm on the outside, but she was falling apart on the inside. She was relieved when Sam, Jamie, and Eli insisted on staying to help clean up.

"I'm not leaving here until we know more about Sean's condition," Sam said. "Even if we have to spend the night."

"I'd appreciate that," Jackie said. "I'd rather not be alone."

Jamie and Eli straightened up and put everything away outside while Sam and Jackie tackled the kitchen. Jackie needed to keep busy, to distract herself from the image in her mind of Sean lying unconscious on the stretcher with that god-awful contraption around his neck. "He didn't fall on his neck!" she'd wanted to scream at the EMTs. At the same time, she was grateful they were being extra cautious.

After everything was cleaned up, and a bag of leftovers had been created for each family, Sam brewed a pot of decaf and set out a tray of her layered brownies on Jackie's pickled-oak breakfast room table. As they watched the sun begin its descent toward the horizon, Jackie told the three of them about Sean's arrest in Athens and about the argument they'd had just the night before.

"I wish you'd told me sooner," Sam said in a soft voice. "Why did you feel the need to keep it from me?"

Jackie had prepared her answer in anticipation of the question. "I thought I was protecting his dignity, but I realize now I was hiding in shame."

"What dignity?" Sam said. "We're family, Jackie. You and I have seen each other at our absolute worst."

Jamie raised his hand. "That includes me too. You've helped me through some dark times, Aunt Jackie."

Jackie looked away, staring out the window as the pink sky faded away. She thought back to the months after the ATV accident in which Jamie had lost his best friend and his will to live. Their whole family, including Moses, had rallied around him. "I know I should have told you. I've felt so scared and alone these past few weeks. But seeing my son kick his father in the face like that . . ." Her voice trailed off.

"We love Sean," Sam said. "We want to help him. Eli and I know firsthand what he's going through. We can offer guidance and support because we know how hard it is."

A lump developed in her throat, and Jackie nodded. She turned to Eli. From the little she knew about his past, he'd been struggling with his addiction for far longer than Sam. "Do you think he needs to go to rehab?"

Eli paused a minute before answering. "I'm not in a position to make that call. Obviously, I'm not an expert. But I do know rehab is more effective if the addict is open to receiving help."

"What if we had a family intervention?" Jamie suggested. "We've all had our problems in the past. Not just us, but Faith too, with Curtis's abuse of her. We need to remind Sean that we care about him, and that he can talk to us, that we can relate to what he's going through."

"I think that's a great suggestion," Jackie said. "The biggest part of his problem is that Sean really misses Cooper. Maybe if we all rally around him, he won't feel so lost and alone."

She glanced at the clock on the mantel in the adjacent family room. Nearly two hours had passed since the ambulance left for the hospital. Excusing herself to go to the restroom, Jackie went to her room and popped another nerve pill. She needed to get hold of herself. But she couldn't very well do that while her life was in such turmoil.

She returned to the family room and reclaimed her seat at the table. Her phone rang with a call from Bill, and she snatched it up. "Thank God. I've been so worried. Please tell me he's okay."

"He's okay," Bill said. "At least for tonight. He'll have a major hangover tomorrow, though. He's conscious and doesn't appear to have suffered any major injuries. Moses is talking with him now, and Mike is signing him out. We should be home soon."

"Okay, honey. Thanks for calling. Be careful, and we'll see you in a few minutes."

Jackie ended the call and repeated the conversation to the three expectant faces staring at her.

"That's wonderful news!" Sam said. "We should let Faith know."

Jackie's skin prickled and she stiffened.

Noticing her reaction, Sam said, "Seriously, Jack. We just talked about how important family is at times like these. Did you fail sharing time in kindergarten?"

Jackie laughed despite herself, feeling her tension subside. Of course she should tell her other sister. For Sean's sake she would need to be better about communicating with her family. He needed his aunts, uncles, and cousins in his life. "You're right. Faith should know. We need to check on Mom anyway. She was hysterical after Sean's fall. Do you mind calling her?"

"I'll text her," Sam said, reaching for her phone. "She may already be asleep, and I don't want to wake her."

"All this worrying has made me hungry." Jamie got up from the table and stretched. "Are there any leftovers?"

Jackie pushed back from the table. "We have plenty of food. No one ever got a chance to eat. I'm sure you're starving. The others will be too when they get home."

The four of them crowded in the kitchen and began pulling containers of leftovers out of the refrigerator and warming up the hamburgers and hot dogs.

"I feel bad for your friends from Charleston," Jackie said to Jamie as they worked. "They drove all the way down here for a party and left without even eating."

"They're fine," Jamie said. "Lizbet texted a while ago. Heidi treated them to dinner at Halls Chophouse when they got back to Charleston."

Jackie smiled an appreciative smile. "Lucky them. Halls beats our burgers any day. Please take them some leftovers anyway."

"Will do," Jamie said. "Leftovers are always appreciated."

A small buffet awaited Sean, Bill, and Moses on the kitchen counter when they arrived a few minutes later. They gathered around Sean, waiting their turns to speak to him. His eyes were red and swollen from crying, and he had scrapes and bruises on his arms and legs from his fall.

"I'm sorry I ruined the party," he said, staring at the floor.

Jackie tilted his chin. "Forget about the party. We're just glad you're okay." She pressed her lips to his forehead. "You scared me half to death."

Jamie clapped him on the shoulder. "We'll forgive you this time, cuz. Just don't let it happen again."

Sam hugged him. "You don't have to go through this alone, kiddo. I would never have recovered from my addiction without my husband's support. We're lucky to have each other. We hold each other together. If you'll let us, we'll hold you together too."

Sean's eyes glistened with tears as he nodded.

Eli offered him a fist bump. "You call me anytime, night or

day. And we're gonna call you too." He poked Sean's chest. "So you'd better answer."

Sean cracked a smile. "I will," he mumbled.

"We just finished putting the leftovers out," Jackie said. "Let me fix you a plate."

"I'm not that hungry," Sean said.

"You'll feel better in the morning if you eat something," Sam said.

Sean shrugged. "Maybe I'll eat a hamburger, then."

Jackie watched her son follow Sam into the kitchen. Her boys had always listened to Sam more than they listened to her. There had been a time when she was jealous of the twins' relationship with her younger sister, but now she'd kiss the ground at the feet of anyone who could get through to him.

Sean took his plate to the family room with Sam, Eli, and Jamie while Jackie, Bill, and Moses ate at the table.

Moses wolfed down his dinner before Jackie had taken the first bite of her burger. She gawked at his empty plate. "I'm glad I don't have to feed you on a regular basis."

Big Mo tilted his head back and cackled. "I apologize for my poor manners. I didn't realize how hungry I was."

Jackie aimed a thumb at the buffet. "Please go back for seconds. There's plenty left."

Moses settled back in his chair and wiped his mouth. "I couldn't eat another bite. But I'd like to talk about Sean for a minute." He glanced over at Sean, who appeared deep in conversation with Sam and Eli. "He's not paying any attention to us," Moses said in a low voice. "After we spoke at the hospital, I understand a little more about where he's coming from. He experienced withdrawal symptoms after flushing his stash of Xanax down the toilet Saturday night. He didn't know how to handle it, and he was afraid to come to you."

"So he started drinking," Jackie said.

"It's my fault." Bill raked his fork through his pasta salad.

"You warned us about the cold-turkey side effects of Xanax withdrawal, but I didn't think it could happen to my son. And I underestimated the extent of his usage. I was thinking like a parent and not a doctor."

"Don't be so hard on yourself," Moses said. "You're his father. The last thing you wanted is to pump more drugs in your son's body. With that said, I think he needs to be on an antidepressant, at least for the short term, until we get him straightened out."

"So I was right about him being depressed," Jackie said.

"There are antidepressants that specifically target anxiety. I'm convinced your son is suffering from acute anxiety. He's having a difficult time finding his way without his twin. I think Cooper looked out for Sean more than any of us ever realized. There were a lot of things Sean didn't have to worry about because Cooper took care of them for him. No wonder he didn't make it at Georgia. A sheltered kid like that would never have survived at a school with nearly thirty thousand students."

Jackie stared at her plate. "I was so proud to have one of my sons attend my alma mater, I never stopped to consider what was best for Sean."

Moses placed his big hands, palms down, on the table. "You guys need to stop beating up on yourselves. Sean admitted to me that it was *his* choice to go to a big SEC school. When it comes to picking colleges, kids don't always get it right the first time."

"Where do we go from here?" Bill asked.

"Well . . . Sean's agreed to meet with me in my office at eight o'clock tomorrow morning. We will come up with a game plan then."

"That's awfully early considering everything that happened tonight," Jackie said.

"I agree," Moses said. "But it's the only available appointment I have tomorrow, and Sean has assured me he would be on time."

"Do you want us there with him?" Jackie asked.

"That's your choice, but I think he feels more comfortable talking to me alone."

Bill shot Jackie a look. He sensed how much she wanted to attend the session. "Why don't you call us afterward and fill us in?" Bill said.

"I'm happy to do that," Moses said. "Sean has given me permission to discuss his case with you. You have a strong network already in place within your family. During the three years I've known your family, nearly every single one of you has suffered a hardship of some sort, and you've survived because you have one another. Sean will be okay. He just needs a little more structure in his life. Making him quit his job at the Roost was a good decision on your part, but he needs something to occupy his time in addition to his crab business."

"Now that you mention it," Jackie said, clasping her hands together. "What do you think about him taking summer school classes at the College of Charleston? We can help him choose something he's interested in that might inspire him to think about his future. He also needs to pull up his GPA. He and I will stay at my house in Charleston on the nights he has classes. I'm in the process of relocating my business. I have plenty to keep him busy in his free time."

Moses smiled. "I like both these ideas."

"Do you think it's too late for him to enroll?" Jackie asked. "Classes start on Friday."

"I can get him in," Big Mo said without hesitation. "Sean and I will look at the course offerings together tomorrow. We'll pick a couple of classes that suit his schedule, and I'll give my contact in admissions a call."

Bill held his hand out to the therapist. "Thank you, Moses. I don't know how we will ever repay you."

Big Mo flashed them a toothy grin. "I'll remind you of that when you receive my bill." He glanced at his watch. "I'd better get going before my wife sends out a search party. Thank you for dinner." He got up and walked his plate to the kitchen.

Jackie followed and gave him a shopping bag of leftovers. "Please extend our apologies to your bride. I'd love to see her again under different circumstances."

"I'll tell her." He lifted the bag. "She'll appreciate this." He started for the stairs. "I'll see you in my office at eight o'clock sharp," he called out to Sean, who gave him a thumbs-up.

Jamie beamed. "Cool! You get to go to Big Mo's office. Wait until you see his shrine."

A tidal wave of relief washed over Jackie. With her family's support, maybe everything would be okay after all.

TWENTY-FIVE

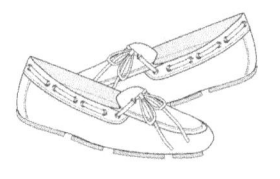

SAM

Heidi called Sam around nine on Tuesday morning. "Can you come to Charleston for lunch today? Annie and I have a proposition we'd like to share with you."

"Today?" Sam looked at the ingredients covering her kitchen counter. She'd planned to spend the morning in her test kitchen perfecting her marinara sauce.

"I realize it's short notice, but this is the only time we can meet. We're booked solid the rest of the week."

"I don't know, Heidi." She hadn't slept well after the crisis with Sean, and she needed to go by Faith's house at some point to check on her mother.

"Please!" Heidi said. "I promise to make it worth your while."

"Since you're obviously not going to take no for an answer"—she looked at the wall clock and made some calculations—"I can be there by eleven. Where should I meet you?"

"Why don't you come to the store? I'll text you the address. We'll show you our operation and then go to my house for lunch where we can talk in private."

Sam cleaned up the kitchen, showered, and slipped on a gray short-sleeved knit dress that flared out at the knees. She brewed a cup of tea in a to-go cup and hit the road. As they'd discussed at the party, she fully anticipated that Heidi would make a formal offer to open a sandwich shop in the new market space. She hated making hasty decisions. But she was meeting with the architect on Friday, which didn't afford her much time to deliberate. Not knowing whether they would ever see a dime from the insurance company made her even more uncomfortable.

But Heidi was a shrewd businesswoman in addition to being a talented event planner. Sam couldn't help but be impressed with her operation, which included the thriving gourmet market Tasty Provisions. Sam had visited the converted warehouse on East Bay Street eighteen months earlier when Heidi was considering buying it. The worn brick walls and random-width oak floors served as a lovely backdrop for Heidi's extensive selection of table goods. Tasty Provisions carried many of the same types of products as Sweeney's—salads and spreads, wines and cheeses and homemade breads—but it focused more on entertaining, whereas Sweeney's was all about the seafood. For a more upscale ambience in the new building, Sam was considering using a variety of materials, much as Heidi had done here, while keeping the same sterile environment she preferred for a seafood market.

Heidi and Annie led her on a tour of the store, including the catering kitchen in the back and the offices on the second floor.

"We're booked through December," Heidi said as she ran a pink-lacquered nail down her twelve-month whiteboard wall calendar. "We even have a few weddings already on the calendar for next summer."

Sam didn't need Heidi to spell it out. She got the message loud and clear. Heidi had not known a single person when she moved to Charleston two summers ago. She'd invested every dime of her meager savings into this warehouse and built her business into a huge success. *Don't you want to be a part of it, Samantha?* was the unspoken question that hung in the humid air as they drove with the top down in Heidi's antique turquoise Mustang to her house on Broad Street for lunch.

Heidi's apartment occupied the second floor of a renovated single house. The kitchen opened up into one main space divided into sitting and dining areas. Her quirky personality was displayed in her decor. A turquoise velvet sofa was the center attraction, with a painting of hot-pink lips in a prominent position over the fireplace. The sexy man in Heidi's bed owned the house and lived, conveniently, downstairs in the ground-floor apartment.

While Heidi set the glass-topped table on the piazza with place mats and silverware, Annie prepared the shrimp tacos and Sam poured three glasses of sweet tea.

"I feel so bad for Sean," Annie said as they stood in the kitchen. "Do you think he's going to be okay?"

"I think so. Bless his heart, he's suffering separation anxiety from Cooper." Sam squeezed her eyes shut when she realized her mistake. "I'm sorry, honey. I didn't mean to bring up a sore subject."

"Oh please!" Annie waved away her apology. "Cooper and I are friends. We text and talk on the phone all the time. I get the impression he doesn't know about Sean. I don't want to tell him, but I think somebody should. He would want to know."

She thought about her sister's words—"*I was hiding in shame.*" Would Jackie keep something as important as Sean's addiction from his twin? "You're right. Cooper would definitely want to know what's going on with his brother. I'll mention it to Jackie."

Sam admitted the tacos were the best she'd ever eaten, with grilled shrimp, avocado salsa, and cilantro dressing. Heidi and Annie had set a trap for her, and she'd walked right into it, but she didn't mind as long as there were more shrimp tacos in her future.

Annie had shown a rare talent in the kitchen when she first

arrived in Prospect with only the clothes on her back and the worn-out dime-store flip-flops on her feet. Her resourcefulness stemmed from having had to raise herself in the absence of a mother and with a father who, as a commercial fisherman, hadn't been a great provider to begin with and was ill the last few years of his life. Annie was grateful for everything she had, and she hadn't minded working hard to get it. Culinary school had honed her skills, broadened her horizons by introducing her to a whole new culture of food, and given her the confidence to let her creative juices flow.

Sam rarely, if ever, had lunch with girlfriends. But this day she was able to relax on Heidi's piazza with a gentle breeze carrying the scent of honeysuckle and enjoy the conversation with two women she respected and had much in common with.

Heidi and Annie nibbled like birds, which allowed them to work around food and still stay trim. Sam, meanwhile, was devouring her lunch and delighting in every single bite.

"You can open a sandwich shop in my seafood market anytime, as long as you promise to put these shrimp tacos on the menu," Sam said, only half joking, when they broached the subject of the sandwich shop again during lunch.

Heidi beamed. "There are many more where that recipe came from. My daughter is a genius, and she has a brilliant future ahead of her. We talked with Lizbet over dinner last night and then well into the wee hours of the morning when Annie and I got home. We believe Prospect is an untapped market in a desirable location, and we want a stake in the game when the economy explodes."

Annie removed a shrimp from her taco and popped it into her mouth. "There are so many more cute shops that have opened since I was last there. I talked to Eli and Mike briefly at the party yesterday. They confirmed that your population has nearly doubled in recent years. Most of these new inhabitants are young families looking for less expensive places to live. In ten years Prospect could be the new Mount Pleasant, with more charm and less traffic. What I want to know is, why are there no restaurants? Where is everyone eating?"

"At home unless they belong to the country club," Sam said. "And from what I hear from Jackie, their food is not very good."

"We'd like to test the market with the sandwich shop," Heidi said. "If it does well, we'll consider opening a waterfront restaurant in a couple of years."

"Are you thinking of moving to Prospect?" Sam asked Annie.

"I haven't gotten that far yet. I will if I need to. But I see myself overseeing the operation and hiring someone else to be my hands-on person."

"Do you have someone in mind?"

Annie tucked a thick hank of honey-colored hair behind her ear. "Lizbet, maybe. Or Sean. Once he gets his act together, he's going to want a piece of the action."

"What if the sandwich shop fails?" Sam asked, reaching for a lemon bar from the plate in the center of the table.

Heidi snickered. "*Failure* is not a term in Annie's vocabulary."

Annie cut her eyes at her mother. "That makes me sound unrealistic, and I'm not. In the event some unforeseen catastrophe happens—which is what it would take for the sandwich shop to fail, considering the success you've already experienced at Sweeney's and the obvious need for more places to eat in Prospect —you will still have the space to use for wine tastings and small events. Having a bigger kitchen will help with your take-out catering. And think of the potential for full-service catering if you decided to venture down that path."

Annie was saying all the right things. Clearly she'd given her proposition plenty of thought.

Heidi folded her arms on the table. "The way I see it, Sam, you are sitting in a pretty position. I advise you to buy the stationery store and build as big a building as you can afford. You won't be disappointed when all is said and done."

"Would you be interested in investing in the building?" Sam asked.

"Not unless you need us to," Heidi said.

"But we will in order to make it happen," Annie added.

"It's a cleaner deal for both of us if we operate the sandwich shop and pay you rent," Heidi said. "In the meantime, we will be putting money aside to invest in the restaurant."

"We know it's a lot to think about," Annie said as she refilled their glasses with tea. "And we don't mean to overwhelm you. We have plenty of time to sort out the logistics while the building is under construction."

"But the decision to buy the stationery store must be made before my architect can start working on the plans," Sam said. "And I'm meeting with him on Friday. It wouldn't hurt to show him the store to at least see what he thinks."

Without the insurance money, she would have to use every dime of her rainy day mad money. And she was hesitant to do that. Knowing she had her own money made her feel secure. Even with her retirement fund, she would still have to borrow a significant sum from the bank. She could always pay herself back if they were to settle with the insurance company later. But if something happened and Sweeney's went bankrupt, they would have only Eli's pension to live on as they grew older.

Annie said, "We want to partner with you, Sam. And with Jamie. And any other Sweeney who enters the picture down the road."

"I know you're worried about doing business with friends," Heidi said. "But that's old-school thinking. We are modern women capable of working together despite any differences of opinion that arise. Mark my words, some will come up. But we'll deal with them in a professional manner because, at the end of the day, we have one common goal. We want to satisfy our clients by offering them cutting-edge cuisine. We want to build a dynasty for the generations in our families to come. We want our clients to get more out of their gatherings, their family holidays and cocktail parties, by taking away their stress."

"That's way more than one common goal, Heidi," Sam said, and they all laughed. "How's this? We strive to enrich our clients' lives with a twenty-first-century spin on traditional southern cuisine, while building a sustainable empire for our families by doing what we love the most."

Annie clapped. "Yay, Sam!"

And Heidi let out a whoop. "That pretty much sums it up."

Sam stood up and walked over to the railing. "Seriously, though. I'm flattered you are interested in going into business with us, and I think we'd make a good team. But I can't make this decision without talking to my son."

Heidi came to stand beside her. "And we totally understand that. We want you to take all the time you need."

Annie joined them. "In the meantime, I made up a list of items, including shrimp tacos, that we should consider for the menu." With a mischievous grin, she handed Sam a folded sheet of card stock.

Sam looked into her big brown eyes. "I'm proud of you, Annie Dawn," she said, referring to the name Annie had used when she first came to Prospect. "I always knew you had talent. But you've become a mature, lovely young woman with a mind of your own. You will go places in life."

"That means a lot coming from you." Annie rested her head on Sam's shoulder. "You and Mom are the best mentors a girl could have."

TWENTY-SIX

JAMIE

Jamie was trimming the ligustrum hedge in the Hornes' backyard when his mother's red Wrangler pulled into the driveway. He set down the hedge trimmers and went to greet her. "This is a surprise. What're you doing here?"

"I hope you don't mind me stopping by uninvited. I tried to call you, but you didn't answer your phone. Now I see why." She eyeballed the ligustrum hedge. "Looks like the Horne sisters have finally put you to work."

He wiped the sweat off his face with his T-shirt. "Those two have no clue what's involved in maintaining a house and yard. Once I started looking around, I was surprised at all the things that needed trimming and fixing and cleaning. So I started doing them. I'm not even sure they've noticed. But that's fine. It gives me something to occupy my time during the day while they're all at work."

Sam cupped his sweaty cheek. "You had to grow up young, didn't you?"

He shrugged. "I didn't mind. Being your little man around the house made me feel important. And I learned a lot of useful skills."

"Your future wife will thank me." Sam looked past him into the backyard. "I'd say Lizbet and Brooke know more about yard work than they're letting on if that garden is any indication."

"That's their mother's perennial garden, the one thing around here they take care of. You won't find a single weed in any of the beds or bugs on her roses. Lizbet sells a lot of her flowers at the market."

Sam walked over to the garden and admired the colorful assortment of perennials. "They're lovely," she said, bending over to sniff a rose.

Jamie planted his hands on his hips. "Are you going to tell me why you're here?"

"I have something I need to talk to you about. Do you have a few minutes?"

"Sure. But let's get something to drink first. I'm dying of thirst," he said as he started toward the house.

Sam followed him inside to the kitchen.

He opened the refrigerator and stuck his head inside. The cold air felt refreshing against his skin. "Lemonade or sweet tea?"

"I'll just have water. I drank enough tea at lunch to fill the Boston Harbor."

He filled two glasses of water from the faucet and handed one to his mother. He guzzled his down and wiped his mouth with the back of his hand.

"Do you think your roommates will mind if I look around?" Without waiting for an answer, Sam took herself on a self-guided tour of the downstairs. "Their mother had a special touch. Can I see your room?" She peered over his shoulder at the stairs behind him.

"No, Mom! I don't think Liz and Brooke would appreciate my mother snooping around their house when they're not here."

"Too bad," she said, heading up the stairs. "A mother likes to be able to picture her son in his surroundings."

"Fine, but hurry," he called after her. "Take a right at the top of the stairs. First room on the left."

He waited for her at the bottom of the stairs. His mother was not a nosy person by nature. She typically respected other people's privacy. What was the real motive behind her visit? Was she hoping to find evidence that he and Liz were sleeping together? They weren't, but he hoped they would soon. He hadn't experienced such a close bond with anyone since Cory died. Almost every night, they talked well into the morning hours without ever running out of things to say. They shared so many of the same interests and they wanted the same things out of life—a family, a meaningful career, and a laid-back lifestyle, preferably on the water.

To his mother's credit, she didn't stay upstairs long. "Now I can envision where you lay your sweet little head on the pillow at night," she said, mussing his hair when she came back downstairs.

"Yeah. So Mom, you mentioned you needed to talk to me about something. I'm curious why you're in Charleston? And I can't remember the last time I saw you wearing a dress, except of course for church. What's going on, Mom?"

Her face grew serious. "Is there somewhere we can sit down?"

He led the way out onto the porch, and they sat down side by side on the bench swing.

"Annie and Heidi invited me to lunch today," Sam said, crossing her legs. "As you're already aware, they are interested in opening a sandwich shop at Sweeney's. I have to admit their enthusiasm is contagious. But I would feel better about it if I knew we'd eventually receive some sort of settlement from the insurance company."

Jamie had given his mother's financial situation a lot of thought. He hoped to get married one day and have a family. Selfishly, he wanted his mother to maintain her financial independence. "I would too, Mom. Honestly, I hate the idea of you using your rainy day mad money."

She furrowed her brows. "That's not exactly the response I was hoping for."

He looked away, watching a pack of adolescent boys cycle down the road and drop their bikes haphazardly in the front yard of the house next door. The brothers who lived next door reminded him of himself at that age, when Cory and he had been inseparable.

"Sorry, Mom, but it's the truth. What if you and Eli want to travel when you get older or buy a sailboat and cruise around the world? What if, God forbid, one of you gets sick? Any number of things could happen. We can't predict the future. Knowing you have Mack's money to fall back on gives me peace of mind. It should you too."

His mother fell silent and a faraway look appeared on her face. "I hear what you're saying, and I agree with you to a certain extent. But with or without the sandwich shop, I have every reason to believe the market will perform as well as, if not better than, before the fire. We've been killing ourselves these past two years, barely able to fulfill all our catering orders on major holidays. The bigger kitchen will allow us to hire more staff and work more efficiently. If the sandwich shop fails, we'll rent the room for ladies' luncheons and bridge clubs and office parties. If that doesn't work, we'll seal up the wall that separates the two areas and lease it out to another business. With Faith and Lovie out of the picture, the market will only have to provide for you and me. Which means we can pay off our debt quicker. My question to you is, are you still interested in coming to work for me?"

His jaw dropped open. "Why wouldn't I be?"

"Because you seem so happy here." She uncrossed her legs and shifted on the swing to face him. "I'm glad you've gotten a chance to spread your wings. I've always worried you would never experience the world outside of Prospect. If this is what you want, I'll back you up one hundred percent."

"I considered living in Charleston for about a minute when I first started working for Heidi." He hung his head, staring into his lap. He wasn't ready to admit to his mother that his attraction was more about the girl than the place. "But this city is crowded and expensive, and there's no real future for me here. The market is saturated with excellent restaurants. The best I could ever hope for would be to manage one of those restaurants. There's nothing wrong with that, but it's not right for me. I want more out of life. And what happened with Sean yesterday made me realize how important my family is to me."

"I hate pressuring you, son. I wish you had more time to be absolutely certain that this is what you want, but whether or not you're committed to Sweeney's impacts my decision greatly."

"I can tell you right here and right now"—he tapped the arm of the swing—"with absolute certainty that I'm moving home to Prospect after graduation. I think buying the stationery store would give us a chance to put Captain Sweeney's Seafood on the list of hot places to visit in the South. Annie's the bomb, Mom. I'm telling you, she's determined to make a name for herself one way or another. I think joining forces with Heidi and Annie is a no-brainer.

"But I can't make the decision about you using your retirement fund. I'd never forgive myself if something happened to you and you needed that money and didn't have it. You and I have been through too much to take anything for granted."

Sam was silent for a long time after he finished talking. Finally she rubbed his thigh and thanked him for his honesty. "Your perspective has given me much to think about."

"Why don't you show the bank our finances from the past few years and talk to the architect about the possibility of throwing the stationery store in the mix? Do some more investigating before you make your decision."

Sam exhaled a deep breath. "You're right. Even if it means delaying construction, I need to be comfortable with my decision."

Sawyer's white Land Rover pulled up to the curb. She was still dressed in surgical scrubs. With shoulders slumped, she trudged up the sidewalk. Who knew when she'd last slept?

Jamie introduced his third roommate to his mother, and they exchanged pleasantries. Sawyer wasn't a head turner like Brooke, but she was equally pretty in a more subtle way. Today, though, she just looked tired.

"Did you work a double shift?" Jamie asked, and then explained to Sam, "Sawyer is in the pediatric residency program at MUSC."

"I had a patient in surgery." Sawyer collapsed onto the love seat. "I didn't want to leave until she got out."

"Is she okay?" Jamie asked.

"She will be eventually. You wouldn't believe this kid." Sawyer's face lit up. "Eight years old. Total tomboy with short dark hair and piercing blue eyes that look straight through you. She was brought in by rescue squad yesterday afternoon. She'd chased her kitten up a tree and fallen onto the pavement from a really high branch. Her body was a mess. She had a number of broken bones and a concussion. Her little face was scrunched up in pain, but she never once cried. She went into shock while they were stitching up a laceration on her forehead. Our trauma team discovered internal bleeding and rushed her into surgery."

Out of the corner of his eye, Jamie noticed his mother sitting perfectly still with her hand pressed to her mouth as she listened to Sawyer's story.

"I saw her just now in recovery," Sawyer continued. "I told her how brave she was and asked her if she was scared. You wouldn't believe her answer. She said, 'Heck yeah, I was scared. I'm only eight years old. I don't want to die. I just started living. But I knew God wanted me to fight, and he would take care of me no matter what. So I concentrated on fighting and let him do the rest.'"

Jamie glanced at his mother and saw a tear rolling down her cheek. He gave her a half hug. He knew she was remembering his accident and how close he'd come to dying.

"Thank you for sharing your story. That's an eight-year-old I'd like to meet," Sam said, rummaging through her bag for a tissue.

"A lot of our patients are tough like that." Sawyer spoke with a faraway look in her eye. "They have to be to survive. They're so young, but the funny thing is, I'm learning so much about life from them." She hung her head. "I'm sorry to be so dismal when we've only just met."

"Not at all. You've had a tough day. I'm glad you felt comfortable sharing it with us." Sam nudged Jamie. "I really should be going, so you can get back to your yard work."

"Okay, Mom." Jamie slid off the swing and pulled her to her feet. "I'll walk you to your car."

"It was a pleasure meeting you, Sawyer. My son is a lucky young man, having three lovely ladies for roommates."

"We're the lucky ones." Sawyer rose slowly off the sofa and wrapped her fingers around Jamie's bicep. "It's nice to have a strong man around to do the heavy lifting," she said, and they all laughed.

Sam and Jamie walked down the steps and rounded the house to the driveway.

"We can all learn a valuable lesson from that little girl," his mother said as she climbed into her Jeep. "God gives us life, and we owe it to him to give that life everything we've got."

TWENTY-SEVEN

FAITH

As Faith had expected she might, her mother took a turn for the worse after the Memorial Day disaster at Moss Creek Farm. Lovie appeared agitated all the time. She hardly slept, barely ate, and fought Faith at every turn. She was becoming increasingly incontinent, and Faith found herself faced with tasks she'd never dreamed she have to perform. She'd made a terrible error in judgment in thinking she could take care of her mother at home. She was ready to admit she was in over her head, but there was no one around to admit it to. Sam was deep in discussions with her architect about the designs for the new market. And Jackie had taken Sean to Charleston to register for summer school at the college. Although they might be back in town by now. Sean would be getting ready for Saturday's farmers' market. She'd give Jackie a call later.

Bitsy had been out of sorts since the party as well. Today was her last day of school. She'd gone home with her friend Chloe Cook, who was having a few of their girlfriends over for an end-of-the-year swimming party in their pool. Faith couldn't pawn her daughter off on friends all summer, any more than she could expect Bitsy to sit around the house while her mother took care of a grumpy old woman who didn't recognize her. Faith considered begging Irene Davidson for another chance, but she knew she lacked the courage for the job. The image of her mother's terrified face when she'd tried to leave her at Creekside Manor last week haunted her at night.

"Let's face it, I'm a spineless wimp," Faith said to Snowflake, who lay on the floor beside her feet as she folded yet another load of laundry.

Even if she was able to arrange for Jackie to make the drop-off, today was Friday, and nothing would happen before the weekend. Which would make for a long two days of taking care of her mother's needs. She longed to spend the weekend with her husband and daughter out on the boat or at the beach.

To add to her angst, the hang-ups had started again on Tuesday morning. The phone had rung all day long until late that afternoon, when Curtis finally spoke to her. "I want to see my daughter, Faith, and you can't stop me. Watch your back. I'm coming for you."

She immediately called Eli, who contacted Emmett Reyes, who assured them that Curtis was currently at his job on a highway paving crew in Columbia. The phone calls had stopped, and she'd received no word from him since. The eerie silence was almost worse.

Eli stopped by several times a day to check on her, which brought her some comfort. Her doorbell would ring as though she'd used otherworldly powers to summon him. While she appreciated his dutiful visits, she sometimes resented the interruption—like now. She wanted to finish with the laundry before her mother stirred from her nap. She flung open the door, expecting to see Eli on her door stoop. But there stood Curtis instead. Before her brain could register his sudden appearance, he shoved her backward and slammed and locked the door behind him. "I want to see my daughter."

His time in prison had not served him well. He'd lost weight, if it was even possible for him to be any skinnier. Lines were etched on his face, and the top of his head was practically bald now. His teeth had yellowed, and she noticed he was missing his top left incisor. His dark eyes, once wild from anger and excessive drinking, had grown cold and hard in prison, full of pure hate.

Faith gulped. "She's not here."

"Don't lie to me, bitch. I know for a fact that she only had a half day of school today."

Faith experienced a rush of adrenaline. She refused to let this monster destroy her life again. She took slow steps backward as she calculated the distance to the console table on her right. She envisioned the bronze statue of the little girl with bare feet Mike had bought for her from a friend's art gallery because he said it reminded him of Bitsy. She sensed an object in Curtis's right hand, but she didn't dare look to see what it was. From the position of his arm, elbow bent and hand near his shoulder, she concluded it was a knife and not a gun.

The console table appeared in her peripheral vision. In one swift motion, she grabbed hold of the bronze statue and crashed it against her ex-husband's skull. He stumbled backward, but she didn't wait to see if he fell. She took off at a sprint down the hall, praying her mother would sense the danger and stay in her room. When she reached her bedroom at the end of the hall, she slammed and locked the door. She was grateful she'd purchased the gun safe with the quick-access digital lock. She removed it from the top shelf of her closet and, willing her hands to stop shaking, wrapped her fingers around the metal pistol handle. She heard a door click shut in the hallway and envisioned Curtis going from room to room looking for Bitsy. She couldn't let him get to her mother. She threw open her bedroom door and marched down the hall toward him.

He eyed the gun in her hand with a condescending sneer. "Put the gun away, Faith. You and I both know you don't have the guts to shoot me."

"Like hell I don't. I've been taking lessons to sharpen my skills. Thanks to my daddy, I'm a pretty good shot." She aimed the gun at his left shoulder and pulled the trigger.

His eyes grew wide, but he barely grimaced at the pain. When he raised his right arm, she saw that the object in his hand was a switchblade. He charged her and she pulled the trigger a second time, shooting him slightly left of his sternum. His knees buckled and he dropped to the ground, a large pool of blood spreading from beneath his body.

The sound of Eli banging and shouting at the front door snapped her out of her trance. She dropped the gun and rushed to let him in. She flew into his arms, sobbing hysterically. "I killed him, Eli! Oh my God. I shot him dead."

Gripping her by the shoulders, Eli shook her until he got her attention. "We need to be certain he's dead, Faith. Where is he?"

She pointed at the body on the floor at the other end of the hall.

Eli called for backup on his radio and removed his gun from his shoulder holster. "Don't move," he said, but she followed him down the hall anyway. He knelt beside the body and felt for his pulse. "He's dead all right." He stood to face her. "Who else is in the house? Where are Bitsy and Lovie?"

"Bitsy's at a friend's swimming party. Mom was taking a nap. Surely she heard the commotion. Thankfully, she had enough sense to stay in her room." As the words left her lips, her stomach rolled and she suddenly had trouble breathing. In her confused mental state, Lovie would not have had the sense to stay in her room. "Something's wrong." She crossed the hall to her mother's room. She opened the door, and afraid she might wake her, she tiptoed to the side of the bed. But as she stared down into her mother's peaceful face, she feared Lovie would never again wake up.

Eli was at her side, searching for a pulse and calling for an ambulance. "She's breathing. That's a good sign."

The ensuing hours passed in a blur. The crew of EMTs offered little encouragement as they rushed her mother off to the hospital in their ambulance. Eli made the necessary phone calls—to Sam, who left her meeting with the architect to go straight to the hospital, and to Mike, who arrived home within minutes.

"We can't let Bitsy find out about this until we talk to Moses and figure out how best to break the news," Faith said.

"It'll be a challenge keeping this from her," Mike said. "The press is already lined up at the end of the driveway. I'll call Chloe Cook's mother and explain the situation." He went outside to the porch and returned five minutes later. "The Cooks are going to the beach for the weekend. They invited Bitsy to go with them. She assured me they would keep her away from social media and not let her watch the news on TV."

"What if something happens to Mom?" Faith's hand flew to her mouth. "What if she—"

Mike knelt down beside Faith's chair. "We'll worry about that if it happens. I'll drive to the beach and get her if need be."

Her throat felt thick and her voice sounded hoarse when she said, "Thank you. Having her taken care of for the weekend will give me a chance to figure things out." She gestured toward the hallway, where a team of crime scene investigators were collecting evidence. "We'll never get the blood out of the carpet."

"They have professionals who will do that for us. I'll get the number from Eli and schedule them to come tomorrow." Mike rubbed her arm. "You're in good hands here with Eli. He'll bring you to the hospital later. After I take an overnight bag to the Cooks' house for Bitsy, I'm going back to the emergency room to check on your mom. Unless you want me to stay."

"No, you go. I'll be fine." She ran her hand down his cheek. "I don't know what I would do without you. I'm so sorry, Mike."

"What do you have to be sorry for?"

"For killing my ex-husband in cold blood in our home," she said, her voice tight with unshed tears.

"You did what you had to do, Faith. You saved your own life, and you would've saved Bitsy's too if she'd been here. You did a damn fine job of defending yourself, and I'm proud of you. You're a much stronger woman than when we first met. It's over, honey. Curtis will never hurt you again."

She nodded, unable to speak. A torrent of tears came with the wave of relief that washed over her. Mike seemed torn, not wanting to leave her, but she waved him on.

During the hours that followed, Faith answered the same questions over and over again from the detective Eli had assigned to the case. Even though he'd recused himself from her case, her brother-in-law never left her side.

"Am I going to jail?" she asked Eli when Detective Hamilton finally finished his interrogation.

"Not a chance. We have a clear-cut case with the evidence to prove that he's been stalking you for weeks and you were defending yourself."

"I don't understand how he pulled it off," Faith said. "How was he able to come and go from Columbia without anyone missing him?"

"As you suspected, he had help on the ground here in Prospect. We found his cell phone in his pocket. Since he got out of prison in early May, Curtis has been in constant communication with his good buddy Earl Sessions."

"I knew Earl was somehow involved in this."

"We've already picked him up. He's on the way to the station as we speak, singing like a canary, or so I'm told. He's owned up to planting the pig and fish. He claims Curtis mailed him the recipe cards. But he swears he had no knowledge of how the fire started."

"Will his word be enough to force the insurance company to settle?" Faith asked.

"That's my hope." Eli got to his feet and peeked into the hallway. "They're wrapping things up in there. They'll get the body out of here soon." He disappeared into the kitchen and returned with a ham sandwich. "Here." He handed her the plate. "You should eat something."

It was past five o'clock, and Faith hadn't eaten a bite since breakfast, but the thought of her ex-husband's body being carried out of her house in a body bag made her feel nauseated. "I'm not hungry."

He pointed at the sandwich. "Eat. You're in for a long night at the hospital."

She'd been too preoccupied with the police to think about her mother. She patted the pockets of her khaki pants. She had no idea where her phone was or if Mike had tried to call. "Have you talked to Sam?"

"Several times." He lowered himself to the arm of her chair. "I hate having to tell you this in the wake of what you've already been through today. Your mother suffered a major stroke. She's in a coma. The doctors have little hope of her ever regaining consciousness."

TWENTY-EIGHT

JACKIE

Jackie, Sam, Sean, and Jamie had been waiting several hours, and so far not a single doctor or nurse had been in to speak with them. Mike had arranged a private waiting room that offered comfortable seating and a view of the hospital gardens through a row of large windows. She wondered if her mother's medical team had forgotten about the family tucked up on the second floor, away from the hustle and bustle of the emergency room.

When Bill appeared in the doorway, she pulled him out into the hall. "Give it to me straight."

He studied her face as though trying to decide if she could handle bad news. "It's not good, Jack. This is the end for your mother. I've always respected Lovie. She was as good a mother-in-law as a man could ask for. This is hard for you to hear, and hard for me to say, but this is the best-case scenario for Lovie and your family."

Jackie knew enough about Alzheimer's to know he spoke the truth. "How much time are we talking?"

He lifted a shoulder. "A few days. A week tops."

"Will they keep her here in the hospital?"

"For the time being," he said. "If she lingers, we may need to make other arrangements."

Jackie pressed her forehead to his chest. "Thank you for being honest with me."

He kissed the top of her head. "Lovie was one of a kind. The world will be a lesser place without her." He held her for a minute before pushing her away. "I need to check in with my office. I'll be back in a few minutes. Can I bring you anything?"

"No," she said. "We're fine for now. When do you think we'll get to see her?"

"Soon, I imagine. They were taking her in for a CT scan when I was down there a few minutes ago."

Jackie watched her husband walk to the end of the hall and disappear inside an elevator. Returning to the waiting room, she locked eyes with Sam and shook her head. Sam nodded her response, an unspoken agreement between them. They would wait for confirmation from the doctors before telling the boys. Just as they'd agreed earlier not to tell them about Curtis's death until the sisters had heard the whole story from Faith.

She sat down beside Sean, who smelled like sweat and fish. From what he'd told her, they'd had a particularly successful day on the water. How would these latest family crises affect tomorrow's farmers' market?

The four of them sat in silence in a row of chairs facing the windows. Over the course of the next half hour, the sky darkened as storm clouds rolled in from the west. A bolt of lightning followed by a loud clap of thunder brought the boys to their feet.

"I'm sorry, Mom," Jamie said to Sam. "I hate to leave you here like this, but we need to get on these crabs."

"Mom?" Sean's eyes met Jackie's. He'd been humble, helpful, and considerate since Memorial Day. "Is it okay if we go?"

Jackie smiled at him. "Yes, son. There's nothing you can do

here, and your grandmother would understand. She'd never forgive you if you let those crabs spoil."

The sisters got up and walked their boys to the door.

"We'll call you as soon as we know anything," Sam said.

"There's leftover chicken parmesan in the fridge and plenty of sandwich meat. I trust you can fend for yourselves for dinner. You two look out for one another. This storm looks like a doozy."

"We will, Aunt Jackie." Jamie smiled at her. She didn't need to spell it out for him. He understood. She was asking him to take care of his cousin.

With each day that had passed since Memorial Day, Jackie had seen more of her son's true personality emerge from beneath the layer of anxiety and gloom. The antidepressants seemed to be working, as did his daily sessions with Moses. Sean had gone to Moses's office on Tuesday and Wednesday mornings and spoken to him by phone on Thursday and Friday. Big Mo was counseling him on how to live his life independent of his twin.

She'd driven Sean to Charleston Wednesday afternoon so he could register for his summer school classes at the college. He seemed genuinely excited about the courses he'd selected—a detective fiction class that fulfilled one of his freshman English requirements and an upper-level course in hospitality and tourism, which he was auditing to explore the subject as a possible major.

After leaving the registrar's office, they'd run into a friend of Sean's from Georgia in the bookstore. Jeb Watson was a cute boy with a head of wavy blonde hair and bright-blue eyes.

"I'm glad to see a familiar face," Jeb said. "Are you transferring here too? Georgia was way too big for me."

"I'm thinking about it," Sean said. "I'm taking a few classes this summer to see if I like it."

Jeb eyed the paperback novels by Arthur Conan Doyle and Agatha Christie in Sean's shopping cart. "Looks like you'll be studying a lot, same as me. I'm taking physics and accounting. We should hang out together in the library."

Sean's face brightened. "Yeah, bro, let's do that. And maybe we can finally take that fishing trip we've been talking about."

"Was he in your fraternity?" Jackie asked on the way to the car.

"No, but we lived on the same hall in the freshman dorm."

"He seems like a nice boy. Is he?"

The irritated expression that crossed Sean's face told her he saw through her questions. He understood what she was asking. She didn't care about his manners. She wanted to know if Jeb was into drugs.

"I don't know, Mom. The few times we hung out, we mostly talked about fishing. His dad owns a sport-fishing boat he keeps over in Mount Pleasant." He deposited his bag of books on the back seat and climbed into the front of her Escalade. "At least I'll know someone here."

Jackie was all for his attending the college. She could establish a strict set of boundaries in the beginning and slowly loosen the reins as he proved himself and earned back her trust. But she wouldn't pressure him into staying for the fall semester if he didn't like it. She'd learned her lesson the last time. He had Moses to guide him now. She'd leave the important decisions to them.

She'd never before given any of the four guest rooms at her house on Lamboll to either of the boys. The house was strictly for show. Decorated with luxury Italian linens and designer fabrics, the rooms were not suited for a twenty-year-old boy who never made his bed and left his sweaty clothes piled in a heap on the floor. She stripped off the bed linens and removed all the decorative knickknacks from the tabletops in the room closest to her. She designated the bathroom across the hall his. She wanted to be able to hear him if he moved around during the night.

Sean wanted something more to occupy his time when he

wasn't in class on Monday, Tuesday, and Wednesday mornings. He interviewed for a job with Heidi, who was fully staffed but promised to keep him at the top of her list if anyone quit or called in sick. Jackie thought he was trying to do too much—he'd committed to helping her move the business when she closed on the warehouse property in two weeks' time—but she reluctantly agreed to let him work for Heidi as long as he kept up with his studies.

"Why are you worrying about this now, Mom?" Sean had said when they were discussing it on the way home to Prospect on Thursday afternoon. "Heidi doesn't even have a job to offer me."

"But she will eventually, mark my words," Jackie said. "Catering jobs are fluid."

"Whether I work for her or not, I plan to spend a few hours in the library every day after class. That's plenty of time to get my work done."

Jackie smiled over at him. *At least you'll be working with Jamie, who will keep you in line,* she thought to herself.

It was almost six o'clock and rain was pouring down in torrents when Faith finally arrived at the hospital. She burst into tears when she saw them and sobbed hysterically for a full ten minutes. Jackie and Sam nestled her in the chair between them and consoled her by rubbing her back and arms and cooing words of encouragement while she cried.

When the sobbing finally subsided, Faith said, "It's all my fault if Mom dies."

You mean when Mom dies, Jackie thought, but she didn't have the heart to break the news to her sister just yet. Instead she said, "Mom suffered a massive stroke. Why on earth would you think that's your fault?"

"Based on the peaceful expression on Mom's face, Eli thinks the stroke happened before Curtis got there," Sam said.

"She was supposed to be at Creekside Manor," Faith said in a quivering voice. "The nurses there would've gotten to her in time."

"That's crazy talk, Faith," Sam said. "Mom has an illness. This was bound to happen one way or another."

Jackie saw no point in discussing the what-ifs and might-have-beens. The sooner they accepted reality, the better off they would all be. They could make plans for their mother accordingly and be strong for their children, who would undoubtedly be devastated by this loss. "This might sound morbid to you, but in a way I think we're lucky. Alzheimer's is an unkind disease. Yes, we'll be deprived of years spent with Mom, but we'll also be spared having to watch her mind deteriorate bit by bit. Mom was a proud woman. She'll die with most of her dignity intact. And I, for one, am grateful for that."

"I agree. These last few weeks have presented some challenges, mostly for you." Sam patted Faith's leg. "But Mom and I shared some lucid moments that I will always cherish. In her state of mind, she reminded me of a much younger Lovie, of the mother from our childhood. We never owned material things of value, but we shared a lot of love in our family. Our little cottage on the creek was a happy place because Mom and Dad made everything fun."

"That's so true," Faith said. "I remember the bonfires and the afternoons spent floating down the creek in our inner tubes."

Sam added, "The ghost stories at bedtime and the watermelon-seed-spitting contests."

"Dad never did teach me to bait a hook," said Jackie. "I hated touching those slimy old worms. I never got into the hunting and fishing like y'all did either, but I always enjoyed that time with Dad. What you learned from him saved your life today, Faith. If you feel like talking about it, we'd like to know what happened. If you never want to mention it again, that's okay too. It's your call."

Faith paused as if gathering her nerve. "I don't necessarily *want* to talk about it, but I *need* to talk about it," she said, and walked them through everything that had happened that afternoon.

"I admire your courage," Jackie said when she finished. "I couldn't have done what you did. I hope you're proud of yourself, because I'm proud of you." She gave her baby sister a big squeeze.

"Do you have any suggestions on how I can break the news to Bitsy that I killed her father?" Faith asked.

"I certainly wouldn't give her specifics," Sam said. "She's way too young to understand it."

"She thinks of Mike as her father now anyway," Jackie said. "I doubt she has any good memories of Curtis."

"It's all over the local news." Faith gestured at the television suspended from the ceiling in the corner. The volume was muted, and they'd ignored the footage of Curtis's body being removed from Faith's house when it aired on the six o'clock news. "You know how kids are. Someone in her class will delight in bullying her."

"You have the whole summer to let the dust settle," Sam said. "The kids will have moved onto someone's else's tragedy by the time school starts back in the fall. I don't feel one ounce of guilt admitting I'm glad Curtis is dead. I only wished it'd been me who put the bullet in his heart."

Jackie too was glad Curtis was burning in hell where he belonged. He was evil through and through.

"I guess this means you'll be getting your money from the insurance company," Faith said.

"And just in the nick of time." A sneaky grin spread across Sam's face. "This morning, before all this happened with Mom, I made an offer to buy the stationery shop behind the market. We're joining forces with Heidi and Annie. We're expanding the business to include a sandwich shop. As of this moment, I'm rebranding our image. In the spring we'll reopen as Captain and Lovie Sweeney's Seafood. That's a mouthful, I know. I'll use the full name on the logo. I can see it now—a ship's captain and his plump-cheeked wife. But we'll always be known to our customers as Sweeney's Seafood."

TWENTY-NINE

FAITH

Faith and her sisters took turns keeping vigil at their mother's bedside, making certain someone was always with her in case she opened her eyes. Or worse. The doctors had called in hospice, who assured them there would be signs when Lovie neared the end. They alternated taking the overnight shift through the weekend, but when Jackie left for Charleston on Monday, Sam and Faith agreed to cut their hours back to avoid exhaustion. They took turns sitting with her for four hours at a time from six in the morning until ten at night.

Faith had been waiting on the front stoop when Bitsy arrived home from the beach on Sunday evening. Her daughter's sunburned shoulders and the freckles dotting the bridge of her nose attested to time spent frolicking on the beach. She hated for her daughter's fun weekend to end on a sad note.

"I have something I need to tell you." She took Bitsy's overnight bag from her and set it down on the bench in the hallway outside her bedroom. The cleaning company Mike hired had done a remarkable job of removing the crime scene evidence, including the large pool of Curtis's blood from the beige carpet in the hallway. "Let's go out on the porch." Draping her arm across

Bitsy's shoulders, she kissed the top of her daughter's brown head. "I missed you, kiddo. I'm glad to have you home."

"What's wrong, Mama?" Bitsy asked when they were seated side by side in the rocking chairs. "Did something bad happen?"

Faith placed her hand on top of Bitsy's on the arm of the chair. "Yes, sweetheart. I'm sorry to have to tell you that your father . . . that Curtis died."

Faith waited for her daughter's response, but Bitsy's expression remained impassive.

"Am I supposed to feel sad?" she asked finally. "Because all I feel is relieved that he can no longer hurt us."

Faith squeezed her daughter's hand. "You can't control your emotions, honey. You feel what you feel. After what Curtis put us through, there's no right or wrong way to respond to his death."

"I thought Mike was my father now anyway. Where is he, by the way? I want to show him this new trick I learned to do with the Frisbee."

"He and Snowflake are getting the grill ready to cook the steaks. He'll be up in a minute."

"Steaks, yay!" She did a little booty dance in her seat. "When are we eating? I'm starving."

Should she be concerned at how easily Bitsy dismissed the news of her father's death? *No,* Faith thought. *I should be grateful.* Curtis had put them through enough. And now that he was out of their lives for good, neither of them should waste another agonizing moment obsessing about him. Moses had advised, and Faith and Mike had agreed, to give Bitsy the details of her father's death only if she asked. Faith was relieved that she didn't.

"In a little while, sweetheart. I have some other bad news. Lovie is in the hospital."

"Oh no!" Bitsy fell back in her chair. "Is she gonna be okay?"

Faith tucked a lock of hair behind her daughter's ear. "Not this time, honey. She's very sick."

Bitsy sucked in her lower lip as tears welled in her eyes. She moved from her rocking chair to Faith's lap and buried her head in her chest as she cried.

Faith rested her head against the back of her chair. "I'm sorry, sweetheart. I know how much you love your grandma." She rocked her daughter until she stopped crying.

"Is God going to punish me?" Bitsy asked, wiping her nose on Faith's cotton blouse.

"Why on earth would God punish you?" Faith said against her cheek.

"Because I prayed for him to either make Lovie better or make her go away." Her confession brought on another round of tears.

"Hush now, sweetheart," she whispered. "It's only natural for you to feel that way. Your grandmother has a very bad disease. She'll be much better off when she can be herself again in heaven."

Faith didn't like to think about life after death. She'd been led to believe that all pain and suffering ended when a person died. Would her mother's memory return to her once she passed through the pearly gates?

"Curtis won't hurt Lovie in heaven, will he?"

A vision of her ex-husband's soul burning in hell flashed before her eyes. But she didn't want to give her daughter nightmares. "No, sweetheart. Curtis will have to repent his sins before he's allowed in heaven."

Bitsy looked at her with wide eyes. "You mean he'll be made good again?"

Faith nodded. "Something like that."

The answer seemed to satisfy Bitsy, and they spent the rest of the evening like a normal family—tossing the Frisbee and playing with the dog while they cooked steaks on the grill, and discussing their summer vacation plans over dinner.

Kathy Cook called first thing on Monday morning. "I heard about your mama. I know you're dealing with a lot right now, and we'd love to have Bitsy stay with us until . . . well, until everything is sorted out."

Faith had breathed a sigh of relief. She'd been torn about leaving her daughter with a sitter. Bitsy was putting on a brave face, but Faith could tell she was upset about her grandmother. Chloe would help take her mind off her troubles. "That would help so much, Kathy, at least during the day. Mike will be here with her at night. I don't know how to thank you."

"No worries, hon. You'd do the same for me."

Faith stood against the wall outside the hospital room and eavesdropped on Sam's one-sided conversation with their mother. She'd had similar discussions with her mother over the past few days, only hers were along the lines of asking how she would survive without her. Sam, on the other hand, offered words of gratitude for Lovie's having been such an amazing mother.

One of the hospice nurses had encouraged the sisters to talk to their mother. "She can't respond to you, but she's aware you're here. Your presence offers her comfort."

Faith questioned whether this was true in her mother's case, considering the massive stroke that had left her in a coma. But who was she to argue with a hospice worker?

She strained to hear Sam's voice. "You and Daddy created something special for our family, and I vow to continue to build on that foundation, for Jamie's children and generations to come. You can die with peace of mind, Mama. You did right by us. You always supported and seldom judged. We were blessed to have you in our lives."

According to the hospice nurses, a dying person oftentimes needs reassurance that it's okay to let go.

"The police in Columbia recovered your recipe box from Curtis's things when they cleaned out his room. Eli brought the box home to me last night, but your pimento cheese recipe isn't in the box. If you could open your eyes for one brief second, I'd love to know your secret ingredient. No matter what I try, I just can't get the pimento cheese right."

Faith shook her head at her sister's dogged determination. Sam never stopped working. If only Faith could find such a gratifying career.

She entered the room and set her purse down on the floor beside Sam's chair. "Has there been any change?"

"You missed the hospice nurse by thirty minutes," Sam said. "I was going to call you, but I knew you were on your way. I figured I'd wait until you got here to tell you. Mom's body is showing signs of shutting down. As you know, the doctors and nurses can't predict how much longer it will be."

Faith lowered herself to the foot of her mother's bed. "Should we call Jackie?"

"I already did. She's with Sean in Charleston. They're driving in later tonight. I convinced her to go ahead and call Cooper. He's on the way home."

Faith thought about Jackie's reluctance to call Cooper home from Virginia. His internship was important to his career, and while she knew he would want to say goodbye to his grandmother, there was no point in his missing more work than necessary.

Sam got to her feet. "I need to take care of some market business. But I'll be back in an hour. Call me if anything changes. Do you want me to bring you some dinner?"

Faith gestured at her purse on the floor. "Thanks, but I brought a sandwich. I don't have much of an appetite anyway. Be careful out there. We're supposed to get bad storms this afternoon. The sky was nearly black when I came in."

"I know." Sam eyed the radar moving across the screen on the wall-mounted TV. "That's all they've been talking about this afternoon. I got tired of listening to it and muted the volume."

Faith rose from the bed and walked her sister out into the hall. "I'm happy for you, Sammie, that everything is working out with the market. I have to admit I'm envious that you and Jackie have found careers that give your lives meaning."

"It's not too late, Faith. Say the word. We'd love to have you back on board."

"I wish it was that simple. The seafood business doesn't light my fire the way it lights yours." When she realized what she'd said, she added, "Poor choice of words. Sorry."

Sam smiled. "The fire. Curtis. All that is in the past. I'm concentrating on the future." She fell back against the wall. "I'm heartbroken over Mom. She's been such an important part of our lives. I'm going to miss her something awful. Does it make me a bad person to be planning for the future at a time like this?"

"Not at all. I think it makes you a lucky person. It doesn't mean you loved her any less."

"Hang in there, Faith. You'll discover your passion. You just have to keep looking."

"I turned forty-five yesterday. I'm a little old to be finding myself."

"Our birthdays!" Sam said, snapping her fingers. "How did I forget our birthdays?"

Jackie's, Sam's, and Faith's birthdays fell on June first, second, and fourth respectively. Ever since they were children, they'd celebrated all three of them with one party on June third.

"Because you're preoccupied with more important things. Don't feel bad, Sammie. None of us remembered. This is as good a year as any to skip the party."

"You're probably right." Sam pushed off the wall. "Happy birthday, sis." She wrapped her arms around Faith. "You have so much to offer. Look at the way you've taken care of Mom with patience and kindness. Jackie and I could never have done it. You have a special way of handling people. Couple that with something that excites you and you'll find your happiness."

Faith squeezed Sam tight. "That's good advice. I'll give it some thought."

Sam drew away from Faith. "Let me run this errand so I can get back. Text me if anything changes."

Her sister started down the hall, and Faith called after her. "By the way, Sam, it's garlic powder."

Sam turned around. "What do you mean it's garlic powder?" she asked, walking backward toward the elevator.

"The ingredient you're missing in your pimento cheese."

Sam palmed her forehead. "That's it! I knew it was something simple." The elevator doors opened, and she disappeared inside.

She returned to her mother's bedside and drew the covers up tight under Lovie's chin. This would likely be her last hour alone with her mother. She'd spend the summer with Bitsy, going to the beach and visiting the tourist attractions in and around Charleston that she'd always wanted to see and never made the time for. But then what? What Sam had said was true to some extent. She had a soft way in dealing with certain kinds of people. She felt compelled to help those in need. Those who were sick or in trouble. *Or being abused,* she thought as a thousand-watt light bulb switched on inside her head.

Faith nearly shot up out of her chair. *That's it! I'll open a shelter for abused women.* Years ago, when Curtis was at his worst, she'd tried to run away from him, but there was no safe place in Prospect for her to go. During the years that followed, she'd often reflected on that time in her life. And she'd never let herself forget how terrified she'd been. She would help women find the strength to protect themselves. So what if she knew nothing about running a safe home? She would hire a staff of professionals who did. Moses would help in that regard. And Mike would use his contacts at the hospital to help her raise funds. She would use her inheritance from Mack if need be. It was a mammoth undertaking, but one that energized rather than intimidated her.

She felt a warm glow settle over her as she experienced for the first time the sense of purpose her sisters knew so well. She reached for her mother's hand, feeling Lovie's cold, clammy skin against hers. *When one door closes, another door opens.* She too would miss her mother terribly.

"Sam was right, Mama. You always supported us, but you rarely judged us. You taught me how to love unconditionally. Now it's time for me to pay it forward."

THIRTY

JAMIE

What had started out as a blissful day was heading south at a rapid rate. Jamie had woken that morning with Lizbet in his arms. On the porch after work the previous night, he'd opened up to her about his grandmother dying, and she'd comforted him right into her bed. She'd held him while he cried and then made sweet, passionate love to him. They melded together perfectly as friends and lovers, giving him the hope that she was *the one* for him. They faced a year of separation while he finished his last semester at Carolina and she attended culinary school in New York. He was grateful they'd have the summer together. Being with Lizbet softened the blow of his grandmother dying, and he would need her emotional support in the months ahead.

His mother had called around three thirty, suggesting that he should come home. "No one can predict when it will happen," Sam said. "But I have a feeling you'll be too late if you wait until tomorrow."

"I can't bail on Heidi at the last minute. This party is important to her. I'll drive home tonight afterward."

Rupert Maki, a top executive at Boeing, had invited everybody who was anybody in the Lowcountry to a large cocktail party to celebrate the completion of extensive renovations he'd made to his home on the Battery. Jamie remembered his Aunt Jackie grumbling about not getting the job when Maki requested a proposal from her eighteen months ago. If she saw what he'd seen of the house, she'd be glad Maki had hired a top decorator from New York. *Tacky*, from his perspective, best described the new furnishings—über-contemporary and ultramasculine, a playboy pad decked out in marble, suede, and leather. Miles of carpet covered the floors in streaks of pale grays that reminded Jamie of an impressionistic work of art.

It was this carpet that was the cause of their current dilemma.

Rupert insisted the party be held outside in his courtyard—which was more like the gardens at Magnolia Plantation than a courtyard—to avoid red wine spillage on his custom carpet. Heidi had pleaded with him to rent tents to cover his terraces, but he was convinced it wouldn't rain. And he was a man used to getting his way. Even from Mother Nature.

For the past half hour, Jamie had been setting up tables on the terrace with his coworker Monte while Heidi studied the darkening sky and the radar app on her phone. The phone rang in her hand and she answered it.

"Heidi Butler." She paused to listen. "You've got to be kidding me." Another pause. "No, you're right. You can't work under those conditions. Thanks for letting me know."

"What's wrong?" Jamie asked when she ended her call.

"That was Jeremy. He and Russell got food poisoning from eating a bad batch of oysters for lunch. They're at the emergency room getting fluids." Heidi scrolled through her contacts. "I'll never find anyone to take their place at the last minute."

"What about Sean?"

She looked up from her phone. "Perfect! Get him over here. Tell him this is his chance to prove himself."

Jamie felt Heidi's eyes on him as he placed the call. The call went straight to voice mail, as did his three subsequent attempts. "He's not answering. He only lives a couple of blocks away. Do you want me to run over and get him?"

"Yes, but hurry." She waved him on. "I'll try a few others while you're gone."

Jamie took off running down the middle of the street. He arrived at Jackie's house as a midnight-blue LR4 was pulling up to the curb with his cousin in the passenger seat. The window rolled down and Sean stuck out his head. "What're you doing here, cuz? This is my friend Jeb, by the way."

Jamie exchanged nods with Jeb.

"We need you to work a party tonight, dude." Jamie opened the car door and pulled his cousin out. "We're in a serious bind. Two of our servers called in sick with food poisoning. The location is two blocks away. We need to hurry."

"Why didn't you call me?" Sean asked.

"I tried, but I got your voice mail."

Sean removed his phone from his back pocket. "My phone is dead. I've been in the library all afternoon." He reinserted his dead phone back in his pocket and turned to his friend. "Thanks for the ride, bro."

"Sure thing, man." Jeb leaned across the passenger seat. "Oh, and Sean, I left you a little present in your backpack."

"Whatever, man. I'll see you tomorrow." Sean waved at Jeb as he started to the house.

The hairs on Jamie's neck stood to attention. "What'd he leave you?" he asked as he followed Sean up the front steps.

"Who knows? Probably some porn magazine or something." Sean eyed Jamie's shorts and T-shirt as he unlocked the door. "Is that what you're wearing for the party? Heidi told me to buy black pants and a white shirt."

"What you have on is fine for now. But bring the black pants and white shirt with you. We'll change after we finish setting up."

Jamie waited in the entry hall while Sean sprinted up the

stairs. He returned in less than a minute with his clothes tucked under his arm. He locked the door again, and they jogged side by side down the block. Between breaths Jamie explained the crisis with the impending line of thunderstorms and absence of tents. They found Monte loading cases of red wine into the rear of the van when they arrived back at Maki's house.

Heidi rushed over to them. "You're a lifesaver, Sean. Thank you for coming on such short notice. I couldn't find anyone else. You'll have to do the best you can."

Sean nodded with more enthusiasm than Jamie had seen from his cousin all summer. "Yes, ma'am. I won't let you down."

Heidi was going out on a limb hiring Sean after witnessing his behavior on Memorial Day. But that was Heidi, always willing to help the underdog.

Her face softened for a second. "I'm sure you won't." She clapped her hands. "All right, listen up. I was watching the local forecast while you were gone. We have no choice but to move everything inside. Rupert will get over it."

"Why not set up one of the bars on the piazza?" Jamie asked, gesturing at the second-floor veranda.

"I thought about that," Heidi said. "But I think it's too risky. Conditions are favorable for tornadic activity with this storm system."

"Maybe some of the guests will stay at home due to the storm," Sean said.

"That seems logical, doesn't it?" Heidi said. "Unfortunately, partygoers view a storm as an opportunity to eat more, drink more, and stay later. We'll push the furniture out of the way, crank down the air conditioner, and serve them clear beverages."

Jamie saluted her. "Aye aye, Captain."

She clapped her hands again. "Okay, then. Let's get to work!"

Jamie took Sean to the laundry room adjacent to the kitchen, where he stashed his clothes in a cabinet out of the way. Annie and Lizbet were busy preparing food trays. Neither of them had seen Sean since Memorial Day. They both stopped what they were doing long enough to give him a hug, which visibly set his cousin at ease.

For the next hour, Jamie and Sean rearranged furniture and set up tables at various points around the house. The sky finally broke as the first guests began to arrive. Sean and Monte greeted them with trays of prosecco. The guests drained their flutes and reached for more, seemingly oblivious to their drenched clothing and dripping hair. Heidi was right. These hard-core partygoers were determined to have a good time, thunderstorms and tornados be damned. Jamie inhaled a deep breath. It was going to be a long night for the servers.

THIRTY-ONE

JACKIE

Jackie reached for her bag on the passenger seat beside her. She removed a bottle of Tums, popped open the lid, and shook three directly into her mouth. Her nerves were frayed. She would have an ulcer before it was all over. A bleeding ulcer. She was exhausted from worrying about her loved ones. Her mother. Sean. And now Cooper, who was driving through a line of severe thunderstorms on Interstate 95, his mind preoccupied by thoughts of his dying grandmother. She envisioned him speeding over the limit, racing to get home in time, and crashing head-on into a tractor trailer. She shook the image from her mind. Cooper was a safer driver than his twin. He was the good son. The one who'd never caused her any trouble. Except, she reminded herself, that time eighteen months ago when he'd gotten Annie pregnant.

Why was life so complicated? Why did loved ones die and children get themselves into trouble? She and Bill would be ninety years old before they became free of worry. Too old to enjoy life. Too old to do anything except drool in a paper cup.

She'd spent the afternoon with Hugh, going over her renovation plans for the new house on Church Street. The meeting had taken much longer than she'd anticipated because she wanted to get it right. This was no show house. This one was hers to keep. She fantasized about the future as she drove the rest of the way home. Bill would cut back on his hours and spend more time with her in Charleston. They would make new friends, dine in all the top restaurants, attend cultural events, and have passionate sex on their living room floor. Her daydream came to a screeching halt. There would be no sex on the living room floor with Sean living with them.

She drove into her driveway and slammed the SUV into park. She pulled down her visor and flipped open the mirror. She'd aged ten years in the past month. Gray hairs lined her part and wrinkles were etched deep around her eyes. Wrinkles that had appeared on her face since yesterday. She snapped the mirror shut and cast her eyes to the dark sky. "Why can't I have one carefree day? Just one day—that's all I'm asking for." Her words were meant for the powers that be in heaven, but they sounded hollow in the empty car and made her feel selfish and ungrateful.

She'd been wavering all afternoon between going home to Prospect that evening and spending the night in Charleston so Sean could attend his classes in the morning. Cooper would not arrive until late, and Bill was planning to meet him at the hospital. She wanted Sean to succeed in summer school. The syllabus covered a lot of material, and he would fall behind if he missed class. She felt certain his professor would understand. His grandmother was dying. But what if she didn't die tonight? What if she hung around another week and he missed more classes and more classes and then he failed? "Ugh!" She pounded the steering wheel. "This is what I'm talking about. How can I win for losing?" The reserve light on her gas gauge flashed on. "If that's supposed to be some kind of answer, I don't appreciate your sense of humor," she said as she looked skyward.

Just in case the inevitable happened, she'd said her goodbyes to her mother when she left Prospect on Sunday night. But the sudden urge to see Lovie one more time took her breath away.

The first raindrops pelted her windshield, and she turned off the ignition. They would need to hurry. They would pack up, lock up, and gas up at the BP station on Rutledge on their way out of Charleston.

She made a dash to the piazza and entered the house through the kitchen door. She went to the bottom of the stairs and called up to Sean. "Grab your things, son. We're going home."

Silence echoed throughout the cavernous entry hall.

"Sean, are you up there?" She slipped off her high heels and padded up the carpeted steps in bare feet. She searched the entire second floor, but the only sign she found of Sean was his backpack, lying on the floor at the foot of his bed.

She'd spoken to him after his class at noon. He had been on his way to grab a bite to eat for lunch and planned to spend the afternoon in the library. She'd given him explicit instructions to come straight home after that. She sank down on the bed. More trouble from Sean was the last thing she needed right now. She reached for his backpack. She'd grown accustomed to searching his room and the pockets of his clothes and the medicine cabinet in the bathroom. She unzipped the front pocket, stuck her hand inside, and removed a plastic ziplock bag. There was a lone white rectangular pill inside, which she now recognized as a bar of Xanax. Where there was one pill, there were more pills. She placed the bag on the bed beside her and buried her face in her hands.

Why, Sean? You were doing so well.

Her bare feet hit the floor and, pocketing the bag, she bolted out of the room and down the hall to the stairs. She found her phone on the kitchen table beside her bag, where she'd left it. She tapped Sean's number. When the call went to voice mail, she left an urgent message for him to call her back. She followed up with several texts; all of them went unanswered. She called everyone she could think of who might know of his whereabouts. Bill hadn't heard from him, and Jamie's phone rang and rang before going to voice mail.

"I talked to Jamie around three this afternoon," Sam said. "I told him what the hospice nurse told me, the same thing I told you. He's working an event for Heidi this evening, and driving straight to the hospital afterward."

Jackie felt a glimmer of hope. "Do you think Sean might be working the event with him?"

Sam paused. "If so, he didn't mention it."

"Do you know where the party is?"

"At one of the big homes downtown. That's all I know."

Jackie hung up with her sister and went to the corkboard above her desk where she pinned her important correspondence. She received countless invitations, not only to informal gatherings of friends but to galas and benefits and gallery openings. Networking at these events was vital to the success of her company, but there was nothing on the board for tonight. She paced in small circles as she racked her brain. She didn't recall any of her friends' mentioning a party, and she couldn't remember the name of Sean's friend from Georgia whom she'd met in the bookstore. Jed, she thought, although she couldn't be sure. The last name escaped her completely.

It was conceivable that Heidi had called Sean at the last minute to fill in at the party. She grabbed her phone and her keys. It was a long shot. But the only shot she had. The first wave of showers had passed, and it was only drizzling as she hurried out to her car, but it began to pour as she drove down the block toward Meeting Street—a torrential, driving rain that made it impossible for her to see through her windshield. She could make out the stop sign and cars parked on the side of the road but not much else. Using her GPS for guidance, she crept along the streets of the Battery. Eventually she got disoriented, and when her engine spit and spurted, she pulled over to the curb. "This can't be happening to me right now," she said as her engine burned the remaining gas fumes in her tank.

Don't panic, Jack. This is why you have Triple A.

Only she'd left her bag at home along with her wallet and Triple A identification number. She Googled the number for AAA using her cell phone. They could access her account by address and phone number. She waited thirteen minutes for someone to answer and was told it would be at least another forty-five minutes before a roadside technician could come to her aid.

"Never mind!" she yelled at the operator and then hung up.

It had gotten hot in the car, and the windows had steamed up. She couldn't turn on the air conditioner without running down her battery. She stuffed her phone into her pocket, retrieved her umbrella from the floorboard of the back seat, and slid out of the car into ankle-deep water. Bracing herself against the hood, she made her way around the front of the SUV to the sidewalk and headed in the direction she prayed was toward home. She made it a hundred yards before the heel of her shoe broke off and the wind inverted her umbrella. She took off her other shoe and abandoned the pair, along with the umbrella, on the sidewalk. Her head tucked against the wind and rain, she ventured another block before she stepped on something sharp.

"Ouch! Damn that hurts!" She hobbled over to a nearby building where a dome-shaped awning offered protection from the rain. The bakery had been closed for hours, according to the sign in the window. Jackie collapsed against the glass door and slid to the ground. Blood seeped from a gash in her foot, but she couldn't bring herself to inspect it. She fainted at the sight of blood. She'd never been good at providing first aid to her sons' wounds, not when they got fishing hooks stuck in their fingers as boys or when they became addicted to drugs as young adults.

Her clothes were soaked through, and her hair was dripping

wet. Chill bumps covered her body despite the humid air. If only she'd taken the time to put on her raincoat.

She dug her phone out of the back pocket of her jeans, hoping for word from Sean, but it too was waterlogged. She hurled the damaged phone into the street. "Could this day get any worse?"

Panic gripped her chest at the thought of Cooper and Sean weathering the storm alone. She could count on Cooper to make safe decisions. He would pull off the highway and wait for it to pass if the weather got too bad. Sean was another story. She imagined him slumped over, doped up on Xanax, in the corner of an alcove in an alleyway in a rough part of town.

Jackie could use that bar of Xanax in her pocket right about now, but using her son's drugs was stooping to a level she wasn't willing to go to. Her own prescription had run out. She would call her doctor's office for a refill in the morning. She would need it to get through the days ahead. To get through her mother's funeral. She'd been borderline abusing the medication of late, but that would all stop when . . .

When what, Jack? When your mother dies? When Sean goes to rehab?

Her children's lives were far more complex than hers had ever been. The peer pressure, complicated exponentially by social media. The competition to get into college and then to get a good job. It made sense they would suffer from anxiety, only they were too naive to the ways of life to understand what they were experiencing.

It had been only a couple of hours ago, though it seemed like a year, that she had been whining about her own level of stress. She'd wished for one carefree day. If something happened to Sean and Cooper, her future would be filled with carefree days. She would have no one to care for. No daughters-in-law or grandchildren. No loved ones for her to worry about. But life was nothing without family. And with family came worry. Bring on the worry!

THIRTY-TWO

JAMIE

Hours passed before Jamie stopped pouring drinks long enough to check his phone again. He had multiple missed calls and texts from his mom and Aunt Jackie. Why the urgency? Had Gran died? He scrolled through the texts. Jackie was looking for her son. He remembered then that Sean's phone battery had died. Had his cousin forgotten to tell his mother where he was? They'd been in such a hurry to get back to the party . . .

He turned his back on the guests waiting impatiently for a refill. Hadn't this crowd already had enough to drink?

His call to Aunt Jackie went to voice mail, but his mother answered right away. "I've been trying to reach you, son. Jackie is worried sick about Sean. You haven't by chance seen him?"

Jamie stuck his finger in his ear so he could hear her better. "He's with me, Mom. Two of our servers got food poisoning, so Sean filled in for them at the last minute. We set the party up outside, then had to move everything inside because of the storm. Sean's phone is dead. We both forgot to call Jackie in all the chaos over the weather. I feel bad for making her worry."

"It's Sean's responsibility to communicate with his mother. Not yours. I'm worried about Jackie, though. She went out in this horrible storm looking for Sean, and now she's not answering her phone."

Jamie turned back around, searching the room for his cousin. He spotted Sean next to a chest by the front door in the foyer, loading up a tray with dirty glasses and plates that guests had deposited on the way out. He'd been keeping an eye on Sean all night. As far as he could tell, he'd done a good job—and without anyone's having to instruct him. In addition to passing trays of hors d'oeuvres, he'd kept the buffet on the dining room table replenished and tidy.

"I'm sure she's at home," he said. "She probably fell asleep or something. We should be able to leave here soon. We'll go to the house and check on her. How's Gran, by the way?"

"Hard to say. Faith and I keep encouraging her to hang on by telling her that y'all are on the way and to wait for you."

"I hope we make it in time. Especially Cooper since he hasn't seen her." He caught sight of Heidi heading toward him. "Listen, Mom. Let me talk to Heidi. I'll call you back when I know something about Aunt Jackie."

Heidi asked Jamie to pour her a glass of Chardonnay. "I need something to take the edge off. That man has nearly driven me insane tonight." Her gaze shifted to the front door, where Rupert Maki was saying goodbye to the last of his guests, who were making an exodus to a hot spot on Upper King.

"Come with us, Rupie," cooed one particularly drunk woman as she ran her hand across his chest.

"Sure! Why not?" Rupert said and left without so much as a backward glance at the catering staff.

Heidi lifted her glass to the door. "Good riddance."

"Say, Heidi," Jamie said, busying himself with loading unused glasses in a plastic crate for transport. "I was wondering if Sean and I could maybe take off a few minutes early tonight. We need to get home to Prospect. My gran . . ." His voice trailed off.

"Of course, honey, you go on. I'll finish up here." She set

down her wineglass and elbowed him out of the way. "I'm so sorry about your troubles. Your grandma is such a dear. You send her my love."

"Thank you. That means a lot." Jamie locked eyes with his cousin across the room and motioned him over. "We're finished here for tonight. The crew is going to cover for us, so we can leave. Gran isn't doing so well."

Heidi finished loading the glasses in the crate and turned to Sean. "You did a stellar job tonight, young man. I like a guy who can jump right in without me having to hold his hand. Jamie has my cell number. Text me your schedule and I'll see what I can do about getting you more hours."

Sean beamed. "That'd be great. Thanks, Heidi!"

They started toward the back of the house, and Heidi called after them. "Stay in touch, Jamie. About your grandmother, I mean."

He responded with a thumbs-up.

Lizbet and Annie were transferring food from the platters to plastic containers when they entered the kitchen. "I'm sorry for cutting out on you," Jamie said. "But Sean and I really need to get home."

Annie's head shot up. "How is she?"

"Not good, honestly. Cooper's on his way home from Virginia, if that tells you anything." Jamie questioned whether it was appropriate for her to come with them to Prospect. But what the hell? Lovie was the closest thing to a grandmother she'd ever known. "Do you want to come with us?"

Tears glistened in her eyes. "It means a lot that you asked. But I can't leave Heidi with all this to clean up." She spread her arms wide at the mess in the kitchen. "Will you squeeze her hand for me and tell her I love her?"

He drew Annie in for a hug. "You know I will." He held her for a minute before turning to Lizbet. He kissed her cheek and whispered in her ear. "I'm going to miss you tonight."

"Me too, you." She ran her finger down his cheek. "I'll be thinking about you and your family."

Sean and Jamie gathered the clothes they'd been wearing earlier and left via the kitchen door. It had stopped raining, but the streets were still flooded, and a mist had settled over the area.

As they started down the street on the sidewalk, Jamie said, "Dude, you forgot to call your mom. It's my fault for not reminding you. She freaked out when she couldn't find you. She went out looking for you, and now she's not answering her phone."

"Shit! She's gonna kill me," Sean said, increasing his pace.

They walked half a block in silence. "Are all the parties like that?" Sean asked as they turned the corner onto Meeting Street.

"Are all the parties like what?"

"I've been to plenty of parties where heavy drinking was involved. Obviously. I was in a fraternity. But I've never seen grown-ups act that way. Sloppy drunk women. Men hitting on other men's wives. I even saw one dude offer a woman a key bump right there in the middle of the dining room. It was gross. I don't want to be like that when I grow up."

"Then don't! You have control over your future." Jamie glanced over at Sean. His cousin's face was tight, as though he was deep in thought. "I know what you mean, though. The crowd tonight was out of control. Most events we cater are for people like our parents, people who drink a couple of glasses of wine and go home before nine o'clock."

The closer they got to Jackie's house, the better the view they had of her driveway. And there was no sign of her SUV.

"She's not here," Sean said, raking his fingers through his copper hair. "Where could she have gone? Maybe she went back to Prospect, thinking I will ride with you."

"She doesn't know you're with me," Jamie said with a sense of dread. He explained the sequence of events with the texts he'd received from Jackie and his phone call with Sam.

"Great! She's gotta be freaking out. She has no idea where I am. I need to call my dad. Maybe he knows where she is." He held out his hand. "Can I use your phone?"

Sean was punching in his father's number when a figure emerged from the mist. The shape and size of the woman's body resembled Jackie's, but the way she carried herself was off somehow. Was she limping?

Sean looked up from his phone and caught sight of her. "Mom!" He shoved the phone at Jamie and hurried to her side.

"Thank God you're okay," Jackie said as she threw herself at her son. "I've been out of my mind with worry."

Sean patted his mother's back as one might a small child's, oblivious to the mascara being smeared all over his white work shirt. "What happened to your foot?"

"I stepped on a piece of glass. It's a long story. When I found the drugs in your backpack I thought maybe—"

"What drugs?" Sean pushed his mother away so he could see her face. "What're you talking about?"

"I say drugs, but it was only one pill. I assumed there were more, and that you'd taken them. I found this in your backpack." She removed a small plastic bag from her pocket and held it out to him.

Jamie had seen his share of drugs at Carolina, enough to know it was Xanax.

"That's not mine." Sean stared at the bag as though it might bite him. "I have no idea where that came from."

"Yes, you do," Jamie said in a nonaccusatory tone. "Remember your friend who gave you a ride home from the library? He mentioned leaving a present in your backpack."

Sean's blue eyes grew wide. "That's right! That asshole! I swear, Mom, I didn't know he put that in my backpack. I haven't had anything to drink nor have I done drugs since Memorial Day."

Jackie squinted as she studied him. Jamie could tell she wanted to believe him, but part of her remained skeptical.

"He was with me tonight, Aunt Jackie. Working for Heidi. Two servers called in sick with food poisoning at the last minute." He walked her through the evening's events, including the part about Sean's phone being dead and the stress of moving the party indoors. "We screwed up by not calling you."

Jackie's shoulders slumped as the tension left her body. "It's not your responsibility to call me, Jamie. It's Sean's." She looked over at her son. "You have no idea how much you scared me tonight."

"But I do," Jamie said. "I've been through this before with my mom. You naturally assume the worst when someone you love has an addiction. And that's not a good feeling. Aunt Jackie, you can't give up on Sean, and Sean, you have to work harder to earn back your mother's trust. You can start by keeping your phone charged."

They shared a laugh. Jackie smacked Sean's arm with the back of her hand. "Don't do that to me again. I'm old. I can't handle the stress."

"I'm sorry for worrying you, Mom. I promised to do a better job of staying in touch."

Jamie checked his phone for the time. "It's almost ten o'clock. We need to get going. Aunt Jackie, where's your car?"

"I ran out of gas over near Colonial Lake."

Jamie's mind raced as he sorted out the logistics. "Sean, take your mom inside the house and bandage her foot. In the meantime I'll go get my truck from the Hornes'. They have a gas can we can use."

He started off at a jog down the street. When he heard a squeal, he looked over his shoulder in time to see Sean lift Jackie off her bare feet and fling her over his shoulder like a sack of flour. He shook his head and smiled to himself. They had their problems, like everyone else in the Sweeney family, but their love for each other would see them through.

THIRTY-THREE

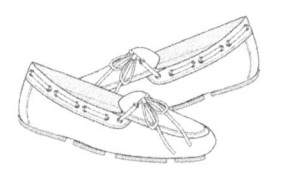

SAM

Sam could count on one hand the times she and her sisters had agreed on something important with little deliberation. And the planning of this day had been one of them. Lovie would have a traditional funeral as was befitting of a classic southern lady.

Her grandsons and sons-in-law served as pallbearers. They carried her mahogany coffin, adorned with a spray of hydrangeas and roses cut from Jackie's garden, down the center aisle of the First Methodist Church. Every pew was filled, with standing room only in the vestibule. Folks had come from across the state to pay tribute to the woman who, for decades, had supplied them with fresh seafood and offered tips on how to prepare it. Lovie meant more to them than that, though. She was a friend they'd visited with every Saturday during the summer. And now they had come to say goodbye.

The service was uplifting. No one was there to mourn. They had gathered to celebrate the life of a very special lady. Lovie would not want anyone to be sad about her passing. She would want her family and friends to pause for a brief moment to reflect on the past, to count their many blessings, and to look forward to the future.

Each of the three sisters gave a eulogy. Faith greeted everyone with a few remarks. Sam provided the history of Captain Sweeney's Seafood Market, outlining Lovie's accomplishments during her decades as proprietor and sharing anecdotes from daily life at the market. And Jackie concluded the lineup, delivering with eloquence comments both heartfelt and witty. For the first time ever, she had worn flats to a social function. "These are the only shoes I own that I can cram this big bandage into," she said of her pewter Tory Burch ballet flats. The gash in her foot had required eight stitches, which Mike had sewn himself when she arrived at the hospital on Tuesday night.

The entire family, including Cooper, had made it home in time to say goodbye to Lovie. She never opened her eyes again, but had been surrounded by all her loved ones when she drew her last breath.

Saturday was the obvious first choice for the funeral, but the church was already booked for a wedding. Friday afternoon proved to be a splendid second best as most folks took off work early for the weekend to attend.

Jamie and Sean were planning their own special tribute to their grandmother. Starting at dawn on Thursday morning, aside from a few hours for sleep, they'd worked nonstop until it was time to shower and dress for the funeral. They'd tripled the size of their usual haul, bringing in so many crabs, Sam feared for the inlet's crab population. Steamed and spiced and packaged by the dozen, the crabs were stored in the cooler at the marina awaiting tomorrow morning, when Jamie and Sean would give them away, while supplies lasted, to locals and vacationers on their way to the beach. Sean and Jamie didn't fret over the loss of income. They viewed it as a gesture of goodwill, in honor of their beloved grandmother, to all the customers who'd remained loyal to the Sweeney family over the years.

After the service everyone gathered in the small cemetery adjacent to the church, where Lovie would later be laid to rest beside Oscar. Reverend Webster read a few Bible verses and said a prayer before extending an invitation to those gathered to join the family for a reception afterward. Police officers on motorcycles led the caravan of cars out to Moss Creek Farm, where a crew of workers valet-parked them.

The picture-perfect weather boosted the spirits of all in attendance. The temperature was cooler than usual for the Lowcountry this time of year, with highs in the mideighties and low humidity. Fluffy white clouds dotted the periwinkle sky, and a gentle breeze rustled the moss in the oak trees.

With only two days to prepare, Heidi had pulled together a reception fit for a royal wedding. They offered a few choices for the landlubbers, but the focus of the cuisine was seafood. Sam made a point of tasting every item, and her seasoned palate confirmed she'd made the right decision in going into business with Tasty Provisions.

Strangers and friends waited in line to speak to the sisters, to express their condolences and tell funny stories about their mother.

Sam held her breath when Donna Bennett appeared in front of her. "I never much cared for you, Samantha, but I always had the utmost respect for your mother."

Sam laughed out loud. "One thing about you, Donna—I always know where I stand with you." Her lips grew thin. "Seriously, though, I owe you an apology. I should never have accused you of setting the fire."

Donna nodded her acceptance of Sam's apology. "And I owe you an apology as well. We should have validated our source before we printed the recipes."

Sam waved a hand at their surroundings. "This seems like as good a time as any to bury the hatchet. What say, Donna, should we try to be friends?"

A moment of silence filled the air between them as they considered Sam's suggestion. Finally they looked at each other, shook their heads in unison, and laughed.

"Why ruin a good thing?" Sam asked.

"Exactly," Donna added. "I like our relationship just fine the way it is."

Sam realized that she too liked their relationship as it was.

Moses was next in line. He had tears in his eyes when he told her how much he'd thought of Lovie. "She was one of a kind. A true lady with a rare grace and beauty."

He kissed Sam's cheek and moved on to speak to Jackie. Sam couldn't help but overhear their conversation.

"Watching Sean suffer with his addiction has opened my eyes to my own Xanax usage," Jackie said. "Of course, mine is prescribed and monitored by my doctor, but I'd like to learn some techniques for coping with anxiety without medication. Is that crazy, Big Mo? Am I too old to change?"

"Not at all. Don't ever give up the fight, Jackie. When you stop trying to better yourself is when you grow old."

Sam spotted Sean in the crowd—standing beside Cooper but at arm's length, no longer in his twin's shadow. Cooper's attention was on Annie, who stared up at him with as much adoration as he bestowed upon her. Annie had gone to New York ready to set the world on fire, but she'd returned immediately after finishing culinary school when she realized how much she loved the South. With any luck Cooper would have the same realization and move back to the Lowcountry, if not to Prospect then to Charleston.

Sam saw Lizbet heading her way and smiled at the pretty young woman as she approached. "Mrs. Marshall, can I get you a glass of sweet tea or lemonade?"

"I'm fine, but thank you," Sam said. "I'll tell you what you can do for me, though."

Lizbet's face lit up, she was so eager to please. "Name it!"

"I'd really like it if you'd call me Sam."

Sam was looking forward to getting to know Lizbet better. She was hardworking, with a good head on her shoulders. She and Jamie had so much in common. One only had to look at them together to see the chemistry between them. Love was in the air for two of the Sweeney boys, and she suspected Sean would soon find someone special as well. He was getting his life back on track. Sam prayed he'd learned enough from his mistakes to prevent him from making the same ones again.

As the crowd began to dwindle, Faith cornered Sam on the terrace. "I've decided what I want to be when I grow up."

"Hmm, let me guess," Sam said, pressing a finger to her lips. "You're going to open a home for abused women."

Faith's jaw dropped to the bluestone. "How'd you know? Did Mike tell you?"

Sam chucked her sister's chin. "No one told me. You forget, baby sister, that I know you. Sometimes better than you know yourself. It's the obvious choice for you, but you needed closure from your relationship with Curtis in order to move forward with it."

A small group of close friends, old and young, lingered until almost dinnertime. Thanks to Heidi, they had enough leftovers to feed the family all weekend. The sisters stood in the driveway, waving goodbye to Heidi in her Tasty Provisions van.

With the exception of the sisters, everyone who remained at the farm—the cousins, their dads and stepdads, Lizbet and Annie—changed into bathing suits and headed down to the dock to swim.

"Wait here! I'll be right back," Jackie said and disappeared inside.

She returned five minutes later with a blanket tucked under her left arm and two wine bottles under her right, her fingers gripping three crystal champagne flutes.

"Now you're talking!" Faith grabbed the blanket and spread it out on the ground on the hill.

Jackie handed each of them a glass and popped the cork on both bottles—prosecco for Jackie and Faith and a nonalcoholic sparkling wine for Sam.

They stretched out on the blanket and sipped their bubbly in silence while they reflected on the day.

"I can't believe she's gone," Faith said finally. "The world is a smidgen less bright without her presence."

"She set a shining example for sure," Sam said. "She lived clean, worked hard, and recognized the best in every one of us."

"Even when that best was buried beneath layers of ugliness," Jackie added.

"We'll miss her like crazy, but her legacy will live on," Sam said.

Jackie rolled onto her side to face Sam. "It's easy for you to say, Sammie. You have the market. Every time one of your customers walks through your front door, they will think of Lovie."

"That's true enough, but the real legacy is them." All eyes traveled to the water, where the boy cousins were gathered around their girl cousin, who was currently holding position as queen of the inner tube. "Every time you look in the twins' eyes, you see Daddy. And Bitsy is destined to look more like Mom than any of us ever did. And Jamie? Well, he doesn't really look like either one of them," Sam said of her son, who was the spitting image of his father.

"Maybe not," Faith said. "But he has Mama's generous spirit and iron will."

"Just think." Jackie rolled onto her back and stared up at the darkening sky. "Mom and Dad, Oscar and Lovie, are together forever now. What do you think they're doing?"

"Watching us and smiling," Faith said. "They can rest in peace knowing that no matter what happens to us we'll always be here for one another."

A NOTE TO READERS

So many lives are affected in some way by Alzheimer's disease. Our husbands and wives, mothers and fathers, brothers and sisters. This cruel and debilitating disease strips our loved ones of their memories and their dignities. I'd like to extend a heartfelt thank-you to my good friend Alison Fauls for sharing her personal experiences with me as I wrote the final drafts of the novel.

Most of us reach the stage in our lives when we are forced to cope with aging parents. We make grave sacrifices to tend to our loved ones. Oftentimes, those sacrifices continue for years. I admire you for your courage, strength, and perseverance. Remember to be kind to yourself. Take time out to reset. Take a long walk, have coffee with a friend, or cook a healthy dinner for your family. Most of all, keep reading. Nothing provides escape from our problems like women's fiction.

ACKNOWLEDGMENTS

I'm grateful to the many people who helped make this novel possible. First and foremost, to my editor, Patricia Peters, for her patience and advice and for making my work stronger without changing my voice. To my literary agent, Andrea Hurst, for her guidance and expertise in the publishing industry and for believing in my work. To my faithful readers for their love of the Sweeney sisters and for encouraging me to write another installment in the series. And to Damon Freeman and his crew at Damonza.com for their creativity in designing this stunning cover.

I am blessed to have many supportive people in my life, my friends and family, who offer the encouragement I need to continue the pursuit of my writing career. I owe a huge debt of gratitude to my advanced review team for their enthusiasm of and commitment to my work, and to my family and friends for their continued support and encouragement.

ABOUT THE AUTHOR

Ashley writes books about women for women. Her characters are mothers, daughters, sisters, and wives facing real-life issues. Her goal is to keep you turning the pages until the wee hours of the morning. If her story stays with you long after you've read the last word, then she's done her job.

Ashley is a wife and mother of two young adult children. She grew up in the salty marshes of South Carolina, but now lives in Richmond, Virginia, a city she loves for its history and traditions.

Ashley loves to hear from her readers. Feel free to visit her website or shoot her an email. For more information about upcoming releases, don't forget to sign up for her newsletter at ashleyfarley.net/newsletter-signup/. Your subscription will grant you exclusive content, sneak previews, and special giveaways.

ashleyfarley.net
ashleyhfarley@gmail.com

CPSIA information can be obtained
at www.ICGtesting.com
Printed in the USA
LVHW09s1338280818
588389LV00001B/206/P